Clay

19 November 2015

Comment A Paris Apartment

Parisian Belle Epoque

PARIS

TIME CAPSULE

Movie: My Old Lady

Avec Kevin Kline & Maggie Smith

Ella Carey

This is a work of fiction. Names, characters, organizations, places, events, and incidents are either products of the author's imagination or are used fictitiously.

Published by Lake Union Publishing, Seattle

www.apub.com

ISBN-13: 9781477829936
ISBN-10: 1477829938

Cover design by Elsie Lyons
Library of Congress Control Number: 2014921618

Printed in the United States of America

For Ben and Sophie, with all my love, always.

CHAPTER ONE

The parcel was wrapped in brown paper and tied with an unblemished silk ribbon. This was quite a feat, given that the package had traveled all the way from Paris to New York. A tiny bow perched on top, its ends snipped short—almost, Cat thought, as if the person who had wrapped it was attempting to be economical. The sender's details were written in faded sepia pen: Monsieur Gerard Lapointe, ninth arrondissement, Paris. Cat had never heard of him.

She gave the parcel a gentle shake. Something solid rattled inside, but just as Cat was reaching for her kitchen scissors, there was a knock on her front door. Christian was right on time. Cat put the parcel down on the kitchen bench, picked it up again, put it back, and went to answer the door.

Christian wore a new suit. His fair hair was slicked back, Gatsby style. "You haven't changed yet?" He looked at his watch.

"Do I need to?" Cat laughed.

Christian strolled through Cat's tiny Brooklyn apartment, looking half as if he owned it and half as if he couldn't wait to return to the Upper West Side.

"How about that little black dress I bought you last week?"

Cat hid her smile as Christian paused in front of her latest treasure, a vintage peacock-patterned shawl that she had picked up at a flea market for a song. Cat had spent hours fixing the tiny rents in the fabric and combing tangles out of its ancient fringe. Now it was draped over her red sofa.

Christian seemed to be conducting an internal debate over whether he should be polite about that shawl or not.

"I had to rescue it. It was in such a state of disrepair . . . I suppose I could get changed." There was no doubt that the minimalist black dress Christian had bought for her last week would be far more suitable for the evening ahead than the pale green 1940s trouser suit that Cat had chosen. He did so love to buy her clothes. It was something that was both endearing and yet a little awkward at times. She'd been crazy about vintage since her late teens, but the main thing, of course, was not to hurt his feelings. She moved toward her bedroom.

Christian caught her hand on the way. "Michael and Alicia chose tonight. The Lemon Tree. Apparently they have a new menu. But—" He adjusted his suit sleeve and glanced at his watch again.

"We'll be on time." Cat slipped the new dress over her head. She handed Christian the silver necklace that he had bought her for her thirty-fourth birthday, turning her back to him and raising her honey-colored hair so that he could slide the clasp together.

"I love you in this."

Cat turned and eyed him. "Don't think I plan to make a habit of it."

"Never."

She dabbed some perfume on her wrists. "A charming little package came in the mail today. From Paris. I'm dying to see what it is."

Christian held the door open. "Last time I was in Paris, all I saw was the inside of the bank."

The package would have to wait.

It was probably nothing at all.

• • •

Although The Lemon Tree was full, the elegant restaurant didn't feel hectic at all. Cat chatted with Tash, Alicia, and Morgan, all of whom were married to Christian's oldest friends. The idea of being a permanent part of this close-knit circle was more appealing than Cat would admit to anyone who cared to ask—it was precisely what she had always wanted but had never had. Even after two years with Christian, she still had a sense of being a little on the outside. After all, Tash and Scott were married with two toddlers, Michael and Alicia had three children and a weekend house, and Morgan and Adam had been together for a decade. They had been planning their wedding since Cat first met them. Christian had been friends with Michael, Scott, and Adam since they were in grade school.

Conversations ranged from the jaw-dropping process of applying for prep schools in Manhattan and the desperate need for the children to speak several languages before they were five to the considerable stresses of shopping on Net-A-Porter and the fact that there was never time for any of it, anyway. It was delicious and a little irreverent, and Cat knew that she was beguiled by them all.

Christian caught Cat's eye and winked, and she smiled right back at him. This had become a little ritual between them whenever they were out. He would check to see that she was happy; she would reassure him that she most definitely was.

"I mean to say"—Alicia placed her wine glass on the table as if she were about to make a grand announcement—"it makes no difference for Annabelle that I'm an alumni. There should be limits to how egalitarian they can be. How far does it go?"

"We should start a campaign," Tash said.

"And you can coordinate it, Alicia." Adam laughed. "You'd be brilliant."

Cat caught Christian's eye again. He raised one of his blond brows.

"Cat," Tash said, "tell me, where did you go to school?"

"Yes, Cat, tell us, where did you go to school? Will the little Carters be following in their mother's footsteps?" Michael asked.

Cat felt a flush rise through her cheeks at the question—and the assumption that her children would be Christian's. "Oh, Mumbai High."

There was a silence, until Christian chuckled and everyone else followed suit. Cat sat back in her own seat and took a gulp of wine. Laughter, the ability to shake things off—it was one of the things she adored about Christian. He had been the only person to come to her rescue the first time she met him. He and several colleagues from the bank had come to have group portraits taken at the photography studio where Cat worked. When Cat's camera had refused to play ball, Christian had hopped out of position, helped her retrieve new equipment, and then, afterward, insisted on carrying it all back to her boss's rooms. The fact that he had asked her out for a drink that very evening had seemed like a foregone conclusion after half an hour spent flirting among the tripods. His green eyes and blond hair were a tantalizing mix, and he seemed confident, so very confident, as well as kind. Now, it was as if they were a pair of birds building a nest, already assuming they would spend their lives together even though they had never formally discussed it.

Now, Cat pushed familiar and intrusive thoughts of her father—and what he would no doubt have had to say about Christian and his successful "bourgeois" friends—out of her head. There was no point in worrying about Howard Jordan now.

"You seemed distracted for a while there tonight," Christian said, as they left the restaurant together.

Cat leaned into the familiar comfort of his arm around her shoulders while they waited for a cab. "Did I?"

"Did you have a good time, honey?"

"Of course."

Outside the fog-smeared car window, the city lights sparkled. Back in Brooklyn, the cab came to a stop in front of her building

"Do you want to come up?" Cat asked.

"I'd love to, but I have to get off to an early start tomorrow."

Cat leaned over and kissed him.

"You know"—he glanced out the car window at her Vespa, which was parked in its usual spot—"you should part with the scooter."

"Don't be ridiculous," Cat laughed. It had been her very first purchase when she got her first job.

"It's too dangerous. If I had my way, it'd be gone tomorrow."

• • •

As soon as she'd closed her door behind her, Cat went straight to the package from Paris. She had only visited France once, during a whirlwind trip right after college. Her time in Paris had been brief, but she had taken more than a thousand photographs during her stay. Upon her return to New York, she had started her job as a photographer at a studio, the same one where she still worked now. She had nearly left countless times, but she knew she was fortunate to have a job during a recession. Besides, every time she had tried to quit, her boss had reeled her back in with pleas so convincing that she had resigned herself to staying a little longer.

The way the bow was tied on this package brought back memories of the sort of elegance that had enchanted Cat when she was in Paris. She slipped her scissors back in the drawer and began to ease the pale ribbon out of its elaborate knot with the tips of her fingers; it seemed a shame to wreck the beautiful silk.

The loft had turned colder during the evening, but her fingers, despite being cold, were deft with some strange energy tonight.

She finished untying the ribbon and slid her fingertips under the brown tape that bound the package together. A small cardboard box lay inside the paper wrapping.

A gust of wind caused the windows to shake. Cat shuddered. A mug of hot chocolate was in order. Cat slipped across the kitchen and poured milk into a saucepan. Stirring the warm milk in the pot soothed her. She broke up two thick slabs of dark chocolate and watched them melt into the liquid, then poured the hot drink into a blue and white china mug that had belonged to her mother. Her sweet, innocent mother.

Cat was determined to live the happy life that her mother must have dreamed about. One thing was certain: Cat's mother would have been far happier with a kind man like Christian than with Cat's opinionated and domineering father. Her mother had, it seemed, loved desperately when she was young, only to spend the rest of her life regretting her horrible mistake.

Difficult relationships were something Cat was determined to avoid.

She took a sip of the heavenly chocolate, put the mug down, and lifted the lid from the cardboard box. There were two things nestled inside: a typed letter and an old brass key.

Cat moved across the living room to sit on her sofa, scanned the letter once, and then reread it a second time. It had been typed on a typewriter. It made no sense at all.

Cat's full name was at the top of the page: Catherine Laura Jordan. Below this, in capital letters, was the name around which the letter appeared to revolve—the name of a woman of whom Cat's father had disapproved so deeply that he turned puce whenever it was mentioned—Virginia Brooke, Cat's utterly unacceptable maternal grandmother.

The letter was formal and brief. Monsieur Lapointe, a lawyer based in Paris, wrote that Virginia Brooke had been the sole inheritor of the estate of the recently deceased Isabelle de Florian. After the passing of Virginia Brooke in 1978 and the subsequent passing of Virginia's daughter, Cat's mother, Bonnie, in 2003, the estate was now left entirely to Cat.

Cat knew that her grandmother Virginia had traveled solo in Europe for six years just before the Second World War, only returning to America when her family insisted that Europe was unsafe. Virginia had remained single for a long time. She had gotten a lowly job in New York's garment district, despite her middle-class family's protests, and had apparently enjoyed the company of several lovers. She had been married late, to a far older man: Cat's grandfather, a Harvard professor whom Virginia, by all accounts, had adored. She hadn't given birth to Bonnie until she was well into her forties.

Bonnie had been wonderfully neglected as a child, left to ramble around the family's old farmhouse and its wild gardens alone while Cat's grandfather and Virginia went about their lives doing exactly as they wished.

As a result, Bonnie had cultivated not only a deep imagination but also an appealing yearning for romance that had captivated Howard Jordan, a former student of her father's. Howard went on to become a public servant with strident political and moral convictions. His primary passion in life was apparently to shape both Bonnie and Cat into something prosaic and suited to his own needs, which revolved around order, efficiency, and the unyielding belief that his opinions were always correct.

It wasn't until Cat was in her late teens that she learned to respect her mother's stoicism, her determination to make something of the situation in which she had placed herself. By the time Cat was twenty, Bonnie confessed that she had been a young romantic and had allowed herself to be swept away by the idea of love rather than really considering Howard as a person. Bonnie's decision to stay with Howard was, Cat knew, for Cat's own sake, and there was definitely something to admire in that.

Bonnie had told her whispered stories about Virginia frequenting Parisian cabarets and bars during the Jazz Age. She had been a regular at society events, openings, exhibitions, the theater. So where did Isabelle de Florian come into this? Amid all of Bonnie's stories, there had never been a mention of an Isabelle. Cat was sure of it.

Cat had half expected—and hoped with all her heart—that her own trip to Paris might hold a hint of that bygone era's cachet, too. Instead, her own European tour had seen her careering around several countries on a crowded bus along with forty inebriated students. By the end of it, Cat had decided that romance was best left in the past.

She had returned to New York and started working in the photographer's studio, and now, with Christian, she was happier than she had ever been in her life.

Paris was six hours ahead of New York. In a few hours, this mysterious Monsieur Lapointe's office should be open for business.

Cat would be businesslike herself. She would give this Monsieur Lapointe a call, even if she had to stay up all night to catch him first thing, and she would sort the situation out. Fast.

CHAPTER TWO

Cat picked up the phone and dialed Monsieur Lapointe's office just after nine o'clock in the morning, Paris time.

The receptionist was firm. "Monsieur Lapointe does not begin for one more hour. I will give him your message, Mademoiselle."

Cat slumped back down on her bed. It was Christian's parents' wedding anniversary today, and she had promised him that she would celebrate with his family this evening. But now she was exhausted.

At four a.m. New York time, Monsieur Lapointe still had not called back. Cat held her hand over the phone. It would not do to appear desperate, but she would just have to call again.

This time, the woman on the end of the phone put her straight through to Monsieur Lapointe.

"Mademoiselle Jordan?" he asked, placing a strong emphasis on the last syllable of her name.

"Oh, bonjour, Monsieur."

"I am afraid that I am going to be abrupt. There is no other way around this. Mademoiselle Jordan, you must come to Paris."

Cat drew in a breath. "Well, would it be possible for us to discuss this over the phone?"

"It would be best for us to speak in person, Mademoiselle."

There was a silence.

"I really can't get to Paris. My work . . ." Her work? Taking portraits of well-to-do New Yorkers, businesspeople—and often their equally well-to-do babies and pets—could hardly be called crucial work. But there was no question of her going to Paris.

"Mademoiselle. Please."

"But, the fares, Monsieur." Although . . . she could probably afford a cheap flight to France. She had some savings built up.

"I cannot come to you."

"No." He had a point.

Cat took a couple of laps around the living room. "So you're saying you cannot do this over the phone or in writing?"

"You could put it this way indeed. The circumstances of this will are . . . not ordinary . . . you will have to come to Paris to sort it out. And, Mademoiselle, I would prefer to meet you before we go ahead with the reading of the will. There are formalities, many formalities. These are very important, you will see."

Cat sat down where she was. "I . . . assume you'd want me there as soon as possible?" Now she sounded like she wanted to go. She cleared her throat. "I mean, I would have to work it out with my boss, you know. I can't just drop everything." What was she saying? She had months of vacation time accumulated. She never went anywhere.

"I will be here when you come." Monsieur Lapointe gave her precise directions to his office. "And do not forget the key, Mademoiselle Jordan."

"Of course." Cat took a breath. "Look, can you at least tell me what this Isabelle de Florian had to do with my grandmother?"

"Please make the appointment with my personal assistant. Au revoir, Mademoiselle."

Four hours later, after trying and failing to fall asleep, Cat emailed her boss requesting some time off. When she received a reluctant yet positive reply from his phone while he was apparently out on his morning jog, she booked herself a flight to Paris the following day. With the help of Monsieur Lapointe's assistant, she found a small hotel near the Palais Garnier opera house, right around the corner from the legal office.

Only when Cat hung up the phone for the last time and the first signs of light appeared through the gap in the curtains did the full impact of the entire situation hit her. Her grandmother had been a wild card. Cat was nothing like her. Why on earth had she allowed herself to be persuaded to fly to France the very next day?

• • •

The small family anniversary dinner for Christian's parents turned out to be a party for fifty. Even if Cat had wanted to discuss her ridiculous grandmother's situation with Christian, it was clear from the moment she stepped out of the elevator into his parents' crowded apartment that there was not going to be a chance to be alone with him all night.

And anyway, what Christian or anyone in his family would begin to think about Cat's crazy family story was anybody's guess. The chic people at this party wouldn't give a damn about Virginia Brooke.

By the time Christian had introduced her to enough charming people to fill a ballroom, in addition to his endless cousins down from Boston, it was almost impossible for Cat to remember why her little trip to Paris with a rusty key and a letter was of any importance at all.

There had been only a handful of occasions when Cat had mingled with Christian's wider family, and having everyone here at once was like being an outsider at a party for *Vogue*. Thankfully, many of Christian's relatives found Cat's vintage 1940s tea dress "interesting" or "quite charming, my dear," and what might have caused her to feel out of place had become an attribute that seemed to endear her to his endless aunts swathed in pearls and Chanel.

Had there been a chance to think about the utter contrast between all this elegance and Cat's own childhood in Durham, Connecticut—her parents had hardly ever had company—Cat would have had to pinch herself to believe she was here. But there was no chance for thinking. That was all part of being in Christian's world. It was all about being in the right place with the right people at the very right time. She gave herself over willingly to the seductive appeal of it all.

After a couple of hours, Cat had convinced herself that even if she had found the chance to discuss the matter of the estate with Christian, she wouldn't have bothered. He wasn't into travel and wouldn't understand why she hadn't insisted that the lawyer just send her an email with all the particulars. Christian often said that everything you could ever want was in New York and you could use a laptop to experience the rest. His grandparents had a comfortable house in the Hamptons for holidays. Why would anyone bother going anywhere else? So. She would simply tell them she was going to Paris. They would accept this and would not require a reason.

"It's a little early for the shows, dear," Christian's aunt pointed out.

"I'm going for work, actually." Cat had to stop herself from chewing at her lip.

"Would you like me to book you on a nice flight?" Christian asked.

"I had the most divine caviar in first the other week. They are improving. Finally." Christian's uncle on his father's side had a moustache and a permanent pleasant expression on his face.

"Caviar and champagne for Cat. Sounds like a plan," Christian said.

"No, no. I've got it all arranged," Cat said and smiled.

Honestly, she didn't care about first-class this and luxury that. She hadn't known about Christian's family's wealth when they had first started dating. It was the little things he did that mattered, like the fact that from the very first time they went out for a drink, he had called her most days, just to see how she was, just to find out how her day was going.

"Surely not coach?"

"No?"

"No."

"I've booked it. Business class, so it's fine." It was only a small white lie, but the thought of telling Christian that she had grabbed a last-minute deal on a budget airline that left at nobody's business of an ungodly hour would, no doubt, send him into a spin.

"The firm's paying," Cat went on. "They insisted." The firm? What firm? But Christian had trouble seeing beyond his own world.

"Call me the instant you land, honey."

Cat slipped into the elevator. When Christian was out of sight, she pulled off her high-heeled 1940s pumps and let her sore feet absorb the cool of the patterned marble floor.

• • •

A few hours later, Cat found herself in the middle row on a budget flight to Paris—about as far from patterned marble floors as she could fathom. She had spent most of the flight with a three-year-old on her lap, attempting to dodge fountains of vomit and chocolate milk while protecting her ears from repeated assaults by sibling squabbles that had caused people several rows in front of them to turn and shake their heads.

Late, very late at night—or early in the morning, depending on how one chose to regard time above the clouds—her small companion had finally crashed into a deep sleep. Cat had spent the remaining hours turning Isabelle de Florian's brass key over and over in her fingers. For some reason, it seemed vital that she keep that key right on her person. She had moved it from her jacket pocket to her money belt, and now here it was, out again. It was as if the cool slip of metal might hold all the answers. What on earth was it going to open?

An armoire, perhaps? It was unlikely that Isabelle de Florian had left anything of any great value to Virginia. Surely there was some sort of mistake; Isabelle couldn't possibly have left an entire estate to some friend she had only known during her youth.

But still. Why was Monsieur Lapointe so insistent that Cat come to Paris? Why would there be formalities if she had inherited nothing much at all?

And would Cat ever find out what Virginia had really gotten up to in 1930s Paris?

As the jet slowed over the city and passengers in the window seats gazed out at the skyline, *ooh*ing and *ahh*ing with delight, Cat imagined Virginia arriving in Paris for the first time. Had she come straight from Boston, where she grew up? What would Paris have been like back then? And when had she met this Isabelle de Florian? And where? At one of the infamous jazz clubs her mother had told her about? If only Cat could ask her . . .

As the plane began to descend over Paris, the child next to Cat stirred and rubbed his chubby hands across his face. When he turned his gimlet-eyed gaze toward her, Cat tucked Isabelle's key into her pocket. She smiled at the small boy and prayed silently that this trip to Paris would be better than her last.

• • •

When Cat woke early the next morning to the sound of shop vendors pulling open their shutters and calling boisterous "Bonjours!" into the cold morning air, it was impossible not to smile.

It was also impossible to resist wandering over to her own set of wooden shutters and opening them wide. She had felt immediately at home in her cozy hotel room, warm against the winter chills outside with its white-painted floorboards, its cream covered chair below the window, and its double bed piled with cushions.

Now, she was tempted to linger, to watch the activity unfurling right outside the window in one of Paris's narrow market streets. There was a sense of being so close to the pretty building opposite that it would have been easy to carry out a conversation with its occupants from where she stood looking through the double-glazed glass.

Indeed, the early morning activity was so invigorating that once Cat had inspected the boulangerie opposite her window and taken in the florist and its roses in buckets on the sidewalk next door, she simply had to hop into a warm shower, bundle up in her coat, and set out to find breakfast on this fresh winter's morning, before her meeting with the enigmatic Monsieur Lapointe.

It was a tentative first sojourn onto the Right Bank—hard to know exactly what she was looking for in terms of breakfast—but walking early in the morning was such a pleasure after all those hours spent huddled in a plane that Cat found herself wandering, practically oblivious to the cold.

Her meeting was not until ten o'clock—in order, Monsieur's assistant had suggested, to give Cat time to get over her jet lag, an idea that had seemed civilized at the time and now had given her a delicious bit of time to herself. Every now and then she simply stopped to marvel at the sheer line of pink sky that ran between the beautiful old buildings. Sunrise over Paris.

At last, a small patisserie not too far from the hotel caught her eye. Cat was still on the Right Bank, having not ventured across the Seine, and she knew that she was still close to the Opéra Garnier. Rows of exquisite creations were lined up in the full-length windows in front of her, their icings and intricate decorations glistening in a multitude of pinks, chocolates, and limes. Several locals sat inside reading their morning papers; the smell of roasting coffee drifted out toward the sidewalk.

She was more than tempted to choose something rich and wicked to accompany her coffee, but the effects of the long flight, and dizzy nerves about what on earth lay ahead this morning, meant that a plain croissant seemed the wisest choice. Cat sat down at one of the small round tables and let the strong espresso work its magic on her tired mind, which was starting to run in circles about Isabelle de Florian.

What was the protocol for inheriting an estate from a stranger? And an estate here in France? For the first time, it was tempting to call home and ask for some advice. But everyone there would still be asleep. The situation had not seemed real until now. And yet here she was, alone in Paris, a croissant crisp and melting buttery soft at the same time on her tongue. She could get used to this.

At precisely ten o'clock, Cat sat opposite the reception desk in Monsieur Lapointe's office. Her hands kept burrowing into her handbag, seeking out the key, clasping it. It was impossible to know what to expect.

Monsieur Lapointe appeared through an interior door exactly ten minutes later. He went to the reception desk first and spoke to the woman sitting there for a moment. His three-piece navy blue suit was impeccable, and he wore highly polished tan shoes. When he turned to face her, Cat couldn't help but notice the red flower in his lapel and the immaculate silk handkerchief in his front pocket.

But when Monsieur Lapointe stepped forward, he seemed more harried than dapper, and he nodded at Cat in the briefest of ways before indicating that she should follow him into the corridor and then into a room furnished solely with a large antique table and chairs. A woman he introduced as his assistant sat at one of the middle chairs.

Monsieur Lapointe adjusted a stack of papers on the table, arranging the immaculate white sheets into a perfect fan. Then he walked around the table and held out a chair opposite his own for Cat. The sound of her chair scraping against the hard floor seemed incongruous in the serious, silent room, and Cat felt herself redden as she sat down.

Monsieur Lapointe seemed to glide into his own chair.

"Mademoiselle Jordan. First, I must see your passport for the verification."

Cat was prepared for this and handed it over. "Monsieur Lapointe, I am so intrigued by all of this. The fact that Isabelle de Florian left an estate to my grandmother. Do you know anything about the friendship they had?"

Monsieur looked up and then simply looked back down. For what seemed like several minutes, he turned the pages and filled out a pile of seemingly endless white forms.

"The formalities. This is important. Most important."

Cat felt a heady mixture of jet lag and heightened sensitivity. The best place for her hands seemed to be folded in her lap.

"It just seems so extraordinary. I wonder if there's any correspondence that you know of between my grandmother and her friend. They must have been so close, and yet I've never heard of Isabelle before. I'd love to learn more about how they knew each other."

"Café, Mademoiselle Jordan?" Monsieur Lapointe's assistant's words made Cat jump in her seat. Monsieur had not looked up from his papers.

"Oh! Sure, that would be great."

The assistant slipped out.

After several more minutes had passed, Monsieur Lapointe screwed the lid back onto his fountain pen. Cat had had plenty of time to notice that it was filled with the very same sepia ink on the package that had arrived in New York.

"Now," he said. "We will wait for my assistant and the café."

"This situation is so odd. I hardly know what to make of it, Monsieur Lapointe."

"We have some more formalities, Mademoiselle Jordan. It is the requirement, you see," he said, as his assistant arrived, wheeling in an elaborate coffee cart with tiny green cups.

While the assistant poured, Monsieur Lapointe began filling out yet another set of forms, this time handing every sheet of paper across the table for Cat to sign. With each form came a detailed explanation.

"Your inheritance tax will be sixty percent of the total value of the estate," he said. "It is a flat rate for nonrelatives in France. I will help you with this once we have done the *attestation immobilière*. Do not worry about it now."

"Oh?" Her head was spinning with French legal terms, and the reams of paper were starting to blend into one continuous blur. The last thing to do would be appearing impatient. Any attempt at conversation had been rebuffed with such firmness that further questions were clearly not a good idea. It was tempting to check the time, but Cat felt almost stuck to the spot. It was impossible to know how long she had been sitting in this office, but it seemed as if hours had passed, and it was hard to know if she was ever going to find out anything at all.

Mademoiselle, it seemed, had no such qualms about checking on the time. "Excusez-moi, Monsieur?" she asked. "C'est l'heure du déjeuner? Non?"

Could it really be time for lunch? Cat's French was limited to two years of dubious study in high school, but she understood the word for lunch.

Monsieur Lapointe sat back in his seat and appeared to consider most seriously whether it was lunchtime or not.

"*Oui*," he said, finally. "It is time. Of course. Mademoiselle Jordan, we will meet again in three hours."

Three hours? Cat sat up in her seat. Surely they could order in sandwiches? But Monsieur Lapointe had already pulled back his chair, while Mademoiselle handed him a tan coat—cashmere, by the looks of it. Not a surprise.

"Are you sure . . . did you say three hours?"

"But of course. We take time to eat properly in France." He rattled off some quick witticism in French.

His assistant tittered

Cat busied herself with her scarf. "All right, then," she said, as they stood by the door. "I'll see you back here at three."

"This is all excellent." Monsieur Lapointe smiled. He looked more relaxed now. "It is all very good."

• • •

It only took a minute for her to walk back to the hotel to pick up her camera. As Cat wandered through the Tuileries gardens toward the Seine, she set up several shots of iconic Paris scenes. In one, she captured the Eiffel Tower in the corner of a long-distance shot at the end of the gardens, with the Orangerie in the left-hand side of the frame. Next, she ambled down to Pont Neuf, with its charming lamps, almost like mini Eiffel Towers themselves.

She wandered across to the Left Bank and was entranced by the tiny streets there. She became lost wandering through the maze-like alleys. Enchanted, she took countless photos of old-fashioned specialty boutiques with their unusual displays, artisan wares that looked to have been made with such love that Cat was tempted to wander inside every shop.

Cat was so absorbed in what she was doing that two full hours flew by before she even realized it. She hadn't had that experience for a while.

With only half an hour to go, Cat bought a *jambon* and *fromage* baguette from a stall back in the Tuileries gardens. She ate it sitting on a green metal chair and watched children play with miniature sailing boats on the ponds in front of her. They were all dressed warmly, bundled up in their regulation down jackets and hats. Even though the trees lining the wide paths that led out toward the Place de la Concorde were bare, the winter sun shone on the water and radiated a little warmth onto her chair. There was so much history in every part of Paris, and it was easy to become lost in imagining the people who must have strolled through these palace gardens once, long ago.

• • •

"I trust you had a satisfying *déjeuner*?" Monsieur Lapointe was ready at exactly three o'clock.

"It was perfect, actually." Cat hid her camera under the mahogany table.

"*Maintenant*," he said. "We come to the reading of the will, Mademoiselle Jordan."

"I'm ready."

Monsieur Lapointe seemed to be thinking for a while.

"Mademoiselle de Florian's will was written in 1940."

"What did you say?"

"*Alors*," he said, finally. "Our instructions are clear. Her entire estate is left to you. In a moment, I think you will understand."

"But . . . Isabelle de Florian left everything to my grandmother when she was how old?"

"She was in her twenties, Mademoiselle."

"But her parents?"

"Mademoiselle de Florian's parents both died of—how do you say it—the Spanish influenza, according to my late predecessor's notes."

"Oh," Cat whispered. So Isabelle had been alone. Just like Cat. A sliver of something rippled through her insides. It was never a good idea to think about her parents, never a good idea to remember that. But it was impossible not to, sometimes. The period after they had been killed in that accident had been the hardest of Cat's life. How must it have been, then, for Isabelle de Florian, alone in Paris with the war looming in Europe?

Cat turned her full attention back to Monsieur Lapointe.

"People did not assume they would live through the invasion. I think if you consider that—"

"She had lost both her parents already. She had no way of knowing whether or not she would survive." Cat's voice was soft.

"So. We are ready to read out the will?" Monsieur Lapointe glanced at his assistant. "There is nothing that you require, Mademoiselle Jordan? A café perhaps?"

"No. No café." Cat felt a jolt of sympathy for this Isabelle de Florian. Being alone with no family in New York had been tough for Cat. Surely, though, Isabelle de Florian had found love, had a family since then? What had become of her descendants? Or had Isabelle lived alone all her life?

Something seemed to shift in the room as Monsieur Lapointe reached for the will.

He paused for a moment, looked at Cat. "Friendships formed during the war years, even during the inter-war years, were often unusually intense. The previous generation had been . . . lost, so . . . it is impossible for us to understand."

"You don't think they were . . .?" She inhaled. "I mean, do you have any evidence that Isabelle and my grandmother were lovers?"

"Mademoiselle. Really. I am not in a position to say." He raised his eyes to the ceiling.

Instantly, Cat slumped back in her seat. "Sorry," she said. "Irrelevant. It just seems so sad. I mean, the only person she had to leave everything to was my grandmother, even after all this time?"

Monsieur Lapointe tented his fingers on the table. "Mademoiselle. Isabelle de Florian died two months ago. We were notified of her death when we received a copy of her death certificate that was sent anonymously. We have an updated document signed by Isabelle de Florian, along with an approved witness advising us to carry out the instructions as they exist in the will from 1940." Monsieur Lapointe reddened. He seemed agitated again, just as he had seemed when he first brought Cat into his office.

"We have a copy of the death certificate. There is no record of any living descendant of Isabelle de Florian. Furthermore, my junior colleague contacted the *mairie* of the village of Saint-Revel in Provence, where Isabelle died. We have had no response to our further inquiries regarding living relatives for six weeks."

"Well, yes," Cat said. "In that case, yes." An anonymous source? No relatives at all and no response from the mayor in her village? Cat sat back in her chair and fanned her face with a piece of paper.

CHAPTER THREE

Small cars and scooters zipped along the narrow street outside Monsieur Lapointe's office. Pedestrians walked purposefully through the now steel-gray afternoon while Cat stood on the legal building's stone steps, turning the key over in her hand. The idea that it belonged to an apartment in Paris had not settled properly in her head. The idea that the apartment was hers seemed stranger still. Right up to the reading of the will, Cat had been sure that the inheritance was not going to be of any real significance.

She reached into her bag for her phone, but as she worked out the international dialing codes to call Christian, the lights came on in the street. Shop windows sent blades of yellow out onto the sidewalk. The buildings' interiors seemed so inviting that Cat put her phone away and pulled out her camera instead.

Well over an hour—and fifty photographs—later, Cat checked her watch. If she were sensible, she would wait until the next morning to see the apartment. But if she had been sensible, she would have stayed home in New York.

The apartment's mere address had enchanted her from the moment Monsieur Lapointe read it out, even in his prosaic way. rue Blanche. Cat had conjured images of girls in white muslin dresses tripping along the nineteenth-century Parisian streets as soon as the word *blanche* was uttered. She signaled a passing taxi.

In the backseat, she called Christian's mobile. When she was put straight through to voice mail, she pushed away a tiny twinge of relief that she could put off an explanation for a few more hours. She left a brief message and told him all was well.

"Rue Blanche, Mademoiselle?" The taxi driver asked. He pronounced his words with great emphasis, giving the flutters that were already in the pit of Cat's stomach another kick start.

He stopped the taxi after several minutes and turned around. "You are sure?"

Cat burrowed in her bag for the fare. "Oui, oui," she said, her words coming out more abruptly than she had intended. She didn't look at the building until she had paid the driver and gotten out of the cab.

"Oh, my," she breathed, when she looked up. "Oh my goodness, help."

• • •

The building appeared to be different from all the others in the street. An elegant black iron fence ran the entire length of it. The fence was waist-high and spiked. There was a gate right in the middle, in front of the closed front door.

But it was the building that made Cat gasp. It did not have one of Paris's typical old facades with several rows of windows sitting flush to the front. Nor did it appear to be one of Haussmann's elegant grand dames. This building was in a style all its own, its windows curved at their tops, with massive decorative ironwork fanning out over the street above the black front door. The oversized upstairs windows were shuttered. Even the size of the heavy stone bricks was unusual. It was three floors, and the entire building looked as if it had landed from another world.

Would Cat's key open the front door? It was more than obvious that this apartment was not going to be just some ordinary flat.

She couldn't contain her curiosity. She would have to go inside and have a quick peek.

Cat had just closed the gate behind her when she heard a voice.

"Catherine Jordan?"

Even as she turned around to see who had spoken her name, she was struck by the fact that the words were uttered with no French accent at all. In fact, the speaker sounded charmingly British. Slowly, Cat turned around. A tall man stood behind her on the sidewalk He wore a black cashmere coat. A gray scarf framed a feature that any girl would notice: a superb jawline. His brown eyes looked straight at her own and held such a sense of confusion that Cat found herself frowning right back at him.

Who was this? One of the lawyers from the office? Had she left something there? Was she missing a document? He certainly could be a lawyer—he looked like quite the dapper professional. But how on earth did he know her name? Or had he said her name after all? Had jet lag befuddled her brain?

The man was so strikingly handsome that she felt a little frisson, a buzz that almost compelled her toward him. This would not do. The proper thing to do was to say something back.

"Excuse me?" That was ridiculous, but it was the best she could manage.

"The very words I should be saying to you, I think?"

"I thought you said—" Cat placed her hand on the gate.

"I did say your name." He blocked her, stood right in her path. Whether this was intentional or not, it was hardly comforting. He placed his own hand on the gate too, just next to hers.

"Excuse me," she said again.

He didn't move. "You see, unfortunately, I can't let you go."

Cat pulled her hand back.

"You have a key in your hand in which I have a great interest, no matter who you are—or who you say you are."

Cat felt her jaw drop. She looked around the street. There were not many people about now. The sky had turned from pale gray to indigo, and the lights in rue Blanche were scarce. The man reached into the pocket of his coat and pulled out a wallet, not taking his eyes off her for a second. Cat swiftly pulled out her phone and stole a quick glance at it. It was either off or the battery was dead.

He handed her a small white business card. "This should help, I hope."

The mad sense that there was some sort of tension—some . . . something in the air between herself and this stranger—persisted. Did he sense it too? Oh, how awkward and ridiculous! Cat reached out and took the card. She would pretend to be businesslike. That was what she would do. "Loic Archer," she read aloud. "Mas d'Amiel, a vineyard. You're the proprietor? I'm sorry, but is this supposed to mean something to me?"

"Keep reading, Mademoiselle Jordan."

"Cat. It's Cat." She didn't look up.

"Cat."

In spite of the entire situation, she felt a smile coming on.

"The fine print. Here." He reached out toward her fingers and placed his own over hers, turning the card over, gently.

Cat took a step backward.

"Saint-Revel, Cat. Does that mean anything to you?"

Cat stared at the name of the village. Monsieur Lapointe said he had contacted the mayor about living relatives but had no response.

"Isabelle de Florian was my grandmother, Cat."

"Impossible." No! That was ridiculous. This was all surreal.

Loic reached into his wallet again and produced his driver's license. "Anything else you'd like to see? Birthmarks? The scar on my left knee from when I fell into a river when I was ten? Or would you prefer my grandmother's pension card?"

Cat passed back the license.

"How about this?" He put a hand into his coat pocket and pulled out a photograph. It was of him with an old woman whose gray hair was swept into a soft bun and whose brown eyes were a mirror image of his own. There were vineyards behind them, the vines heavy with fat purple grapes that looked ready to pick.

"Yes?" Cat asked. It would hardly do to admit that she wouldn't know a photo of Isabelle de Florian if she fell over such a thing.

"Yes."

Cat glanced up and down the street. There was no one in sight. Not a soul.

"Could we go somewhere and talk, Cat?" He seemed to struggle for a moment. "You can choose where we go, if it makes you feel better."

Cat sighed. If this Loic Archer was Isabelle's grandson, then none of this made any sense. How could Isabelle have a grandson who didn't inherit anything? What must Loic think of her, if he was telling the truth? How on earth was she supposed to explain her relationship to Isabelle? She wondered fleetingly whether he could be a con artist—but if so, how had he gotten her name? No, she needed to hear him out.

"There's a good bar just down the street," he said.

Cat nodded. He stood aside for her to pass.

"This way." Loic stopped outside a modern bistro, all stainless steel. A couple of tables were free near the windows, and the bar area looked busy. Soft strains of jazz drifted out into the evening. He held the door open and waited for her to enter first.

"Can I get you a glass of wine?"

She probably looked a wreck. Jet-lagged, stultified after hours of lawyer's meetings, she was hardly in the best state to be going out for a drink with a devastatingly handsome French man who had a mysterious British accent.

He reappeared quickly with a platter of cheeses and a baguette.

"Thanks." Well, if he was a con artist, at least he was a thoughtful one.

"You look exhausted."

The wine and cheese were fortifying, and to his credit, Loic stayed quiet while she nibbled at the baguette.

When he finally spoke, his voice was gentler. "I only heard about this . . . situation this morning." He seemed to be struggling with what to say. "I came straight up to Paris. I just finished with Monsieur Lapointe."

Cat watched him.

"Sorry if I frightened you."

"The thing is, Monsieur Lapointe said that he had written to Isabelle's village six weeks ago, but he had heard nothing back. He said that there were no living descendants." Cat toyed with her glass.

"He did write to the mairie—the mayor's office—and they forwarded his letter to my mother. But I was away, in Italy, and the letter just asked us to contact Monsieur Lapointe in Paris over a legal matter to do with my grandmother. My mother was—grieving, of course, for my grandmother—emotional, understandably. She didn't feel up to dealing with legal letters and lawyers, and she had no idea why they would be writing to her. So she waited until I arrived home and asked me to deal with it. She didn't want to bother me while I was away. This is typical of her, I'm afraid. Sort of considerate to the point that she can sometimes end up in a mess."

"It's terrible timing, though, for your mother, if what you're telling me is true."

"So it seems."

"So, you've been in Italy?" Cat asked, unsure what to say.

"Yes. I love opera."

"Oh?" So, perhaps not such a hardheaded businessman, then.

"You don't like it?"

"I . . . really couldn't say."

"I've been in Milan and then Lake Como."

"Oh." She needed to steer the conversation back to the will. Loic seemed to be watching her now. Was he sizing her up? Cat busied herself with another slice of baguette.

"You've never been there?"

"I confess, I haven't."

"The Lakes are a soothing place to mourn. And opera? Italian opera—well, you know, Cat, sometimes I think it explains our humanity better than anything else on this earth."

Cat put her glass down. The wine had gone to her head.

"I mean, think about it. We strive so hard to be rational, confident, thinking human beings, but at the end of the day, I wonder whether that's the last thing any of us are—especially when it comes to relationships. You know, opera captures the magic that exists between some people."

"Do you talk to every stranger like this?" Cat laughed.

"Sorry. It's the effects of Italy, and . . ." He looked away.

What a curious mixture he was: he may have a British accent, but he seemed so European in every other way. There was one question Cat had to ask. "Tell me. Why do you have a British accent?"

"My father was from the UK. He came down to Provence in his twenties, fell in love with my mother. Never went home."

He poured another glass of wine for them both.

Cat stopped herself from putting her hand out to cover the glass.

"And so your mother is obviously—"

"Isabelle's daughter. Yes, Cat." He spoke softly.

"You won't like my next question."

"Why my grandmother left an apartment in Paris that none of us knew existed to an American girl, a stranger to us all? I assumed you were a fraud. Or an idiot. Someone who likes paying inheritance tax."

"Oh, dear." The words came out almost as a groan.

Loic rested his head in his hands for a moment. Then he looked up at her. "Why don't you tell me a bit about yourself? Maybe we can figure this out."

"Presumably, you weren't ever supposed to find out about me." Cat attempted a smile, and she was relieved to see that he did smile back.

A dimple appeared to the right of his lips. "Timing," he said.

"So it seems."

He seemed genuine. His story made sense. But what was her role in this? Was she now out of the picture entirely? Presumably, if Monsieur Lapointe had sent Loic to the apartment, he was also convinced that his mother was the heir to the estate.

"I don't know any more about your grandmother's will than you do, and I'm as baffled by this as you," Cat said. "The first I heard of the inheritance, and of Isabelle de Florian, was two days ago when I received a letter from the lawyer and the key to the apartment."

Loic stayed quiet.

"All I know now is that your grandmother Isabelle formed a close . . . friendship with my grandmother Virginia Brooke, when they were both young. So close, in fact, that Isabelle left her apartment in Paris to Virginia. In 1940! Virginia was on some sort of grand European tour of her own. She must have stayed in Paris with Isabelle. You know, the strange thing is that I had heard about Virginia's escapades, but I had never heard of Isabelle de Florian. If they were such close friends, why had my grandmother never mentioned Isabelle to my mother? I've always gotten the impression she was pretty . . . wild—if you can use that term for that era—but now it seems she was a complete enigma as well."

"Isabelle was clearly insane, too." His eyes danced as he spoke the words.

"So what now?" Cat asked.

Loic sat back in his seat and folded his arms. "I'll walk you back to your hotel. But I'll be in the lobby at eight a.m. tomorrow, and we'll go and look at this apartment together. I need to absorb this tonight, before I go and see it. Before *we* go and see it together, Cat."

"I'll talk to Monsieur Lapointe," she said.

The walk back to the hotel felt awkward. People strolled past, so many of them couples, arm in arm, most likely off to a wonderful dinner in the most romantic city in the world.

Loic was quiet.

Cat stole a look up at him, but he was staring straight ahead, marching along next to her. A small frown line had appeared between his eyes, and his hands were tucked inside his pockets. His mouth was set, firm. Oh, what was she doing, studying a man's face? A man she hardly knew? The wine, the wine. She would have to go out and find some proper food for dinner after he dropped her off.

Of course, it was just the photographer in her studying Loic's beautiful face. It was what she did—she looked at people, at things too, in ways that helped her see what was truly inside. But still. Wine and cheese and handsome French men were not the best combination for a girl on her first night in Paris, especially not for a girl who had a lovely man back at home. Christian. What would he be doing now?

This should all be sorted out fast. It was all just a big mistake. The apartment belonged to Loic and his family. Then she would head home, back to her life. This business in Paris was the last thing she needed right now, wasn't it?

CHAPTER FOUR

Cat slipped on the pair of tiny diamond earrings that Christian had bought her the previous summer in the Hamptons. The morning sky outside was pink through the old panes of the hotel window. Bare trees were silhouetted in the street.

Cat surveyed her outfits. They were all laid out on the bed. She had dashed out earlier in an old pair of jeans and her favorite old sweater to buy a croissant and had called Monsieur Lapointe's office on the off chance someone would be there early, but there was no answer, of course.

Why was it so hard to choose what to wear? Cat busied herself matching shirts with skirts, taking them away, then lining sweaters up with pants, fake pearls, even a hat.

Nothing seemed to work. Clearly, she could not stand about in her camisole and undies for too much longer. Loic Archer would be in the lobby in a few minutes.

Cat wiped a hand over her tired eyes. She had lain awake half the night. In the end, surely the most sensible decision was to insist on giving the inheritance right back to Loic if he was indeed who he claimed to be. After all, the whole thing had seemed unreal from the start.

The phone in the room rang, and Cat reached across to pick it up. The receptionist announced that her guests were waiting for her in the lobby. Guests? What guests?

Cat grabbed a 1930s silk blouse. It was in perfect condition, and it went well with her flared 1940s trousers. That would do. She grabbed her coat, slapped on some lip gloss, brushed her hair again, and dashed out to the corridor.

Cat paused at the foot of the stairs and frowned. A small party was waiting in the lobby. Monsieur Lapointe was in the thick of it, immaculate in a gray three-piece suit with a pink handkerchief today.

His assistant appeared to be attempting to flirt with Loic.

Loic stood a head above them both. It was hard to read the look on his face, but he caught Cat's eye as soon as she came into the room.

"Ah, Mademoiselle Jordan!" Monsieur Lapointe bustled over to meet Cat.

Loic, who was close behind, leaned down and kissed her on the cheek.

Cat felt herself flush. Still reeling from jet lag, she couldn't help but wonder whether she looked like a train wreck in front of both these dashing French men—not to mention Monsieur's immaculate assistant, who looked as if she had just arrived from a beauty parlor.

"Monsieur Archer has filled me in," Monsieur Lapointe said. "It is all very irregular. Although. This is France."

"Yes." Loic raised a brow. "This is France."

"I tried to call you, Mademoiselle Jordan, several times, yesterday in the afternoon!" Monsieur threw his hands in the air.

"Oh, I'm sorry. My phone was dead. I tried to call you this morning, too."

Monsieur Lapointe looked like a balloon that was deflating fast. "This is a very odd situation. I would never normally, you understand, appear like this in your hotel, Mademoiselle. But Monsieur Archer, he rang me again and . . . we need to come to some sort of arrangement. You will come back to my office now. We will talk."

"Thank you," Loic said. He put a hand on Monsieur Lapointe's back and started to move toward the hotel door. When Loic got there, he held the door open for everyone.

The legal assistant slipped out first, throwing a charming smile up at Loic as she did so.

"Sorry about this," Loic muttered to Cat.

"Look," Cat said to Monsieur Lapointe on the pavement. "It's no one's fault, Monsieur Lapointe. We'll try and sort things out. But at the end of the day, I think that the right thing to do is for me just to give—" She glanced at Loic.

He shook his head.

Cat shot him a look back, but he averted his gaze.

"Yes, yes, is a confusing business. I can help you sort it. We will do that," Monsieur Lapointe said. Then he appeared to gather himself together. "You will come with me now, Monsieur?"

Loic reached out and shook Monsieur Lapointe's hand. "Cat and I would like to go and see the apartment first."

"Oh, no. You must come with me first. We need to discuss the formalities."

Cat had to force herself not to groan.

Loic chuckled softly beside her. "Yes. I'm aware that there will be plenty of those to be had. But, for now, I want to see this apartment for myself. And I think Cat has a right to come along too."

There was a silence as Monsieur weighed this. It seemed clear that Loic was not going to budge. "You will get in touch as soon as possible, please. You mother will be expected to accept her inheritance. That is the law. It will only go to Mademoiselle Jordan if she refuses completely. And . . ." He was muttering now. "I must do some more verifications, Monsieur Archer. I mean, I am sure this is all in order, but—"

Loic patted the older man on the shoulder. "We'll be in touch very soon."

Finally, Monsieur Lapointe nodded at them both and led his assistant away.

"Well," Loic said, turning to Cat. "Now we go and find out what the hell my grandmother has been playing at."

In spite of herself, Cat smiled. She was more than keen to see this apartment belonging to her grandmother's mysterious friend. It was unlikely anything much would be there, of course. It would be extraordinary indeed if anything were left from the 1930s. But it would be fascinating to walk in the rooms where, perhaps, her grandmother and Isabelle had once walked, to see the views they had gazed at out on the street, to have some sense of the lives they had lived here in Paris. The Jazz Age and Paris. What a heady mix.

As Cat and Loic wound their way past the Eglise de la Sainte-Trinité into the ninth arrondissement and toward rue Blanche, Cat couldn't help sensing a gradual shift in the air. She slowed down as they stepped out of the square in front of the church and into the narrow street where Isabelle had lived. Something turned in her stomach as they passed a school for girls. The building was imposing, and the date July 1881 was carved into the front wall. Had Isabelle de Florian swung her schoolbag down the street to this very school every day?

A few doors down, they passed a smart restaurant. Rue Blanche was narrow here but seemed to widen farther up, beyond the apartment. It was as if this part of the street was an enclave all of its own. The restaurant looked a little out of place with its upmarket planter boxes out on the sidewalk. Its bright red front door was freshly painted, and its windows gleamed.

Next, an old theater. This seemed to fit in better.

"There used to be plenty of theaters in this neighborhood. Racy ones. And nightclubs. It was all quite seedy, Cat. We're not far from the Moulin Rouge."

Below the theater was a run-down café, then beyond it a long spiked fence protecting what looked like a private square with a garden in front of an elegant house.

"Paris is full of contrasts, though," Cat murmured, itching to take out her camera. But they had nearly reached Isabelle's building.

"Ready?" Loic asked as they stopped outside the gate.

Cat had the key in her hand. "I am. Are you?"

"I'm fine, Cat."

Cat pushed the heavy oak door open and at once was aware of the sound her heels made on the hard marble floor inside. There was a stairway decorated with a gilt bannister off to the right of the high-ceilinged main lobby. In front of them there was a lift with brass buttons.

Cat stood beside Loic and waited for the elevator to descend. The apartment, Monsieur Lapointe had told her, was number five on the third floor.

The elevator, like so many old European lifts, was not in any hurry to convey them anywhere. It stopped for no reason on the second level. Cat held the old doors open for a moment and peered out on to the landing. There was another marble floor, this one with four solid-looking doors off it.

Loic pressed the button again. The doors closed, and . . . nothing. The elevator was not going to move. It was hard to know what must be going through his mind right now. There were shadows around his eyes this morning that had not been there last night.

"Okay, Cat," he said. "We'll use the stairs."

The top floor was a mirror image of the one below, with four identical doors—two facing the rear of the building, two facing the front. Apartment 5 faced the front of the building, looking over the street. Cat pulled the key out of her handbag and turned to face Loic.

"Would you like to open it?"

His pause was too long.

"Just coming to terms with it, Cat."

"Oh, I've been thinking. There must be another will. You might just have to look through your grandmother's things. Honestly, we'll sort it out." The key felt warm in Cat's hand.

"No. It's not that. Cat, if you had watched someone struggle financially all her life and yet she had this . . . you know what? I need to take a walk."

"Loic—" she said. But he was halfway down the stairs.

Cat stood and waited until she was certain that Loic was not coming back.

She was just raising the key to the apartment's front door when her phone began to ring. She stopped, key poised. Perhaps it was Loic. She had given him her number when they had parted ways the evening before. Now, perhaps he had changed his mind, decided that he should be there after all when Cat opened the door to what should be part of his family's legacy.

But it was Christian. Christian. A comforting thought.

"Honey." He sounded excited.

"Yes?"

"You'll never guess where I am!"

"I probably won't."

"London."

Cat almost dropped the key. "London?"

"Yes."

"Christian—"

"Thought I may as well come over for some meetings the bank wanted me to attend. I'll be in Paris tomorrow night. Spend the weekend with you."

"Oh! Oh, that's fantastic." Cat began pacing up and down the corridor. He was coming to Paris, too. Excellent. Well, that was a good thing, wasn't it? "Right, excellent."

"Send me an email to let me know where you're staying," he said. "I should be there about seven."

"Christian, I didn't get a chance to tell you in New York, with your parents' anniversary and everything. It was sudden, and I . . . I just . . . I'm actually in Paris because of a family thing. It's complicated. Do you really want . . . I mean, it's a bit confusing, not really your sort of thing . . ." She stopped outside the apartment door again. Should she go inside without Loic?

"So you're doing that as well as your work, honey?"

"Well, theoretically, I suppose I am." Cat made a face. She had taken hundreds of photographs yesterday. She could show them to her boss. Not that he would care, but still, technically . . .

"See you tomorrow, then. Can't wait to see Paris with you," he said.

"I'll be excited to see you, too."

She hung up. It would be wonderful to have Christian here. Of course it would. She should have told him why she was here in the first place. He would have understood. She shouldn't underestimate him. Of course he would take her strange family business in stride. Christian took everything in stride. Yes, his coming would be a good thing. But she couldn't think any more about that now. Cat took a deep breath and then put her key in the lock.

"Bonjour!" Cat jumped at the sound of a woman's voice. She turned to see a woman who seemed hardly half Cat's own height standing across the hallway. The woman was eyeing Cat up and down very quickly. "Vous entrez la?" Was she going in there?

"Oh! Oui, oui. Pardon, my French is not good . . ."

"Non, non, non, non, non!" The woman, who wore a maroon skirt and coordinated blouse, eyed Cat again. In the space of a second, she seemed to change her mind and change tactics.

Now, something approaching approval passed across her face. "Américaine?"

"Er, oui."

"Well." With great care, the woman shut the apartment door and came out into the corridor. "You 'ave a key for this one, non?"

"Yes!"

The woman folded her arms. "Zer has been no one in zis apartment since I live here."

"The woman who owned it was very old. She was possibly ill, so—"

"But no one in ze building know who own zis apartment."

"No one knew Mademoiselle de Florian? How long have you lived here, Mademoiselle?"

"I've been here these twelve years," the woman announced. "Never have I seen a person enter zis apartment."

Well then, had Isabelle de Florian been unwell for that entire time? It would hardly have been appropriate to ask Loic about the state of his grandmother's health. After all, she had been ninety-one when she died. So if she hadn't visited for twelve years, then that was hardly unreasonable.

The woman in front of her held her own ground. "I see now. You Américaine, so you never come to Paris. Keep it locked." She shook her head. "So, ze apartment is yours?"

Cat chewed on her lip. "Well . . ."

The woman looked at her, beady-eyed.

"Nice to meet you. I'm Cat Jordan." Cat held out a hand.

"Sandrine." No last name.

"So . . ."

"Your apartment will be full of mice!" This seemed to cause Sandrine great satisfaction. She looked straight up at Cat, triumphant.

"Oh!" Mice? Perhaps. They were the least of her concerns.

"Oui."

Then, the unmistakable sound of the old elevator cranking up to their floor. Loic stepped out into the hallway.

Sandrine locked her eyes on him and didn't take them off. "Zis is your 'usband? *Chic alors!*"

"No! No, no."

But to Cat's complete surprise, Loic threw an arm around her shoulders.

"You know, this is a special time for us. We'll catch up with you, Mademoiselle. Soon. Thanks for dropping by." He was putting on a perfect American accent.

Sandrine seemed to consider this. "You will knock on my door if you need me." She was simpering up at Loic.

"We will." Loic was firm.

"Thank you!" Cat trilled. Her voice sounded tinny and high.

Loic took his arm away from Cat's shoulder as Sandrine melted back through her own front door.

"Best not to get the neighbors involved at this stage," he said.

Cat looked up at him. "Are you sure you're ready to do this? I understand if you aren't."

"It just got to me. That's all."

"Yes . . . I can't begin to imagine. Well, then. Here goes."

Cat tried to turn the key in the lock, but it would not turn an inch.

"Let me have a try."

"Sandrine says it's a long time since it's been used. She's never seen anyone enter the apartment in the twelve years she's lived here."

"I can turn the key, Cat, but the door is jammed shut." Loic leaned his entire body weight into the door, but it was stuck fast. After several attempts, he stopped and leaned against the wall.

Cat pushed at it again. "Makes you wonder whether it's been even longer than twelve years."

"I'm hoping it hasn't been shut up since 1940."

Cat looked at him for a moment, but he was studying the door. Suddenly, she threw her own body weight against it. She felt a searing pain in her shoulder. The door did not budge.

"Martial arts, Cat?"

"Years of living on my own and getting by." Cat felt her face redden.

Loic moved toward her. "So, no live-in man, then?"

"Nope."

She was about to give it another try when he took her arm gently. "Don't hurt yourself."

He shouldered it himself, hard. "It's moving," he said, his voice straining with effort.

"Well, if you say so," she laughed.

Loic raised a brow and looked down at her. "You can't see that clearly this door has budged?"

"Well . . ."

"Okay, then." He tried again. It didn't give.

"You'll have Mademoiselle Neighbor out here in two seconds," Cat giggled.

Loic raised a brow. "Well then, in that case—" He turned and gave an almighty push with the other side of his body. The door sprang open, appearing as light as a soufflé now that it had decided not to be stuck.

Loic held it open. He waved Cat into the apartment.

• • •

Instantly engulfed by dust, damp, and a stench of rot, Cat and Loic both started sneezing. Cat, her eyes closed, sensed Loic striding toward the windows.

"*Merde*," he muttered.

She heard Loic pulling open curtains, then shutters. Finally, there was the sound of a window latch being unclipped. Suddenly, light was flooding in. Even with her eyes closed, Cat could sense its intensity. How long had it been since the place had seen anything like it?

Air swept into the room next, an almost visible swirl of it. Dust spun as if it were furious about the upset of air and light and Cat and Loic arriving all at once. It seemed to fall from the ceiling, bounce off the lights. Cat coughed so hard she thought she might choke. From what she could sense with her grit-filled eyes, Loic was leaning on the open windowsill, half out in the fresh air. Footsteps next: Loic striding around the room, past the spot where Cat stood just inside the entrance.

"Wait there," he said, his voice grim. "I'll open all the windows first."

Every time Cat tried to open her eyes for more than a second or remove her hand from her mouth, she was overcome with thick dust traveling down her windpipe. The first angry dust dance would not abate and was still choking her.

"Sorry." Her voice almost stuck on the words. "I'll be okay in a minute."

"Cat?" There was something in Loic's voice that compelled her to move toward the sound of him. "Can you open your eyes?"

She took a few steps and tried to take some deep breaths, the air still rank with the smell of old grit and God only knew what else.

Loic was by her side, holding her arm. "You're going to have to open your eyes. This is unbelievable."

Cat felt her entire body stirring. She would have to force her eyes open.

With the sort of care she normally reserved for taking a step into the cold sea, Cat opened one eye and then the other. It was all she could do to breathe. She took one step deeper into the room, then another. Shafts of sun bore yellow streams onto . . .

"Oh!" Dust that had grayed into thick velvet with age clung to every surface. Cobwebs spiraled down from the ceiling like ghostly chandeliers, spinning around the real chandeliers that hung suspended from the peeling ceiling.

Between Cat and the floor-to-ceiling curved windows that Loic had opened up was a dining table, set with silver as if guests from a decades-old dinner party were about to reappear, sit down, enjoy dinner, light cigars, chat.

To the left of the vast dining table, a black marble fireplace slept under layers of hideousness that nevertheless could not hide its solid, genteel beauty.

Louis XV chairs sat as if they had been arranged by a servant, ready for their mistress to come home from a day of shopping. Had Isabelle chosen to rest her tired feet on the chaise longue to the right? At one time it wouldn't have had the great rust stain that now ran across its center. At one time, the pink *toile de jouy* would have been immaculate.

A vast cabinet stood against the wall, its wood still gleaming in places underneath the grime. It was filled with the sorts of porcelain treasures that people like Cat only drooled over while window-shopping. And yet here it all was, on location, the real thing.

Loic stood next to an Empire chair that was upholstered, under the dust, in an exquisite Napoleonic pattern of bees.

"You should see this." He led her into the next room through a set of open double doors, their gold gilt still beautiful against cracked white paint.

"Are you okay, Cat?"

There were no words. The apartment was filled with the sorts of treasures that anyone who had even the remotest of interest in the past would die for. Another chaise longue sat in this room, covered in the same tiny pink and green flowers that decorated the pretty wallpaper. The wallpaper peeled in foot-long patches from the walls.

"A lady's private sitting room," Cat whispered.

Loic was silent. He moved across to the open window and stood by the faded green silk curtains, which looked as though they might break into bits at the touch of his hand.

A baby grand piano stood in front of the window next to Loic. There was music still on its stand, open not at the beginning of a piece but at a page somewhere in the middle.

"Debussy," Cat murmured. There was another fireplace opposite the chaise longue, white marble this time, and another vast web-covered chandelier hung from the ceiling.

"Cat."

"Hmm?"

"Come to the bedroom."

She had to stop herself from laughing; the expression on his face was so serious.

"What more can there be?"

"This." Loic took a step through the next doorway.

For the first time, Cat noticed the sound of his shoes on the parquet floor.

"I'm finding this impossible to conceive," he said, moving into the room. "But come in here."

The only thing to do was stare. The living room and exquisite sitting room—which had apparently lain untouched, waiting patiently while Paris surged on through the forties, fifties, sixties, seventies and beyond—had already wrenched at Cat's heart and caused her imagination to fly into orbit. But the bedroom nearly knocked her down flat.

Loic seemed to be watching her. "Keep looking."

Cat took a few steps closer, toward the impossibly enormous four-poster bed that rested in an almost imperious state near the window, its deep red canopy moth-eaten and hanging in strips. A cluster of pale pink cushions was still perfectly arranged on the cobweb-covered pillows. The room looked as if it belonged to royalty.

Cat put a hand out and touched one of the dust-drifted pillows. There was something more. It was as if the apartment had its own lingering smell, a hint of something that seemed to emerge through the dust. It was almost as if some old perfume was trying to reach its ancient and gnarled fingers out to remind her—to remind them both, perhaps—that someone had once lived in these rooms. That, once, they had been loved.

Once, someone had filled this apartment with the most beautiful of things, with the most stunning collection of objects that Cat had ever seen in her life.

"Cat, turn around." Loic's voice was soft.

She could sense him watching her and she knew that what she was staring at now had been more precious to someone than the sum of everything else in the apartment put together.

It was breathtaking.

A portrait of a young woman overlooked the bed. It looked as though she had swept her hair up hastily into a loose arrangement that would fall in cascades down her elegant back if she pulled out even a single pin. Her head was turned to the side. One hand rested on her décolletage, looking almost as if it were holding up her low-cut pink dress, which was frothed with seamy silken brushstrokes not so much to cover her body as to show off its obvious charms. Her other hand hung loose in front of her and was covered with rings.

"Loic . . ."

Loic looked down at the street. "My grandmother came down to the south of France with nothing. She . . . cleaned houses for a living. My mother lost opportunities because there was never any money. Forgive me if I'm a little . . ."

Cat moved toward him. "This belongs to your family. I won't take it. You know I can't take it. Can't you just accept it?" She put out a hand, her fingers reaching of their own accord for the nearest thing to lean on.

"Oh!" Her hand had landed on a dressing table, a beautiful dark wooden affair with an oval mirror covered with antique scent bottles of all shapes and sizes, their silver tops blackened and their glass fogged with age. A set of silver brushes sat alongside them. They were all laid out on a square of gossamer-fine linen edged with lace. Cat shuddered.

Loic still did not move. "It wasn't left to us. I noticed you like vintage clothes, so . . ."

"I may be in my own personal heaven here, Loic, but I'm not a criminal."

"Yes, but here's the material point. How the hell is my mother going to cope with the fact that my grandmother had all this and kept it from her daughter? That's all that concerns me right now, Cat."

"I'll leave you alone for a moment." Cat took another long look at the painting. It was impossible to read the expression on the woman's face.

Cat slipped out of the bedroom. Next to it was a dressing room, as wide as any of the other rooms in the apartment. It didn't seem right to open up any of the elegant armoires that lined the wall. There was an oval mirror in the corner farthest from the window. In spite of the dust, Cat could still see a faded reflection of her astounded self in the glass. She looked like a ghost.

Spare sections of walls were lined with white-painted shelving. Floor-to-ceiling shelves were stacked with ancient shoeboxes. Cat forced herself to move through to the next room, a smaller bedroom. Two single beds were covered in spidery apricot silk. A book lay on the small table between them. A French romance. Inexplicably, Cat wanted to reach out, turn down the bed covers, and see if the beds were made. But she knew what the answer would be. There was no need to check.

Cat moved back through the eerie dressing room, the main bedroom, and the pretty sitting room back into the dining room. There was another door at the end of it, and Cat slipped through into what was a small kitchen. An ancient range sat against the far wall, and the kitchen also held some loose wooden benches and an antiquated porcelain sink. At the very back of the apartment was a final door, smaller this time and with no gilt, just plain wood. It opened into a tiny corridor. A small set of painted wooden stairs led up to Cat's left—almost, she thought, like stairs from a doll's house. The contrast with the rest of the apartment was so great she hardly knew what to think.

Cat tested the first step. It seemed to be safe. She climbed the narrow flight, stopping on the small landing at the top. The ceilings were far lower up here in the attic. A narrow corridor led across the top of the building. Dust floated around, like a subdued mirage, as if waiting for her to react. Off the attic were three rooms. One contained a sink, an old wringer, and a set of irons on a shelf by the tiny, murky window—evidently a laundry room.

The next room was furnished simply with a single bed, its ironwork heavy, practical. A cross hung on the wall above it. There was an iron bedstead in the last room, but it had no mattress. The black springs looked menacing. Cat shuddered and went back to the stairs.

She slipped through the kitchen back into the dining room. There, she did a double take. Was she beginning to go mad, or was she looking at a floppy Mickey Mouse leaning against the wall by the sitting-room door? Cat moved over to it and knelt down in the dust. Mickey was propped up next to a teddy bear. And above them was a stuffed ostrich, draped with the sort of elegant scarf that Cat would have rescued in a heartbeat if she'd seen it at the flea market.

Loic appeared in the doorway. "I have to do something."

Cat blew out a breath. "What did you have in mind?"

"The painting seems a good place to start."

Cat watched him. He seemed calm, but she knew this was probably a front.

"Yes?"

"We need to get an expert out to look at it. Now that the apartment is opened. I'm going to ring Gerard Lapointe. That okay with you?"

"Go ahead." Cat nodded.

Loic took out his phone, dialed, and spoke in rapid French to Monsieur Lapointe.

"He'll be here with an art expert within the hour. I just told him about the painting. He'll see the rest of it soon enough."

"The painting is breathtaking." Cat was tentative. He had zoomed in on it the moment he saw it.

"It's more than that, though, Cat." A flicker passed along his cheek.

"Do you know much about art?"

"Enough." He leaned against the doorframe. "Enough to know we can't leave it here. I don't recognize a particular artist's style, but there's something going on here. I don't know. We need to check it out."

"I wonder who she was."

But Loic seemed to be miles away.

Cat gazed around the exquisite dining room. For some reason, she wanted to protect all of it. It was all about to be sorted. Of course it was. Somehow, it seemed awful to disturb it all, sacrilegious, almost. Cat couldn't shake the sense that these ghostly, beautiful rooms were waiting for their proper owner to return.

CHAPTER FIVE

"Monsieur Pascale Colbert." Monsieur Lapointe stood outside the door with a man wearing red-framed glasses, corduroy trousers, and a deep green vest. A yellow silk tie was arranged in perfect symmetry at the collar of his wide-sleeved shirt. "Monsieur Colbert is a specialist in the Belle Époque. He consults for the Musée d'Orsay and the Orangerie."

"Bonjour Mademoiselle, Monsieur," Monsieur Colbert said, holding out a pale, manicured hand.

"Bonjour." Cat took his hand.

Loic was behind her. He had one hand resting on the apartment's front door handle and he stood close to Cat. "How much is this going to cost?"

"I charge one hundred euros per hour."

"I'll pay."

Cat was about to open her mouth, but Monsieur Lapointe spoke first. "Oui, oui. These are details that Monsieur Colbert is used to dealing with. It is the same all the time . . all the time."

"I'm glad we've got that settled." Loic stayed where he was.

"Monsieur, there is something you ought to know about this particular apartment," Cat began.

"There is something wrong with the apartment?" Monsieur Lapointe asked.

"Well . . ."

"You may as well come on in." Loic opened the door.

Pascale Colbert slipped past Loic and then stopped as though frozen. He covered his eyes with his hands and then pulled them away again, gazing around the room as if in a trance, his eyes wandering slowly over every single thing.

Monsieur Lapointe was right behind him. "*Mon Dieu*!" he said. "This is disaster!"

"I cannot believe what I am seeing!" Pascale Colbert said. "No one has been here since—"

"Nineteen forty," Loic supplied. "Apparently."

Pascale Colbert turned to him. "And you and Mademoiselle Jordan own this?"

"Mademoiselle Jordan owns it," Loic said.

"It belongs to Monsieur . . oh . . . Loic's family," Cat spoke hurriedly. "Would you like to see the painting, Monsieur Colbert?"

"Pascale," he muttered, coming to a sudden halt at Mickey Mouse.

It took several minutes to get him out of the first room. Wonder emanated from Pascale like heat off molten rock. When they entered the bedroom, he went straight to the painting and removed his red glasses. For what seemed like an age, he did not move.

"Mon Dieu."

"Oui," Monsieur Lapointe said, sounding professional again now.

"I will have to do the necessary verifications." Pascale Colbert addressed Monsieur Lapointe.

"Of course." Monsieur Lapointe had a handkerchief in his hand and was wiping his brow.

Suddenly, Pascale sat down, hard, upon the old bed. Dust flew up all around him.

"Pardon!" he said, standing up again. "But, mon Dieu!" He walked right up to the painting again, running a hand over his head. "This sort of thing happens once in a hundred years."

Cat sensed Loic shifting beside her.

Pascale pulled out his mobile phone. "We cannot leave it here. This painting has to go straight to the Musée d'Orsay."

There was a silence.

"I cannot say any more." Pascale held out his card. "I will return in the morning. I will bring a team to look over the entire apartment. Meanwhile, the Musée d'Orsay will be here within the half hour, to pick the painting up. It will be handled with the utmost care. We will arrange all the necessary forms for you to sign and we will arrange immediate insurance. That is, until we are certain . . . I do not wish to say anything more now. I cannot."

"Monsieur Colbert is the best expert on the Belle Époque in Paris," Monsieur Lapointe said. "You have my word."

Cat caught Loic's gaze. He raised an eyebrow.

"Okay, then," Cat said.

Pascale moved toward the beautiful dressing table in the corner by the window and looked at the delicate scent bottles, the silver brushes. "If you would mind not touching anything, I would appreciate this. Until tomorrow," he said.

Pascale peered at the painting again and mumbled to himself in low French.

Monsieur Lapointe took Cat by the arm. "Have you had any indication that Monsieur Archer's mother will claim her inheritance?" he whispered, once they were in the next room.

"I can't possibly keep all of this," Cat said.

"I have carried out even more checks, although I was certain before, of course. He is definitely the grandson. Do not say anything without thought."

"I can't see why they would ever refuse such a thing," Cat said.

"Nevertheless, if they do, it will all be yours. But I do agree with you, Mademoiselle, it would be odd if Mademoiselle Archer were to refuse it. If I have caused a false alarm for you, Mademoiselle Jordan, please forgive me. I am sorry to have put you to so much trouble."

The apartment felt stranger still once the painting had been safely removed to the Musée d'Orsay in a small white van with Monsieur Pascale, looking most serious, in the back. After a long and protracted protest, Loic had managed to convince Monsieur Lapointe to return to his office, with reassurances that they would talk very soon.

Cat gazed at the darker patch on the pretty wallpaper where the painting had hung. The naked space was almost an accusation of sorts. Loic came and stood behind Cat.

"We had to get it looked at," he said.

Cat turned to face him. "I feel out of place here, Loic. I'm intruding. It's your family's legacy. I shouldn't be going through your grandmother's things."

"Aren't you interested in the connection between your grandmother and Isabelle, Cat?"

Yes, she was. Wildly. But the last thing she wanted to do was get in the way.

"You'll have to stay here until we sort things out. You're part of this, too. You can't just go now. I insist."

Cat floundered for words. "I am interested. I am fascinated. I just . . . would you mind if I did help with the sorting of the apartment? I'd love to better understand the connection."

Loic chuckled. "You don't have to ask, Cat. I'll be here tomorrow."

Cat nodded. "So. We'll meet with this team in the morning and help them get to the bottom of this."

"Exactly," Loic said.

• • •

The young woman Monsieur Pascale Colbert had sent to examine the apartment was already standing outside the building in rue Blanche the next morning when Cat arrived at nine o'clock. She wore a red scarf and a smart black coat, and a beret perched on top of her dark curls.

She held out a black-gloved hand. "Bonjour. Anouk Tailler. I will be looking at your apartment today. *Enchantée.*" Anouk handed Cat her business card.

Cat shook Anouk's hand just as Loic appeared next to them. It was hard to ignore the admiration in Anouk's eyes as she took him in.

Anouk's face turned pale when she entered the apartment. "I have the goose bumps."

Even without the magnificent painting—which was now being safely analyzed at the Musée d'Orsay—the ghostly atmosphere of the rooms struck Cat with the same force it had as the day before. It was impossible to know where to start. After several minutes spent wandering around—Anouk almost speechless with wonder as she surveyed the rooms—Cat decided it was time to make a start.

"How about we start in the bedroom, Anouk?" she asked. The day before, she had noticed bundles of papers bound with ribbon and stacked on the floor. There were obviously far more beautiful items in the apartment to study, but Cat was lured to the wrapped yellow papers more than anything else. They would tell her something. They had to.

But Anouk shook her head. "I am going to do this logically, starting from the entrance."

"Would you mind if I had a look through some of the papers in the bedroom?" Cat sensed Loic watching her.

"Of course it would be okay. I will work as I always do." Anouk opened the black suitcase at her feet and pulled out a pair of white gloves and a laptop. "Mademoiselle, we are also looking at the possibility that you had an important late nineteenth-century work in here yesterday. So, please, do not take any papers out of the apartment, even if they do not seem relevant to art."

"Do you know anything about that?"

"Do not remove anything, that is all. I can tell you, they are working around the clock."

Cat turned and walked toward the bedroom. She almost jumped when she sensed Loic right behind her.

"Mind if I work with you?" he asked.

"You seem very calm."

"Oh, as soon as the windfall hits, I'll be chasing after you."

Cat chuckled. She turned to the pile of papers on the shelves against the wall. "Shall we, then?"

"After you."

CHAPTER SIX

It felt almost sacrilegious to touch the wrinkled yellowing papers. Someone had tied ribbons around each pile, but unlike the smooth silk that Monsieur Lapointe had used to wrap his parcel to New York, this ribbon was frayed and stained by the accumulation of damp or perhaps years of reading and rereading. And the reason it seemed intrusive to read the papers was because the papers were letters.

Tentatively, and still with a sense that this was not right, Cat lifted the top letter from its resting place. Even though the paper was dreadfully thin, the handwriting was firm—a man's writing.

"Would you like me to translate them for you aloud, Cat?" Loic asked.

Anouk appeared at the door. "Monsieur, Mademoiselle. I have a problem. I am told this apartment was left in 1940. But, you know, everything I have seen is from fifty years before then."

Cat looked at Loic. Silently, she hoped Anouk wouldn't ask him if he knew why.

"In fact," Anouk went on, "I think that most of the things in here look as if they were from the period between 1890 and 1900. It looks as though it was originally furnished then. But I found a newspaper from June 1940, and I did a quick glance over the kitchen. It was probably altered during the 1930s. But I have to wonder about all the exotic gifts, the furnishings. There were apartments, you know, set up for women, certain women who—"

"What are you saying?" Loic sounded sharp.

Anouk pressed her bright red lips together. "Monsieur Archer, given what I have seen . . . well. It is quite clear to me that we are dealing with an apartment that belonged to a *demimondaine*, a courtesan. You know what I am saying."

Cat's mind spiraled. What did this mean for her grandmother? Had Virginia worked in the house too? She sat back down on the floor with a thump.

Anouk gestured around the bedroom with a sweep of her arm. "The decorations, the seating, the chaise longues, the paintings: everything in this apartment, to me, looks like a gift. Now, the ostentation is not atypical of the fin de siècle in Paris, the Belle Époque. But I think we have something more going on here. Demimondaines were at center stage during the Belle Époque. It was they, not the demure upper-class girls, who were the true representatives of the new *beau monde*."

Loic shook his head. "I can't believe this."

"Monsieur, your grandmother's apartment appears to me to be a perfect and complete representation of the life of a demimondaine. Even without the portrait, the apartment is extraordinary, to say the least. These courtesans were always women from the lower classes who masqueraded as members of high society. They went to the theater, went shopping, sat for portraits, visited couturiers. Some of these courtesans were even known to the public by name."

"So she was infamous," Loic said.

"Of course, prostitution then, as it is now, was a sensitive subject. The courtesan would never be invited into certain homes, for example. And though she pretended to be honest, in reality, everything about the courtesan was make-believe. She was an illusion, an artificial creation of her own making."

"It makes no sense," Loic growled. "My grandmother Isabelle wasn't born until 1919."

"The past generations never do make sense, Monsieur Archer." Anouk moved back toward the bedroom door. "I would say we are talking about someone further back, perhaps another of your ancestors. Whoever she was, she was not a common prostitute, Monsieur."

"Handy to know," Loic muttered.

"What she is saying—" Monsieur Pascale Colbert appeared in the bedroom door. He had on a different pair of glasses today, absinthe green. "What Anouk is telling you is that 'la demimondaine' only would have attended to very . . . wealthy men. Her primary attribute was beauty, her role was to seduce. The theater was growing in significance at the turn of the century, and the demimondaine took advantage of that theatricality."

"Excellent."

Pascale Colbert took a turn around the room. "One of the demimondaine's lovers would have bought this apartment, Monsieur. Other wealthy gentlemen clients would have bought her the exotic gifts—the stuffed ostrich from Africa, for instance. Typically ostentatious and unique. This would account for the vast collection of glass bottles of couture perfume, all her clothes, the paintings, the glassware. Have you looked through the clothes, Mademoiselle Catherine?" Pascale eyed Cat's vintage outfit.

"No, I haven't, honestly. None of it's mine."

"Yes, it is," Loic muttered.

Anouk cleared her throat. "The painting, Pascale?"

Pascale looked triumphant. "We think that the subject was the owner of this apartment, and"—he turned to Loic—"your grandmother Isabelle de Florian's grandmother. If that is the case, Monsieur Archer, your ancestor was one of the most famous members of the demimonde. She was, as Anouk suspected, both an actress and a courtesan. Her name was Marthe de Florian."

"Your grandmother never mentioned her?" Anouk turned to Loic.

Cat closed her eyes.

"My grandmother never talked about the past. I know her parents died when she was young. She'd clam up about anything else. We only have one photograph of her in her youth, and that was taken when she was in her twenties. Sorry, but I can't believe this."

"Well, Monsieur," Pascale went on, "we have discovered that Marthe de Florian's real name was Mathilde Heloise Beaugiron. Mathilde was a seamstress before she, well, changed her profession, and her name. She reinvented herself completely. Mademoiselle Beaugiron no longer existed, and the name died out. She never referred to it or went by anything other than de Florian again. She had two sons, one of whom died young. The other, Monsieur Archer, was your grandmother's father."

Cat chewed on her lip.

"But there is more," Pascale said. "Brace yourself, *mes amis*."

"My great-grandfather was an ax murderer?"

Pascale Colbert shot Loic a look. "Monsieur. We think that Marthe de Florian's portrait was painted by none other than Giovanni Boldini."

"Who?" Loic asked.

"Exactly," Pascale nodded. "Boldini is not seen as an important artist in history. He is not world famous. He has been a little—how do you put it—disregarded?"

"So this is exciting because?" Loic spoke quietly.

"For a long time, he was only viewed as the recorder of an era that disappeared in 1914, an era that was quaint, superficial, and best left in the past. Moreover, Boldini's work was regarded in much the same way. Superficial. But there was more to him than that.

"We know that Boldini worked fast. His wife wrote in her journals that he embraced the period of change in the early twentieth century. He was known as the master of swish."

"Really?" Cat asked. The master of swish. Well. There was a certain amount of . . . swish about the painting.

"Oui. Boldini was on good terms with John Singer Sargent, but Sargent became far better known than Boldini, especially in the English-speaking world. Sargent did not break the rules, you see. He painted debutantes. His work is refined. But Boldini's work was more edgy, more sensual, and more explicit. He did not express gentility, he expressed Belle Époque Paris."

"So he was a part of it all," Cat said.

"Indeed. Superficiality was his specialty," Pascale said. "He turned his subjects into exotic creatures. You could say that he was associated with the early idea of the femme fatale. He wanted to give the viewer an eyeful."

"Did he just," Loic muttered.

"Boldini's women were a party to their objectification. They were displayed in his dishabille style. Their hair always looked as if it were about to fall down, their gowns seemed as if they were barely held up. But their faces were without mystique; he was not interested in their worries. He denies them this."

"Do you think they denied it to themselves?" Cat asked.

Pascale shrugged. "It was all, you could say, stereotyped. He lived in the same world as them. He was commercial, in a time when commerce was replacing the traditions of the landed aristocracy faster than you could blink. His work has often been called kitsch."

"But the painting's so glamorous, don't you think?" Cat asked.

"*Mais oui.* It has been said that he played a role in creating glamour. Think about portraits of Hollywood stars. Think about how they were portrayed in the thirties. The thing about Boldini is that he embraced the new mix between classes. Boldini embraced courtesans and the theater as rising stars. He helped to create the cachet that still exists around them today."

"So this Boldini was one of Marthe's lovers?" Loic's voice sounded dry.

"Boldini did not marry until very late in his life. He had a reputation for being a little . . . risqué with his female subjects. Marthe and Boldini could have been lovers. We have people going through Boldini's wife's writings now. She kept extensive diaries." He paused for a moment, then took a turn around the room. If the Belle Époque was all about theatricality, then Monsieur Pascale Colbert would have fit right in. The thought made Cat smile as he went on. "If this was a Boldini, you would do very well at auction."

"That would be up to Loic," she said.

"No, it damn well wouldn't." Loic almost growled the words.

Pascale held up a hand. "Anouk will continue with her inventory. We will read through the letters and search the entire apartment for any evidence of a connection with Giovanni Boldini, and we will take it from there."

"I'm going out for some fresh air." Loic strode toward the front door.

"Loic!" Cat called after him, but he waved her away.

"It is a lot to think about," Pascale said. He picked up a bundle of letters. "We must, nevertheless, make a start."

Cat sat down next to him. Right then her phone buzzed. It was a text.

Christian was flying out of Heathrow. He would meet her at her hotel this evening.

• • •

At precisely half past five, Anouk came into the bedroom. Pascale and Anouk had not taken an extended lunch; in fact, they had not taken one at all, though Pascale had slipped out for coffee several times. Now, Cat's back and legs were stiff. She had hardly moved all day from one of the dining chairs that had been the quickest to dust. Entranced, she had listened while Pascale read out letter after letter, translating as he did so.

He and Anouk had been right. Marthe de Florian had had countless admirers. Wealthy aristocrats and businessmen, all writing about a theatrical and exotic Paris that had been smashed by the hurricanes that were the First and Second World Wars.

"We will be back on Monday," Anouk said, wrapping herself in her coat. "I can see why Monsieur Loic needed some time to think."

"Yes," Cat sighed. It was hard to know how she would have reacted to such a startling family secret herself. Had he told his mother yet? At least he had the weekend to think about how to break the news to her.

"Given the nature of this investigation," Pascale Colbert said, "I must request that you not move anything over the weekend."

"It's not mine to move." Cat put the letter she had been holding back on a side table. Suddenly, she was aware of traffic noise on the street outside. Christian would already be waiting for her at the hotel.

She let Pascale and Anouk out and walked through the apartment, closing the shutters tight. Cat couldn't help but feel a twinge of envy for those who lived during the Belle Époque. Things had been about to change so dramatically that the world as people knew it at the turn of the nineteenth century would almost have been unrecognizable to those who lived thirty or forty years later.

Was she yearning for the past? The romance of it all, the beauty, the glamour: these would be enticements indeed if one was fortunate enough to have been born in the upper classes. But by all accounts Marthe had been both a victim and a product of her time. Her tale seemed to be that of a curious combination of a woman who was beginning to emerge as a force in her own right while still having to live in a world dominated by men.

Cat locked the apartment door. Halfway down the building's silent stairs, she dialed Loic's mobile. It was no surprise when he did not pick up. Her message became longer than she had planned. She told him about the letters that Pascale had translated, then suggested they talk about the next steps to take. She couldn't help feeling that there were decisions she should not be making. But still. Would she ever find out anything more about the friendship between her grandmother and Isabelle de Florian? One might assume that her grandmother must have met Marthe de Florian, too.

Cat wandered out into the chill Paris evening. How had the street looked when Virginia, Isabelle, and Marthe had walked out this very door?

Not ready to leave Marthe's story behind yet, Cat found herself wandering up through the Pigalle district toward the Moulin Rouge. Had Marthe performed here? Small theaters still dotted the surrounding streets, and a line for the Moulin Rouge was gathering on the pavement outside.

Cat stopped then. Enough of the past. Christian would be waiting for her in the hotel.

• • •

He was sitting in a wing-back chair just inside the hotel lobby, cradling a whiskey and reading the *New York Times*. He looked up just as Cat came through the glass front doors.

"Honey," he said, standing up to kiss her

"I'm so happy to see you. Things have been crazy."

She had attempted to remove as much of the apartment's dust as she could, but it seemed to have seeped through her clothes. "Hold on a minute," she said.

Cat noticed what he was wearing under his coat. It was a dinner suit, with a black bow tie.

"I've checked you into a better hotel."

"I'm fine here! I like it."

"Cat—"

"Did you look at the room? It's just fine."

"I've booked us something much better for the weekend."

"You mean bigger?" Cat asked, but Christian was already walking toward what looked like a town car parked in front of the hotel's entrance. Her suitcase, she noticed, was lined up by the front door. The driver of the fancy car hopped out and was wheeling it toward the pavement.

"Hang on," Cat said, trotting up behind Christian.

But he turned and he just smiled. "Honey," he said. "Let me spoil you. I thought you'd appreciate not having to pack up. I asked the maid to do it all."

"I see," Cat said.

Christian was talking with the driver.

"Wait a minute," she muttered, half to herself. She walked over to the reception desk.

"*Merci,*" Cat said to the girl on duty. "Thank you for everything."

"Merci, Mademoiselle." The girl smiled. "It was a pleasure having you to stay with us."

Cat took a step toward the door, but then she turned back around. "You know what, I'll be back on Monday."

The receptionist checked her computer. "For how long would you like to stay with us?"

Cat looked out at Christian. He was watching the driver load up Cat's luggage. "You know, I'm not exactly sure."

Three minutes later, they were in the elegant black car, cruising toward the Seine.

Cat sat back in the leather seat. She hadn't even looked to see what it was—a BMW, or a Mercedes-Benz, perhaps? How different

Paris felt now that Christian was here. It was amazing how rapidly he had taken charge in a city he professed to hardly know at all.

"How was your flight?"

"Caught up on some work. It was fine." Christian pulled out his iPad. "In fact, I just need to check one thing. A business hasn't responded the way we thought. It won't take more than a second."

Ten minutes later, they swept into the curved entrance of their new hotel. Cat had to wake herself from her thoughts about Marthe de Florian. She took in the flags at the grand entrance, the uniformed porter who opened the car door. The hotel overlooked the Seine and was not far from the Louvre.

"Thanks," Christian said, handing both the porter and the driver a wad of euros. He swept into the lobby, one hand on the small of Cat's back. "Reservation under Carter. New York."

"Bonsoir," Cat added, to the receptionist behind the desk. It was important, in France, to say hello.

"Bonsoir, Mademoiselle, Monsieur," the receptionist said. He was as smooth as the staff at Cat's previous hotel had been friendly. Everything was different—it was worlds apart from her little hotel near the opera house. It probably didn't matter if she didn't observe the social niceties that she had come to love about France. The staff was trying to impress her, not the other way around.

"My personal assistant booked your best suite," Christian said, leaning forward so he could see the receptionist's computer screen.

"Oui, Monsieur."

"Oh, and send a bottle of champagne up to the room. On ice," he added, taking the room keys and handing one to Cat.

"I don't know if they drink champagne cold in this damned country," Christian said, sotto voce, to Cat. "You can never be sure."

"Christian," Cat laughed. "France is the only country that makes champagne, you know."

"Still."

They rose in the gilded elevator to the second-to-top floor and found their room.

"Now, honey, this'll be a surprise."

"Oh my goodness!" Cat wandered through the exquisite sitting room to the window. "The Eiffel Tower and bridges are all lit up. Look at the palaces along the edge of the river!"

Christian came up behind her and wrapped his arms around her waist. "See those little boats down there?"

Cat nodded. She gazed at the riverboats, decorated with lights that seemed to float above them, as if they were miniature cruise ships.

"Well, I've booked one, the whole thing. For a candlelit dinner. Just us."

"Just us?" For a mad moment, Cat almost felt like Marthe de Florian. Is this what the men in her life had done for her? How many cruises down the Seine had she been on in her time? Cat shook the thought away. "You didn't have to do that."

He turned her around and cupped her face in his hands. "Yes. Yes, I did. Because you are the most special thing in my life, and I need to show that to you, Cat."

"Well, then." Cat hugged him. "What can a girl say?"

Having examined every detail of the luxurious room—the tall picture windows and their heavy curtains that cascaded to the floor in pools of gold silk, the bed stacked with luxurious pillows and cushions of every imaginable shape, the antique chairs dotted about the room—she gazed at the slip of a dress Christian had brought from New York. It was brand new, of course, and minimalist black, again. Christian said that Morgan and Tasha had helped him choose it. They had missed her at dinner earlier that week. Cat had laughed this off. She doubted it. But it was kind of him to say so.

Cat slipped her head under the bubbles in her bath. She would wash her hair with the expensive-looking hotel shampoo, and over dinner she would tell Christian all about the apartment.

• • •

But as soon as they stepped out of the hotel an hour later, it was clear that Christian had other plans. He kept up a steady stream of chatter in the car on the way to the river, one hand resting across Cat's shoulders, which were bare in the tiny black dress underneath her coat.

"Cat," he said, after they had set off on the charming little cruiser and were seated in the middle of the cabin, another bottle of Moët in a silver bucket by their side. "There's a reason for this."

"Oh?" Cat said, her eyes not knowing whether to feast on the French architecture lining both sides of the river or admire the inside of their boat, which was decked out in beautiful pale wood and modern furniture.

"There's a reason I came all the way to Paris."

"What is it, Christian?"

But Christian was down on one knee. From out of nowhere, a photographer appeared.

"Mademoiselle, Monsieur. As you requested, I will now take your photograph."

"Too early, dammit." Christian batted the poor man away.

"Christian?" Cat tried to send an apologetic smile to the cameraman.

"Cat," he said. "I'm in love with you. Violently. I can't wait any longer. I want to marry you."

Applause sounded from the far end of the cabin. The cameraman rushed back in. "Now, I take photo? Monsieur, Mademoiselle?"

Another waiter appeared with two more glasses of champagne. "Is for the toast," he insisted. He also placed a bunch of peach-colored roses in the middle of their table and a dish of caviar with tiny water crackers on another plate.

"You stand up," the photographer said to Christian.

"Hang on," Cat said.

But Christian beamed at her. "Honey," he said again as he shuffled around in his dinner jacket pocket.

"Ah! The ring!" The photographer squeaked. "We will be going past the Eiffel Tower in thirty seconds. We take photo outside. Now."

"Shall we?" Christian held out his arm.

The air outside was freezing. Cat snuggled up next to Christian on the deck of the boat. The sound of accordions from other cruise boats was wafting down the Seine. The photographer moved them expertly from pose to pose.

All she could do was gasp when Christian pulled out the most divine diamond ring she had ever seen. She could only nod when he slipped it on the third finger of her left hand.

"Yes," she laughed, as he slipped an arm around her back. "Yes! Of course! I thought you'd never ask!" She beamed for the photographer, and he smiled at them both.

"You make a stunning couple," he said. "Is too perfect for words!"

CHAPTER SEVEN

Cat didn't wake until the sun was streaming through the elegant hotel windows onto the enormous bed. She sat up slowly, gorgeous recollections of the night before still dancing around in her head. She stretched out her finger, looked at the ring. It was beautiful. She was in Paris. She was engaged.

Christian was at the walnut writing desk. "Morning, honey," he said, his fingers dancing across the keyboard of his laptop. "Slight problem. One of our businesses. They don't get the program."

Cat walked over and wrapped her arms around his shoulders. "Breakfast?" she murmured, nuzzling into his neck.

"You go get ready, honey."

Cat spent another wonderful half hour in the bathroom. She could get used to this, she knew. But she must tell Christian about the apartment. The key was in her bag. She would take him up to the Pigalle district this morning.

"What do you want to do today?" Christian asked, as they settled down in the hotel restaurant.

"Have one of these wonderful croissants, for a start."

"Try on wedding dresses, perhaps?"

"There's something else I have to tell you. It's kind of a surprise, but a little awkward too . . ."

Christian had his phone out. “I’m going to have to take this call. You enjoy breakfast.” He left the restaurant.

Cat sat back in her chair. Well. Of course he had to take calls from New York. He couldn’t just stop because they were engaged now, could he? Life went on. Even on a Saturday.

Cat got out her own phone. There was a new message. She sighed and listened to it. Loic. He was sorry for leaving so abruptly on Friday. He would be there on Monday. It was best if they just got on with it.

Cat shut her phone and went to check out the gorgeous buffet. Everything looked so delectable, and she was starving. She had not eaten much last night with all the excitement.

Christian was lying on the bed, working on his computer, when Cat went back up to the suite. She got her coat on and pulled on her gloves.

“Have to get this done, honey.”

“I’ll go out for a while, let you finish it.”

Three hours later, having walked along the Seine and lingered over coffee at one of the cafés overlooking the river, Cat wandered back to the hotel. She felt ready to tell Christian about the apartment, and the sooner, the better. The next time she went into the building in rue Blanche, she wanted to go with her fiancé.

Christian had finished his work and was lying on the bed, flicking the remote at the television, when Cat entered the suite.

“Can we talk?”

Christian crossed his arms behind his head and smiled at her. “Did you do some shopping, honey? Find anything nice?”

“I just walked. Paris is perfect for walking.”

There was a pause.

“Christian, I want to show you something.”

“Sure, honey. We can do whatever you feel like today. I’m all yours.”

“Come with me,” Cat said, and she took his hand.

• • •

The taxi ride to the apartment seemed to go very quickly. Cat had planned to tell him everything once they arrived in the apartment. It would all make sense to him then, being there.

When the taxi pulled up outside the building in rue Blanche, Christian seemed nonplussed. Surprisingly, he had not asked her any questions about where they were going or what she was proposing they do. He probably assumed they were going shopping, or to a gallery, perhaps. Christian wasn't particularly interested in art. At home, if Cat wanted to go to the Met, or to any other exhibition, she always went with a friend.

"What are we doing, honey?" he laughed, as the taxi pulled up outside the extraordinary building. It still made Cat gasp. "Are we visiting a friend?"

"Sort of," Cat said, pulling out her key and opening the front door.

He was quiet as they climbed the staircase. She wasn't even going to start with the old elevator.

His reaction to the place was so unexpected that all Cat could do was watch him. He wandered, enchanted, through each of the rooms, stopping to pick up objects and asking her to repeat the extraordinary story several times.

When they stood in the smaller second bedroom, Cat ran her fingers over one of the dust-covered silk bedspreads. They left shining trace marks across the faded fabric.

"I've been thinking about this room," she said. "If Virginia stayed here—which I am certain she must have, now—then this would have been where she slept. When I first wandered through these rooms, I was so startled by it all that I didn't really take in what was what."

"Now, look at this," she went on, picking up the two novels that sat by the bed. One was Hemingway, the other the romance that she had spotted earlier.

"I wonder if one of these belonged to Virginia," she said.

"Who knows?" Christian smiled. He came up behind her and wrapped his arms around her waist. "It's spooky, though, isn't it? Do you feel comfortable being here alone, Cat?"

She turned to him, rested in his embrace. "Yes," she said. "I feel at home here. Close to my grandmother. Close to the past."

"Come on, though, let's get out to check out today's Paris."

"Today's Paris," Cat murmured as she led him back to the front door. "I wonder how much has changed?"

• • •

The rest of the weekend whisked by in a flurry of shopping trips and plans as well as many phone calls back home. On Monday morning, just as he was about to leave, Christian pulled Cat toward him and kissed her.

"I take it I have your permission to tell everyone about this?" He lifted her ring finger and kissed that too.

"Of course!"

"They all love you, you know."

Cat wound her arms around his neck. "That's important to me."

He picked up his luggage. "I know it is. I love that about you." He hugged her one more time, and then he was gone.

Cat had half an hour to check out of the hotel, move her luggage back to her old hotel near the opera house, and get to the apartment to let Anouk in by nine.

But it was not Anouk who stood outside the apartment door when Cat bustled up the staircase. It was Loic.

He was wearing a black overcoat and scarf, and he had two cups of takeout coffee in his hands. He held one out to Cat.

"Peace offering?" she asked. "Although your disappearance on Friday was perfectly understandable. You'd have to be made of rock not to be moved by all this."

Loic grinned at her and held up the coffee cup. "I heard you Americans like this sort of thing."

Cat took a sip of the coffee. "The fact that it's French coffee in a cardboard cup makes all the difference," she laughed. They entered and closed the door behind them.

Once inside, Loic took her arm and turned her to face him. "Sorry I left you here, though."

"Oh! No, like I said . . . it was understandable." He was looking at her, a curious expression on his face.

"How was your weekend?"

"Fine."

"Hmm." He let go of her arm and walked into the room, then turned around again.

"Have you . . . rethought things?" Cat asked.

"I can't take what isn't mine." He picked up a vase that Anouk had dusted off and placed on the dining table. "But there is one thing."

"Yes?"

He was silent for a moment. "It's my mother."

"She wants to claim her inheritance?"

"She won't do that."

Cat felt an annoyed chuckle rising in her throat. "Look, Loic, wouldn't that be her decision?"

Loic shook his head. "I know her."

"Are you sure?"

He caught her eye again, catching her off guard. This was becoming a habit. Cat felt herself flush.

"Have you ever been to the South of France, Cat?"

"I've only been out of the US once before."

Loic raised a brow. "What are you saying?"

There was the sound of footsteps coming up the stairs. Anouk.

Loic took a step closer. "Come to Provence and meet my mother. It'll be important for her to talk to you. It'll make her feel far better."

"Yes, but—"

Something tightened in Loic's cheek. "At least meet her, Cat."

"Loic—"

A knock sounded on the door, efficient.

"Wait." Loic took Cat's hand as she reached for the door. "My mother needs to see that you're not, to be frank, a gold digger. I don't want any of it, not if my grandmother didn't leave it to us, but I want to make things as easy as possible, under the circumstances, for my mother—for Sylvie."

"I want to give your family their inheritance."

"Please, Cat."

"Hopefully, your mother will just take what's hers." Cat walked toward the door to let Anouk in. But then she turned again. "I find it incredible that Isabelle left all of this to my grandmother. I am . . . stunned, to be honest. I don't even understand their connection. But you must take it all back. And . . . I need to get home."

Loic held her gaze. "It's my mother who you'll have to convince. And you won't be able to do that unless you meet her."

• • •

Two hours later, they were in a steady routine. Anouk appeared to have recovered from the shock of finding the apartment on Friday and was in professional mode. She worked quickly, immersed in making detailed lists on her laptop while simultaneously cross-checking every last piece using her knowledge and online resources.

Cat and Loic had spent the entire morning in the bedroom reading love letters from Marthe de Florian's admirers. Loic read them aloud, translating effortlessly in his clear, confident English. So far, all they had found were the most exquisite letters Cat had ever read in her life. But there was nothing from Giovanni Boldini.

"Oh, mon Dieu," Loic said, pulling a letter out of an envelope. "I think I'm seeing things."

"What is it?" Cat leaned in closer to him. They sat at a little side table by the window, and Cat had made a neat pile of letters already read. Shafts of clear sun warmed the room. "A famous actor? Aristocracy?"

"Not exactly, Cat." He held out the letter in his hand.

Cat read the signature on the bottom. "I've heard that name . . ."

Loic chuckled. "Have you, just? Ring any bells, Américaine?"

Cat folded her arms.

"Georges Clemenceau was one of our prime ministers."

"Oh."

"Yes."

"So"—Cat felt mischief in her bones—"you know what that means."

"Highly unlikely, Cat." But he was grinning.

"But you could be."

Loic put that letter by itself.

Cat smiled. "You know, I'm starving. Can I get you something while I'm out?" But Loic seemed immersed in what he was reading.

Just as she put her hand on the front door, Loic stood up.

"Cat."

"Or . . . do you want to get some lunch with me?"

Loic shook his head. "Don't go."

"What?"

He was frowning over another letter.

Cat waited.

He looked up at her over the faded paper. "You can't go now."

Cat moved to read over his shoulder. It was all there. Boldini. Attached to the thin paper, its once-bold type faded now, was a calling card. Giovanni Boldini. And in the letter—which Loic read fast, translating it into English with the speed of a whippet—Boldini poured out all of his passion for the enchanting young Marthe de Florian.

Anouk was a model of efficiency. As soon as Loic handed her the letter, she was on her phone with the Musée d'Orsay, speaking in rapid French. Then she hung up and spoke, fast, to Loic.

"They are still reading his wife's journals."

"I still can't believe he wrote love letters to Marthe de Florian and had a wife," Cat said.

Loic grinned, his head tilted to one side.

"Typical," Cat muttered.

Anouk went back to her work.

"Don't worry, Cat," Loic said. "Apparently Boldini didn't marry until 1929. He was eighty-six. He painted Marthe in 1898. Anything else you'd like explained?"

Cat shrugged.

"He had no reason not to paint her," Loic said, his voice gentle.

There was a silence for a moment.

"Did you make up your mind, Cat?"

"What about?" Cat felt light-headed.

"You know."

"Loic, surely you can just convince your mother to take it all? I really can't come to the South of France right now."

"It involves your past too, Cat. Aren't your curious?"

"Oh, Virginia," Cat sighed.

"Okay, then, you just take it all and go back to New York."

"You're playing hardball."

"Yes."

Cat stood up and walked toward the door. Just as she reached it, she turned. "Loic, I'm going out for lunch."

"Think about it, Cat."

Cat shook her head and picked up her coat.

CHAPTER EIGHT

The art experts moved quickly once Boldini's letter was found. By the time Cat returned to the apartment, having lunched on a bowl of French onion soup and a warm baguette, Pascale Colbert was there too. He and Anouk communicated all afternoon with their counterparts back at the Musée d'Orsay, who were reading through Boldini's papers, his letters, his wife's memoirs, and anything else they could find.

Loic continued reading the letters while Cat helped Anouk, dusting individual pieces, admiring them, watching Anouk catalogue them.

At four o'clock, Anouk surveyed what she had done in the living room and the kitchen. "Tomorrow, I will bring in another person. We will continue to work through all of this, catalogue it for you, and value it all for the estate. I think it will take about two weeks."

Loic came into the room. "I've read the rest of the letters," he said, handing them to Anouk. "Nothing more about Boldini. But you take them. Read them yourself."

Anouk looked coyly up at Loic. "And were you moved by these beautiful love letters, Loic?" she asked.

"Not in the least." Loic grinned at her. "But my mother will be. I want Cat to come and meet her."

"Loic, please tell me your mother isn't as stubborn as you," Cat said.

"My mother won't accept what wasn't left to her," Loic said. "There must be some reason that my grandmother didn't change her will. After all, she had seventy years to do so."

"So there's no chance, then."

"Well, you'll never know, if you never try—" Loic began.

Anouk's phone rang; she answered it on the first ring. Cat couldn't understand a word.

Loic moved closer to her. "They've done it," he said quietly, listening to Anouk. "The painting's a Boldini. His wife mentions the painting of Marthe in her memoirs. Marthe de Florian was twenty-four when Boldini painted her."

Anouk hung up and turned to face them. And then she stumbled across the room to Cat. She clutched at Cat's arms and twirled her around.

"This is incredible!" she said. "This painting is a once-in-a-lifetime discovery! It will be worth a fortune!"

It was impossible for Cat to know what to say.

Finally, Anouk let go of Cat's arms. "Do you understand what this means? Everyone will go crazy for this painting if you sell! You need to consult with Loic's family as to what do with it. You have a masterpiece on your hands! Now this becomes even more exciting. It is not just an old apartment full of all these beautiful things that were given to a demimondaine, this is now an important discovery in the history of art! It will be famous! Oh, mon Dieu!"

Anouk turned to include Loic. "The team, all of us, we are going out to a wine bar tonight to celebrate! You must come with us! You helped us by finding the wonderful letter. Please?"

Loic looked at Cat. "I'm in, if you'll come too, Cat?"

Cat shrugged.

"I'll translate for you," Loic chuckled.

"Oh, I may as well!" Cat said. "A night alone in the hotel isn't much fun, after all."

"You definitely need a night out."

Anouk was packing up. "I cannot concentrate anymore," she said. "I am going home to wash and get all dressed up!" She picked up her bags and told Loic in French where they would all meet that evening.

Loic turned to Cat. "Shall I pick you up from your hotel at eight?" he asked, as Anouk walked out the door.

Cat picked up her things. She needed some time alone to digest this. This was not her world, her inheritance, her legacy. It was not up to her to make decisions about valuable artworks. She turned to Loic.

"This is getting serious. There's a lot . . . involved here."

"I know, Cat. That's why I think you need to meet my mother. You need to work it out with her. I think you'll like her. And I think she'll like you too."

"But surely you have to see reason," Cat said. "Now you've turned up; just take it over. What sort of claim could I possibly have to any of this now?"

Loic reached out and put a tendril of Cat's hair back in place.

She took a step back.

"It's everything to do with you. Isabelle wanted you involved," he said, his eyes still on her.

Cat bustled about in her bag. "The key. It should be somewhere in here."

"You left it in the door. Here it is." He handed it to her.

Cat didn't look at him when she took it from him. "Did I?"

"Stay in France for a little while, Cat," he said. "There is more going on here than either of us thought at first. You can't just ignore it. Not now. You can't tell me you're not intrigued, either. I can tell by just watching you in here."

Cat felt a small gasp rise in her throat. She turned to him, but he was moving toward the door. What did he mean by that?

• • •

The wine bar was full and noisy. Anouk, Pascale, and several other people sat around a table in the corner of the room.

"Bonsoir!" they called, the men all kissing Cat on both cheeks and shaking Loic's hand.

When they were all settled, Pascale turned to Cat and Loic.

"So," he said. "What is next for you two discoverers of this great treasure?"

Cat waited for Loic to speak. It was his family. His history.

"I'm hoping to take Cat down to Provence. There are still . . . things to work out."

Pascale leaned across the table and held his wine glass up to Loic. "Here's to this wonderful discovery. Words cannot describe my feelings for it. May you work together and revel in all its amazing stories," he said.

"Cat will want to get back to her fiancé in New York soon." Anouk's smoky voice cut through the rest of the chatter, and the noisy group suddenly fell quiet.

Cat was sure her face was turning scarlet. Anouk had admired Christian's ring this morning. Now, everyone seemed to be waiting for Cat to say something. "I . . . got engaged over the weekend."

"Congratulations," Loic said.

Pascale made a comical face.

Loic got up and went to the bar.

After a beat, the conversation started up again around Cat. She stood up herself, then sat back down, then stood up again and walked over to where Loic was.

He stood next to her at the bar, but he didn't turn to face her. "I didn't realize you were engaged," he said, still facing straight ahead.

"I didn't notice the ring today." He glanced at Christian's diamond, then waved at a waiter.

Cat said nothing.

"Do you like wine, Cat?" He sat abruptly on the stool in front of him.

Cat sat down next to him. "Yes, I do."

He handed her his glass. "Tell me what you think of this one."

"Oh, sure!" Suddenly, it seemed imperative that she keep the mood light. She took a sip of the wine.

"Any good?" Loic slid the glass back along the bar toward himself, rolling the stem between his fingers.

"Divine." Was that the right answer?

"Okay. Try this one." Loic took another glass from a bartender who had appeared right in front of them.

Cat watched him and took a deep sip.

"Is it as good?"

"Oh," she murmured. "Easily." She turned to Loic. "Tell me, how is it that you French make the best chocolate, the best wine, and the best patisseries on the planet?"

"Probably because we are idiot perfectionists," Loic said. A twinkle had crept into his eyes. "And we know exactly when to stop."

Cat took another sip of the divine wine and held the glass toward Loic. "Your elegance is in what you don't do, then?"

"Or what we don't say," Loic muttered, taking a sip out of the glass Cat had tried earlier.

"So, which of the two wines did you make?"

"Both."

Cat knew that if she didn't have something to eat soon, she'd start to feel light-headed. The combination of the excitement of the last few days, the wine, everything, appeared to have hit her all of a sudden. "Well, that's great. Well done. You're a talented winemaker." Why could she not say something sensible?

He looked at her for a moment. Was he assessing her again? It felt like it. "Look, Cat, if you're coming with me, I think we should get an early start tomorrow." Loic stood up suddenly. "I'm going to say good-bye to the others." He stood there, looking at her.

Cat blew out a breath. "Look, Loic, I just think—"

"At least meet her. You can't just abandon it."

"The only reason I would come is to convince your mother to take her apartment." The music in the bar had softened, and Cat dropped her voice to a whisper. "That would be my only reason."

"Good." He leaned forward now.

Cat put out her hand, but he kissed her on the cheek. It was feather-light, but the touch of his lips against her skin was startling. She took a step backward and nearly fell over the barstool behind her.

"I'm glad you made things clear," Loic said, his voice barely audible. He tossed his jacket over his shoulder. "I'll pick you up at nine from your hotel." He marched off toward the rest of the party.

Cat sat down on her stool again with a thump. She watched him walk back to the table of art experts, shake their hands, kiss Anouk on the cheek. Of course. That was what French men did. To everyone, including her. That was all that had happened. Nothing else. She sat up a bit taller. It was what they all did.

Cat waited until he was well out of the building. Then she went over to the group at the table and sat down with them. If Loic wouldn't be sensible, she needed to convince his mother to be, and quickly.

• • •

As soon as she was in the taxi, Cat grabbed her phone and called Christian.

"Hey!" she said, beaming into the darkness.

"Cat." The sounds of tapping on a computer echoed down the phone as if he were in the next room, not across the ocean.

"How was your flight?" Cat kept her voice deliberately loud.

"Fine. The flight was fine," Christian said. "Are you almost done over there?"

"Oh, well . . . are you back at home now?"

"I'm at home."

"And working, by the sound of it? So dedicated."

"What?"

"Dedicated. To your work! Is everyone okay at home?"

"I was only gone a few days."

"Great. Excellent." The taxi pulled up outside the hotel. Cat paid, climbed out, entered the building, and stepped into the old caged lift. "So . . . have you told people about the engagement then? Your mom?"

"My mom?"

Cat winced. "Your . . . mother, I mean. And father."

"I'd like to tell them in person. I was planning on taking them out for dinner."

"Oh! Tell them in person when you next see them, of course you should. What a surprise, eh? I hope it's not a shock!"

"What?"

Cat threw herself down on her bed and stared up at the ceiling. "Sorry. I just wanted to . . . hear your voice," she finished quietly.

"Well, here I am."

"So, you want to know when I'll be back?"

"Absolutely, Cat."

"Oh, good." She closed her eyes. After this, she would go out and buy some food. That was what she would do. "Well—"

"Still working on this same damned job, you know. That business I mentioned earlier. It blew up while I was on the damned plane."

Cat spoke in a rush. "Look, I'm just going down to the South of France for a couple of days. Just to . . . sort some of this stuff out. I need to convince the rightful heir that the apartment is, well, hers. And we discovered the painting was a Boldini. I texted you! Did you get my text?"

There was the sound of shuffling papers. "Boldini? Who's Boldini? I'm sure you can sort out the issue of the apartment with the lawyer, Cat. It doesn't need to involve you personally. You don't have to do all this."

"It should only take a day or two." Now Cat felt irritated with everybody. Couldn't Christian get off his laptop and leave his papers alone for five minutes to listen to what she had to say? "Bye."

Christian hung up, and Cat slid the phone across the double bed. It rang again.

"I wanted to say goodnight to you properly," Cat said.

"Any time, Cat."

Cat sat up on the edge of the bed. She felt herself blush. "Loic."

There was a pause. "I've told my mother . . . as much as I could on the phone. I told her that you were . . . that you were a good person. Which you are, you know. I honestly think that. She would love to meet you, Cat."

"Look, what I was saying before was not—"

"Thank you for coming with me." He cut her off. "You need to have something to eat."

"Do I?"

"There's a good little bistro just around the corner from your hotel. Go out the door, turn left, and then take your first right. It's halfway up the street. You won't miss it. Afterwards . . . get some rest, won't you."

"Whatever you say."

"*À demain*, Cat."

"À demain," Cat whispered. She slumped back onto the bed.

CHAPTER NINE

Loic texted to say he would be in the hotel lobby at nine. At least her morning had been efficient. She'd had no difficulties choosing what to wear. Last night, after a dinner of delectable B*oeuf Bourgignon* followed by a melt-in-your-mouth crème brûlée, Cat had packed and laid out an outfit for the train trip to Provence.

If she was going to think about any man, she was going to think about Christian. What had happened last night with Loic was nothing. Nothing at all. She had simply been annoyed with Christian using his laptop while he was on the phone to her, and she had been thrown by a Frenchman. She was certainly not the first girl to fall for this, but she would not let herself be taken in by Loic. She was engaged to Christian and perfectly happy.

But she was in a 1930s mood, and there was nothing wrong with that, so she had chosen a tight, fitted navy jacket and a skirt to match, then teamed this up with a silk scarf. A silk scarf did seem essential in Paris. There was nothing wrong with a little blending in to a place.

"You know, I think I can see you loving the French countryside," Loic said, as the train moved beyond the outskirts of Paris. He had offered Cat the window seat, and he was next to her. He leaned over and pointed out the window. "Look at that village. See, it's so typical of this part of France. Provence is so much more rustic, almost like another country."

"Do you think of Provence as more down-to-earth than the north?" Cat asked. She couldn't help but be aware of his closeness.

"To me, yes." His voice was soft.

There was a silence.

"And where do you think you'll end up living?" Loic asked. "Now that you're—"

"Oh, Manhattan." Cat was quick. "No question about it. I couldn't see Christian living in the countryside." She was flustered. Perhaps she should stand up, go for a walk down the train. But she didn't want to. She shouldn't have to. Oh, honestly.

"And you're happy with that?"

"Yes! Perfectly."

"Poor you."

"Why poor me?" Cat turned to him.

But he was grinning at her. "Poor girl."

She swiped at him with her hand. "Okay, then. What about you? Don't you ever wish you could be in Paris? Being so French, so sophisticated and all?"

"Look." Loic leaned closer and pointed out the window. "See what I mean. The villages are changing already. Stone cottages, less formal. Buckets more charm. So . . . what does your fiancé do?"

"Merchant banker."

"Oh, no," Loic growled.

Cat stared out the window. She would not rise to this.

The food cart arrived. "Even the train food is good in France," Loic whispered. Cat ordered a jambon baguette. She did not look at Loic.

"Not bad," she said. It was delicious.

"So, would your merchant banker ride through France in a train with you and eat jambon baguettes?"

"Stop it!" Cat laughed. She pulled out her headphones. "Now, I need a rest before I meet your mother."

"Yes, she's terrifying." Loic smiled. He sat back in his seat.

Cat put in her headphones. Closing her eyes seemed like the perfect idea.

• • •

"Are we . . . walking?" Cat asked.

"Not exactly." Loic led her out to the cobbled road that ran along the back of the station at Saint-Revel, passing a couple of silver Peugeots. A man climbed out of one of them and greeted Loic. After a brief conversation in French, the driver took their suitcases and put them in his car.

Loic strolled toward a red Vespa and handed Cat a helmet.

"Hop on."

Cat laughed. "That's so funny."

Loic tilted his head to one side.

"No, it is. I have a Vespa at home. Hey, why don't you ride on back?"

Loic glanced up the steep hill that ran behind the train station, toward the impossibly narrow roads that doglegged their way up through the village. The village, in turn, overlooked a spectacular valley bathed in golden sunlight.

"Our gendarmes prefer you to have a French license. Sorry, sweetheart, no go today."

"That's a shame." She took the helmet and tucked it onto her head. "It's okay; I can do it," she said when he reached out to help her adjust the chin straps.

"I'm sure you can," he said, climbing onto the scooter.

Cat didn't move for a moment. "Loic. I'm wondering: How much, exactly, have you told your mother? Sylvie?"

He smiled up at her and shook his head. "She'll love you, Cat. I know that. Just relax."

Cat folded her arms.

He grinned again, settling himself on the seat of his scooter. "Hop on."

"Great," Cat mumbled. But there was no point standing here in the train station. She climbed on the back of Loic's Vespa. Gingerly, she wrapped her arms around his waist.

"Okay?" Loic asked, turning on the engine. He turned to look at her.

"Fine!" Cat shouted.

Loic opened up the throttle. Cars were parked at odd angles right up against the honey-colored houses and the small shops—*patisserie*, *boulangerie*, *boucherie*, *tabac* and *supermarché*—that lined the main street of the pretty village.

When Loic pulled up outside a two-story house, its front door sitting atop a small flight of steps lined with colorful pots of pansies, Cat's insides began to churn with anxiety. What on earth was she going to say?

Loic leaned forward and undid her chin strap.

Cat jumped at the touch of his hands just below her lips. "Oh!" she said. "I was just . . . admiring the view."

Loic raised an eyebrow, then stepped behind her, allowing her to go first up the short flight of steps to Sylvie Archer's pale blue front door.

Sylvie Archer was not what Cat had been expecting at all. For some reason—although she didn't know why, since Loic was clearly stunning—she had imagined a short woman, beady-eyed, who doted on her only son. She would be dressed entirely in black from head to toe, with sensible, flat-heeled shoes.

But Sylvie opened the front door wearing a pair of faded jeans and a loose pink sweater that draped elegantly across her youthful frame. Though she must have been nearly seventy, her hair was still dark and fell in a cloud around her shoulders. Her brown eyes were just the same as Loic's.

"Darling children," she said, her accent far more pronounced than Loic's. "You must be starving. You ate, yes, on the train?"

"Yes." Cat smiled. "It is so nice to meet you, Mademoiselle Archer."

"Oh, Sylvie, Sylvie, please!" Sylvie leaned forward and kissed Cat on the cheek. When Sylvie reached up to hug Loic, Cat took another glance at the older woman. She was smiling, but traces of tears were visible around her eyes.

She and Loic followed Sylvie into her pretty house, past a stairway, then down a narrow hall painted navy blue and covered with dozens of black-and-white photos. Cat was tempted to stop and take a look, but Sylvie marched straight down toward the back of the house.

"Cat's suitcases are upstairs?" Loic called through from behind Cat.

"Of course," Sylvie said.

"Oh, please don't feel you have to have me stay with you. I can find a hotel."

But Sylvie smiled and shook her head at Cat as she entered the bright kitchen at the rear of the house. A farmhouse oven warmed the space, and an adjoining sitting room with comfortable-looking sofas and chairs was framed by an all-glass wall that looked on to a small courtyard. It was clear that Sylvie was a creative gardener. The space was filled with roses in terra-cotta pots, and a high wall with trellised plants backed the garden.

"This is gorgeous," Cat whispered.

"Merci. Sit down," Sylvie said. Suddenly she sounded a little awkward. "We will have a glass of wine, shall we not, and then we will eat later."

Loic had gone upstairs. Cat wished he would reappear. She perched on one of the cream sofas.

Sylvie poured three glasses of wine and leaned on the kitchen counter. "I'm sorry, dear, Cat. Please, relax. Make yourself at home in my house."

Cat sat back against one of the pale cushions behind her. She blew out a breath. "So—"

"Dear—" Sylvie spoke at the same time.

"You two are getting to know each other?" Loic appeared and leaned against the side of the kitchen doorframe. He looked both too tall for Sylvie's small house and perfectly at home.

Cat sensed Sylvie looking at him as if for help and felt herself doing exactly the same thing.

"Let's sit down," he said to Sylvie. "Have a talk with Cat, *Maman*."

Cat put her wine down on the glass table in front of her. "Sylvie," she said, "I hope Loic made my intentions clear. I want you to take your inheritance. It's not mine. It really isn't."

Sylvie ran a hand through her cloud of dark hair. It was much the same gesture as one Loic often made. "I can't. I would simply never do that."

"But why?"

Sylvie shook her head. "My mother was of sound mind when she died. She must have had a reason for . . . not telling us about Paris, for not changing this will. She had decades to change it, but she never did. I don't know why, but I do know that I respected her. I loved her. I won't go against her wishes."

"Maman's right." Loic's voice broke into the room.

Sylvie leaned across and put a hand on Loic's own. "Cat. My mother came down here, one of the many refugees from Paris on the eve of the Nazi invasion in June 1940, with nothing. There is a nunnery, high up on the hill above the village. They took her in when she first arrived. She was pregnant, and she gave birth to me there. The nuns looked after her during the war but—" Something passed across Sylvie's face. "Isabelle, my mother, was poor all her life. Struggling. She worked at the nunnery until she was well into her sixties. Cleaned for them. She never married, just put her head down and worked. My admiration for her is so great that I cannot mess around with what I am sure were her good intentions."

Cat didn't know where to look. None of this made sense. The woman had an apartment in one of the world's most coveted cities. She owned a Boldini. The electricity had been on when Cat and Loic arrived at the apartment. The utility bills had been paid up until Isabelle's death, according to Monsieur Lapointe. There was evidence that someone had been living in the apartment right up to the war, when Isabelle escaped. So it would be safe to assume that she had lived there; it had been her home. The only other possibility was that the apartment had simply been left to Isabelle when her own grandmother, Marthe, died, and Isabelle had never been there in seventy years. But that didn't add up, either. Why would Isabelle keep that gold mine a secret from her own daughter? Cat shook her head. Loic was talking.

"I don't think the fact that Isabelle kept a secret from you meant that she loved you any the less, Maman," he said. "I don't know, maybe it was just the war, all too much; she bottled it up."

"Wait," Cat said.

Loic and Sylvie turned to face her.

"Isabelle's reasons aside, I can't even afford to keep the apartment, you know. And I'd feel guilty all my life. I wouldn't begin to know how to deal with it, what to do with all your family's things. I'd be hit with inheritance tax, which is sixty percent of the value of the estate, apparently. I don't live in Paris, and my fiancé doesn't travel much. It belongs to you. It's yours."

Loic made a sound that was almost a growl.

Cat wanted to throw her hands up. "Please, at least tell me you'll think about it, Sylvie."

Sylvie stood up. "I will show you to your room. We will eat together at eight. You must be exhausted."

Cat avoided Loic's eye as she followed Sylvie up the stairs.

• • •

An hour later, Cat lay on Sylvie's guest-room bed, its white quilt cover scattered with blue cushions. There was a perfect little bathroom next door with just enough room for a bath. Cat had taken a quick shower. Now it was high time she called Christian.

"They won't budge," she told him. "I can't see why they won't just take their inheritance."

"I can see your dilemma." That was the thing about Christian. He always offered support, never advice, which was a relief most of the time.

Now, Cat stood and stared out at the cobbled village street. A young couple strolled outside, her arm tucked into his.

"Yes, but it feels utterly wrong to take this family's assets away from them. Any ideas?" Cat knew she sounded helpless.

"Well, I've got some exciting news, honey." Christian sounded as if he had put something down, whatever it was he was doing.

"Even if I gift it all back to them, after probate, they'll probably send it right back!"

"Honey?"

"Of course, I could donate it all to a cat rescue or something, but that's not going to help the people who should rightly have it."

"You're not listening to me."

"I could leave it all to Loic when I'm dead. Now, there's a plan, just as great as Isabelle's was—"

"Cat. I understand the problem, but I can't see that you can do much about it."

"Oh!" Cat slumped back on the bed.

"I've organized our engagement party. How about that for a change of subject?"

"Oh?" Cat heard Sylvie coming up the stairs and closed her bedroom door. "What?" she whispered.

"And guess what, Cat?"

"Yes?"

"The best time for us all is a week from Saturday. Mother and Father are going on a trip for three months after that, so . . ."

"Oh?"

"The Hamptons, we thought. We've hired someone who can help organize things, honey. Should be perfect. She can do the wedding as well."

"You've already hired someone?"

"We've used her for other family events. Elise. Great girl. Will do an excellent job, keep it tasteful. We won't have time to do it ourselves. It's important to do this right. Mother's sent out the invitations."

Cat closed her eyes. "I'm a little preoccupied. I . . . can we talk about it more when I get home?"

"Yes, details, details. I love you, honey."

"Yes, I love you, too."

Christian hung up.

It was almost time to go down to dinner. Cat moved about the room automatically, pulling on a dress. She couldn't possibly leave everything to the planner. The sooner she sorted things out here, the sooner she could go home and get her life back under control.

CHAPTER TEN

By the time Cat had changed into a 1940s fitted dress, she felt far more able to face Sylvie and Loic. She had heard Loic's Vespa scooting off through the village. Presumably he had been headed home, to his vineyard. But now he was back. He had changed into a loose black sweater, the sleeves rolled up, and a pair of faded jeans. He was opening a bottle of wine in the kitchen while Sylvie tossed a green salad on the counter.

Cat paused at the bottom of the stairs. They seemed so in harmony, Sylvie and Loic. His skin was a little fairer than hers, but he had inherited her dark eyes and her clear, expressive face. When he turned to face Cat, she sensed him starting a little.

"What a beautiful dress, Cat," he said, handing her a glass of white wine.

For some reason, this made Cat feel warm. She took a hasty sip.

Sylvie brought plates of crisp roast lamb, and baby potatoes that had been roasted with rosemary and olive oil, to the table. She placed the large salad bowl in front of them all.

"Help yourself, darlings," she said.

"So, how long have you had your vineyard, Loic?" Cat asked.

"Ten years," he said. "I took it over after the last owner retired. He'd been there forty years. I restored the *mas*—that is, the Provençal house that came with the property—two years ago. Before that, I lived in the caretaker's cottage. It's been hard work, but rewarding. Fortunately, I love what I do."

"And Loic has turned it around." Sylvie smiled. "He is winning awards nationally and is beginning to win awards throughout Europe as well. I am so proud of him," she said.

Cat smiled. "It's great to have a passion for what you do."

"Yes." Loic looked at her. "Your passion is for photography, I can see that, Cat. You must love your job, too, then."

Something told Cat that Loic would probe if she admitted that she didn't exactly adore her current job, so she skirted around this. "It can be a tough profession."

"Every profession is tough," Loic said. "I promised myself years ago that I wouldn't do anything I didn't love. It was a tough decision, but I think it was worth it."

"Once Loic has made up his mind, that is it!" Sylvie laughed. "He knows what he wants, and he goes for it."

Stubborn and determined, then. Were these negative character traits? They could be, in the wrong hands. He seemed to be a feeling person though, too. The fact that he had walked out of the apartment, struck by the enormity of his grandmother's secrets, showed that he was not cold. Cat shook herself slightly. What was she doing? She didn't want to let herself think too much about Loic's character. It was time to change topics.

"The area is beautiful," she said. She stole a glance at Loic. That eyebrow was raised.

"You should take some photographs while you're here. I can show you around, if you like."

Sylvie stood up and started clearing plates.

Cat stood up, too, but Sylvie waved her back down. "No, no, I insist," she said.

The pears in red wine that she brought out next were like velvet, and the mascarpone alongside them was thick and sweet. "If you feed me like this, I'll never want to leave," Cat laughed.

"We could cope with that, couldn't we, Maman?" Loic was watching her again.

Cat focused on the pears. Why was he flirting with her? He knew she was engaged. Or was he just being French?

"Indeed, we could," Sylvie said. "I feel as if you are at home here, Catherine. I hope you might come and visit us again."

"The New York fiancé, though. There is him," Loic murmured.

Sylvie busied herself with her food.

"Well, I'd love to see more of the area, if we have the time," Cat said, keeping her voice bright.

Loic looked at his watch. "Speaking of which, I should get going." He stood up. "I'll call by in the morning. I hope you two can talk," he said, leaning down to kiss his mother on the cheek. He collected the dessert plates, took them to the kitchen, and put them in the dishwasher.

"And Cat," he said, coming back over and kissing her on the cheek too, "thank you for coming down. I hope we can sort this out." He was walking toward the hallway now.

After he left, Sylvie sank back in her chair. "You know, he is the most wonderful of sons. Always has been, ever since he was a child. I am so lucky to have him."

Cat chewed on her lip.

"Well, then," Sylvie went on. "We will talk in the morning. We have had such a lovely evening, and I am going off to bed."

"Of course." Cat smiled. She stood up too, brought her wine glass to the kitchen, and helped Sylvie finish tidying up. What sort of plan was she going to have to make to put things right for these people? Their respect for family—for their late grandmother, Isabelle—and their complete lack of concern for the materialistic aspects of the situation was endearing. But they couldn't seem to see that this . . . steadfastness—that was how Cat was starting to view it—would cause them to lose a legacy that should be passed down to the future generations of their family, not Cat's.

• • •

Cat woke late the next morning. The smell of roasting coffee beans and warm pastry wafted up the stairway. Sylvie had the radio on, softly, and every now and then, Cat could hear the older woman humming to herself.

When Cat arrived at breakfast, the table was laden. But Sylvie was not bustling about the kitchen anymore. Instead, she sat at the table, alone, her chin resting on her hand. She didn't look up when Cat walked in.

"Sylvie?" Cat rushed over to her. "Are you . . . well?"

Sylvie smiled her deep, beautiful smile. She rested her hand on Cat's arm. "It's just . . ."

"You are okay?" Cat sat down next to her.

But Sylvie stood right up. "You need to eat," she said, marching across the kitchen and pulling a tray of warmed croissants out of the oven. She arranged the croissants on a plate and then poured two cups of coffee and set a plate of bright clementines on the table. She sat down, picked one up, and started peeling its thin orange flesh and popping segments into her mouth. Then she put the fruit down with a sigh.

"You must be starving," she said, absently, handing Cat the plate of croissants. "Loic is coming down to the village soon. He phoned me this morning."

Cat took one, mostly just to please Sylvie, and put it on her plate.

"Eat, *chérie*."

Cat broke a piece off the croissant.

There was a silence for a few moments as neither of them spoke. Sylvie picked up and put down her coffee cup several times, then played with her clementine skin, then rested her hands in her lap and looked out the window.

"I must tidy up my garden," she said absently.

"Oh?" Cat turned around to face it. It looked immaculate.

"Yes. My husband loved the garden." She sounded wistful now.

Cat sipped her coffee in silence.

"I lost him ten years ago," Sylvie went on. "And now, my mother. She was a strong woman."

"She must have been."

Sylvie stood up again. "And she did not put up with any . . . how you say it? Nonsense."

"Oh, Sylvie." Cat stood up and clambered around the table to put her arms around the older woman.

In spite of the fact that Cat had only met Sylvie one day earlier, she felt close to her. Sylvie rested her head on Cat's shoulder.

"Yesterday, I thought I had it all under control, but thinking about my mother—and why she did what she did, how she lived her life—well, it's hard."

"No," Cat said, stroking her head. "This has been a terrible shock for you." After a few moments, she held Sylvie at arm's length. "I want to help make it right. I wish you'd make it easier for me, though."

Sylvie rested her hands on Cat's shoulders. "Cat," she said, her accent more pronounced than it had seemed before, "I will not let you hand back what my mother has left to you. I loved her. And I respected her. I respect her choices."

"Oh, but please!"

"No. The only thing—"

"Anything."

"Bah, you are busy," Sylvie said.

Cat smiled and caught Sylvie's hand. "No, please tell me."

"What? No, my dear. I was wondering, though . . . well, I was thinking. Although it is probably a stupid idea. It's just that, you have complete access to her apartment. And, well . . ."

"Yes?"

"You see, oh, I know it is silly. Sounds ridiculous now, like how my husband used to say, sour grapes?"

"But?"

"Oh, well, you see, but you know, the thing is, I always wanted to go to art school."

"Art school?" Cat felt her shoulders slump.

"Oui." Sylvie walked over to the window. Her back was to Cat. "But there was never enough money. So."

"I'm sorry, Sylvie, but—"

"Oh, chérie, I did just fine. I have a little gallery in the village, where I paint and sell to tourists. I am largely self-taught, but you know. It is okay."

"Sylvie, would you like me to give you some money from the apartment and the painting to put toward your work? Is that it, because, honestly, you don't even have to ask."

"Oh, no, no."

"Sylvie, I—"

"No. It's more that. Oh . . . I am too old for secrets."

"Sylvie—"

Sylvie sat down heavily at the table and took a long sip of her coffee. "I respect my mother's choices, but right now I do not understand them. It seems so strange—shocking, almost—that there was an entire side to her that I did not know. And that is what is haunting me now. If I wasn't feeling so fragile, and—I don't know, I admit it, old—I would chase around and find out why she did what she did myself. But I'm not up to it. My mother's death is too raw."

Cat sat down too. At the moment, she was so entranced with Sylvie that she would do anything for her. But she didn't have time to go digging up old family secrets in a country she hardly knew how to navigate. Where would she even begin? Besides, she had to get back to New York.

She took Sylvie's hand in her own. "I would love to help. And I feel for you, I do; it's just that I have commitments and I should be at home."

"Oh." Sylvie was wiping away tears. "I am sorry I asked. Just forget about it. It doesn't matter."

Cat kept hold of Sylvie's hand. The watering system came on in Sylvie's small garden, spraying just short of the French doors leading out to the patio. A bird appeared, dancing in the dots of water that fluttered over the plants.

"Once the apartment is packed up and sold, this will all be in the past. It doesn't matter," Sylvie said.

The bird played for a while, flapping in the water. Then, as quickly as it had appeared, it flew over the high wall at the back of the garden.

Cat gnawed at her lip. A possibility had sneaked into her head while they sat there. It was a slim possibility, but what if Sylvie agreed? It could solve everything. Problem was, it was almost impossible. She waited a beat. "Sylvie, what if I could find a reason, a good reason, for you to take your inheritance? Would you consider taking it then?"

Sylvie drew her hand away from Cat's, wiping it over her still-beautiful cheeks. "Oh, chérie."

"How about if I . . . try and find out why your mother never went back to Paris, why she never told you anything about it? If I do that, and if the apartment, everything, should go to you, will you take it? Can I have your word?"

Sylvie gazed out the window for a few moments. "If it turns out that it is the right thing to do, then, yes, you have my word. Although I will insist on compensating you."

Cat stood up. "I wouldn't hear of it. But given how much is at stake here, you have my word that I'll find out all I can. We have a deal." Cat reached out a hand, and Sylvie held out her own in return.

• • •

Where Cat was going to begin was quite another matter. She stared at herself in the white-framed mirror while she brushed her teeth. What on earth had she taken on? The chances of finding out why Isabelle had abandoned the apartment and never returned to Paris were so low as to be ridiculous. But if she didn't try, and if Sylvie refused to take the inheritance without further investigation, how would Cat live with herself?

The best place to start, of course, would be with a thorough search of Isabelle's papers. Sylvie, or Loic, must have these somewhere. Surely there must be bills, accounts, pertaining to the Paris apartment. But if that was the case, why hadn't Sylvie found them? Perhaps they hadn't been through them yet. The woman in the neighboring apartment in Paris had said that all the bills had been paid, but she didn't know any more, other than that the owner was a Mademoiselle de Florian. Where would an old woman keep her secrets? Where was she living when she died?

Cat slipped a bracelet onto her wrist and went down the stairs.

"Sylvie?"

The kitchen was empty. Cat could sense that the entire house was empty. She jumped at the sound of a Vespa revving its way up the steep street. Obstacle number one.

Then there was the sound of Sylvie, out on the front doorstep. Clearly, she had been waiting for her son. Cat stayed in the kitchen, walked around the room a couple of times, and straightened her hair.

"Chérie?" Sylvie's voice rang through the house. "Come and look who is here, my darling!"

She knew who was here. It was just that she couldn't quite pinpoint whether she wanted him to be here or not. Or whether it didn't matter—which it shouldn't. Not a bit. Loic was Sylvie's son, and that was it. End of story. Except that he had flirted with Cat, and she had to admit she had felt flattered. Or had she imagined that? Was she so easily affected by a couple of kisses on the cheek from a handsome French man? But then, deep down, did she want to rush back to New York? She took a couple more turns around the room. Of course she wanted to go home. Back to sanity—to a lovely engagement party, and to . . . the wedding planner? Oh, dear. She should be there too. She frowned at her reflection in the mirror. She looked pale. Pinched her cheeks a couple of times. What was she, a thirteen-year-old?

Sylvie burst into the room. "Cat!"

"I'm here!" Cat turned from the mirror and almost fell over the sofa.

Sylvie almost bumped into her at the same time. She grabbed Cat by the arm and dragged her into the front entrance hall.

"Look who has arrived!"

"Bonjour, Loic," Cat said. But just as she said the words, she stopped. Someone else was in the entrance hall too. A girl, who was taking off a red helmet and shaking out her long dark hair. Two large brown eyes raised themselves up to look at Cat, and the girl held out a slim brown hand to shake Cat's own.

"Bonjour, I am Josephine."

Loic's girlfriend. Of course! Fabulous. Perfect. Well, that answered that question. Cat had allowed herself to play the blushing schoolgirl, and here he was already taken. How ridiculous Loic must think she was. Although she hadn't behaved like a fool, had she? She shouldn't be too hard on herself. Oh, things seemed far simpler in New York. She held out her hand to the other girl. "Nice to meet you."

Sylvie skipped past Cat and pressed her lips to Josephine's cheek.

"Alors," Loic said. "Let's go through."

"Cat." Loic took off his gloves and left them with the helmets on the hall table. He was wearing a leather jacket, and his dark hair was slightly ruffled.

"Morning, Loic," Cat said.

He indicated for her to go through to the kitchen first.

"Josephine! Josephine!" Sylvie bustled to the espresso machine.

"Let me." Loic went over to the cupboard and got out coffee beans.

"Merci." Sylvie grabbed Josephine's hand and led her to the table.

"How is Maman today?" Loic asked Cat.

Cat set four cups on the kitchen counter. "There's something you should know—"

"I thought bringing Josephine over was a good idea." Loic whizzed the beans like a pro.

"Sure."

"She came down last night on the Avignon train. I picked her up after I left here."

Why was he telling Cat all this? He seemed to want to explain. But there was no need.

"Aha," she said, very casual.

"Damn. Maman should get a new machine." Loic shook his fingers. "In fact, I'll buy her one today. There's a pretty good shop in the village now that sells this sort of stuff. Handy."

"How useful."

Loic stopped and looked at her.

"Look. Cat."

"Loic?" Sylvie called to him. "Josephine has been made a partner in her practice!"

"I know, Maman. It's wonderful news. Excuse me," he said to Cat. He started walking over to them but then turned, his head tilted at an angle. "Was there something, Cat?"

"Oh, later." Cat smiled, waving him off. She let out a sigh.

"Chérie!" Sylvie called. "You come over too. You are part of the family!"

Cat hovered by the counter.

Loic indicated the chair next to him. "Come and sit down, Cat."

Sylvie and Josephine were clasping each other's hands now, speaking in rapid French.

"Mutual congratulation society. Happens every time they get together," Loic said. "Did you . . . sleep well, Cat?"

Cat put down her coffee. "Yes, thanks. But—"

Sylvie turned her smiling face to encompass them all. "*Bien*. Shall we tell them? Shall we tell them our darling little plan, chérie?"

Cat felt her stomach drop. "Oh, I don't know, Sylvie. Is that a good idea? I mean, there's no rush, you know. We can talk about it later. It's nothing, absolutely nothing at all."

"Cat, what's going on?" Loic's voice was low.

"The café is ready, darling." Sylvie smiled at him.

"Oui," he said, not taking his eyes off Cat as he pushed back his chair.

No, please, Cat thought, *let's not discuss this in front of this elegant, beautiful stranger. Not now*.

"What sort of practice do you work in, Josephine?" Cat asked.

She could sense Loic's narrowed eyes not leaving her for a moment.

"*Psychologue*." Josephine's voice was like crystal.

"Oh, congratulations!" Cat said. Of course. Why not? The girl would be psychoanalyzing everyone in the room. She probably knew about Sylvie and Cat's mad plan already. Their body language had probably given the game away before they spoke.

"Oui, chérie, it's a big practice in Paris. So exciting for Josephine. But, still! Cat and I have an announcement!" Sylvie clearly was not going to be put off.

Loic returned with four espressos. He handed one to Cat first. She tipped her head back and drank it.

"Shall I tell them, or you?" Sylvie's eyes danced.

Cat shook her head. "Oh, I don't know . . . we could . . . talk about it later," Cat said, wanting to indicate wildly at Josephine but failing spectacularly to move her head an inch.

"Spill it, Cat," Loic said.

"We're all family, Catherine," Josephine purred.

"Oh!" Cat said. "I'm so sorry, I didn't realize." Loic and Josephine were engaged? Married? Why shouldn't they be? "I—well, that's so great. I . . . you live in Paris, then, Josephine. It would be hard to find work near Loic, I suppose."

"Sit down," Loic growled.

Josephine looked at Cat as if she were a lunatic.

"Oh, sorry, chérie!" Sylvie said. "Forgive me! I thought you knew. I thought Loic would have told you."

Cat ran a hand through her hair. "Sorry?" she said, not looking at Loic.

Josephine appeared to be struggling with laughter. "Sorry," she said. "It's been a big few days."

"Of course." Sylvie leaned forward and patted Cat on the arm. "I should have introduced her properly. Cat, this is my daughter, Josephine."

Cat felt herself redden from the base of her neck to the top of her head.

"Enchantée." Josephine held out her hand again.

"Oui . . ." Cat muttered, surprised at her use of French. She still couldn't look at Loic. Still sensed him watching her.

Sylvie had a beady look in her dark eyes now. "Cat and I have something to tell you both. We have, as you say, a plan."

Cat closed her own eyes.

"What is this, Maman?" Josephine sounded serious.

"Well. Cat and I have struck a deal."

"Pardon?" Josephine asked.

"A deal." Loic folded his arms.

"Oui." Sylvie still sounded confident. "I am too old to chase around Paris. And my feelings for my mother were—and are still—raw."

"Oui, Maman," Josephine said.

"But I have to know why my mother kept this secret. I need to know the truth—before I die. And Cat, Cat has agreed to help."

"Well." Cat cleared her throat. "I'm hoping that Sylvie will take back her inheritance. I think there's been a mistake."

"So Cat finds out the truth—which seems an impossible task—and if she proves that the inheritance should go to Maman, then Maman has agreed to, well, accept it." Loic supplied.

"Well, sort of. Oui," Sylvie said.

"Oh, no, no, no. I have worked all of this out." Josephine stood up and moved behind her mother, resting her hands on Sylvie's shoulders. "It was, how you say it? Post-traumatic stress. *Grand-mère* could not bear to return to the place that she had to flee. It is simple. There are many cases like this one, you see. Most especially with the war. You look at that generation, you will find many, many such cases. It is understandable. Non?"

Loic looked amused and caught Cat's eye.

Cat looked away.

"She then shut it all out," Josephine went on. "Blocked it. As if it had never existed. Maybe she meant to tell you someday, Maman, but that day never came. It happens. Is simple."

"She remembered to let her lawyer know that her 1940 will was to be carried out," Loic pointed out.

Josephine shook her head. "No, no, I mean she refused to acknowledge her life in Paris consciously at the level of her relationships with other people around her. She kept it to herself."

"That doesn't explain why she cut me out from inheriting the apartment, Josephine." Sylvie was serious.

Josephine shot a look at Cat.

"There is something very strange going on there," Cat said.

"Hmm," Josephine said. "I still say deep post-traumatic stress."

"Or maybe there was something she didn't want you to know about," Cat spoke softly. "Something else. Another reason."

They all turned to her.

"But it will be impossible to find out! You will waste your time, Cat. And Maman, it will be way too much." Josephine shook her head.

Sylvie turned to her daughter and reached out a hand. "*Ma petite*. I will not know peace until I know we have tried our best to learn why my mother did this. Her not telling me amounts to . . . a lack of trust? I think? Oui . . . if I don't try to find out why she kept this secret, then I will never know whether it was me or . . . something else."

"Maman!" Josephine threw her hands in the air. "You are catastrophizing and internalizing! You must change your thinking! How could it be you who is the problem here? It would be nice if she had told you, but this is not the end of the world! Non! You had a good relationship with your mother. You must focus on this. She is gone, Maman, you need closure, not this stranger searching through all of her things! It will end in disaster and upset for all concerned! If our grandmother had an apartment in Paris, then that is her private affair. So what? Is not a problem, if you look at it the right way."

"Ma petite, I am not mad. But if I never know why she kept this secret . . . well. It will haunt me. And it could affect all our futures."

"What if you find something that hurts you?" Loic spoke, his voice soft.

Sylvie shook her head. "You see?" she said to Cat. "You are the only one who understands. Thank goodness I have you to help me."

Cat didn't have to see the dagger looks that emanated toward her from Josephine's direction. She could feel them. Loic stood up, went over to the kitchen counter.

"Loic, Maman is not in a state to discuss this now," Josephine announced. She stood up. "I only hope, Maman, that you will soon see sense, but I cannot sit here and listen to any more. I cannot rely on you, Cat, to protect my mother from pain, and she will not listen to me. I am going back to Paris."

"It will cause me more pain not knowing, Josephine," Sylvie said.

Loic folded his arms. "I don't want you to suffer either way, Maman."

"Oh, this is not a problem; she has Catherine to scrounge around for her," Josephine said. "Our mother has found a near stranger to root around in our past, and Maman has made this decision with no input from us. And what good could possibly come of learning about our grandmother's long-held secrets? I don't care about the money, but I do think that this is an invasive plan."

"I don't care about the money either," Loic said, his voice soft.

"But what if its millions? That painting could be worth a fortune!" Cat said. She reached out a hand toward Sylvie, but then drew it back. It had been her idea to find out what had happened. If it was going to cause a real family crisis, she would stop, but it seemed to her that Josephine shouldn't be the one to make that decision. "Don't you think your mother has the right to make her own decisions?"

"But whose idea was this, Catherine? Who is making this decision? You?" Josephine asked.

Cat closed her eyes and shook her head. Josephine clearly didn't want Cat fishing around in her grandmother's past. Perhaps Josephine had enjoyed a special relationship with Isabelle. Did she feel threatened by Cat? Isabelle had died only recently, so the feelings of loss were probably still raw for her, too. But it wasn't as if Cat had sinister motives. She just wanted to give the inheritance back to Sylvie. Thank goodness she had Christian to go home to at the end of all this. She couldn't handle this sort of drama in her life.

Josephine stormed out, and the front door closed.

"Talk to her, Loic," Sylvie said.

He turned and followed his sister out the front door, and the sound of the Vespa shooting off down the hill echoed through the house.

Sylvie leaned closer to Cat. "I am exhausted. I will rest. Start by searching in my attic. There are several suitcases and boxes up there that contain my mother's belongings. I haven't had the energy to go through them yet. It's still too difficult for me. But see what you can find."

"You don't think Josephine is right about Isabelle? After all—"

"She is psychologue, oui," Sylvie finished. "But she is not an expert on the past. She wasn't there. If you can find out the truth behind this extraordinary situation, then maybe we have a chance, all of us, of living in peace."

Cat sighed. "Right. I'll head up to the top of the house right now."

Sylvie leaned forward and hugged Cat, hard.

CHAPTER ELEVEN

Sylvie's attic was as well kept as the rest of the house. The wide, long room sat directly under the eaves, its walls and floorboards painted white. There were dormer windows along the front side of the roof, letting enough natural light in to make the room inhabitable. Cat moved toward the suitcases marked "Isabelle" stacked neatly along the back wall.

There were three suitcases. Cat opened each one gingerly and spread them open on the floor. It was strange going through Isabelle's recent past. The overwhelming collection of exotica in Paris had been replaced with outfits of the most utilitarian order.

It seemed indelicate to search through the pockets of Isabelle's three plain coats, worn and fraying in places; her three felt hats; a few summer dresses kept—Cat suspected because Sylvie or perhaps Josephine could not bear to part with them yet. Perhaps they had been favorite dresses, dresses that Isabelle had worn again and again. Part of her. And yet it appeared that Isabelle had been determined to erase the part of her that had existed when she was young.

There were no hidden documents in any of the old woman's pockets, nothing in the suitcases that hinted at Isabelle's past. Isabelle's papers were stacked neatly in a cardboard box. There was nothing even remotely suggestive of a secret apartment in Paris. Isabelle had covered her tracks like an expert.

It didn't take long to search through the rest of the room. Everything was up to date and labeled with thick black felt pen. After two hours of looking, Cat knew there was nothing there to find.

"Nothing," she told Sylvie late that afternoon. They sat in the living room, sipping glasses of wine. "Your mother did a good job."

"I thought so, chérie. So. Where do we look next?" Sylvie's determination and unwavering belief that Cat was going to be able to find something out were at once endearing and worrisome.

Cat looked at the hopeful expression on Sylvie's beautiful face. Her mother had only died recently. Was this determination to find out about Isabelle's past about more than she realized?

"The nunnery, I thought. She may have . . . confided in them, Sylvie."

"Yes, I suppose she may have talked to them." Sylvie passed the back of her hand across her forehead. "Look. Why don't you go up there tomorrow? I think it would be best if Loic went with you. Josephine will be on the next train back to Paris. I have potential customers coming to look at some paintings in the morning. They are coming to the village especially from Aix. And I would probably become emotional if I learned that my mother had shared things about herself with the nuns while she kept it all from me. I would not be an asset to your investigations. Let us put it like that!"

"Sorry."

"No, no. Loic's vineyard is in the valley below the village. It is a short walk down the hill. You won't miss it. I shall tell him to go with you and talk to the nuns. He can translate. And we will see. Oh, this is hard, you know. But, well. We must deal with it. I cannot die, chérie, without knowing the truth about my mother."

"No," Cat said, her voice coming out quite absently. "I don't think I can, either."

• • •

The next morning was clear, sunny, and crisp. Cat stopped just as she left the village, following Sylvie's directions onto a narrow shepherd's path that wound its way down into the valley below, and looked back at the picturesque village that sat on the side of the hill. Cat could now see, perched above this, the old convent that Sylvie said had been there for centuries. On the next summit across were the ruins of a medieval castle.

Sylvie had called Loic during breakfast and battered out instructions in rapid French. There had been an argument.

"He claimed to be busy! I did not accept this."

Cat had felt a chuckle rising in her throat. "I don't need Loic with me, Sylvie."

"Bah! He is being very stubborn, chérie. As you know, Josephine is worried that this search will find nothing and I will be upset. Go through the whole grieving process again. Apparently, I am just getting better, and this could tip me over the edge. Now Loic has started to listen to Josephine. I want answers! All I want is the truth!"

"As long as you're sure, Sylvie . . ."

"As long as we have tried, I will not mull it over in my mind like—how you say—a whirlpool. But, I cannot rest, not properly, until you have done all you can."

Cat had nodded. "In that case, Sylvie, I'm off to the nunnery."

"Go to Loic first, chérie. Make him drive you up the hill."

Cat leaned down and kissed Sylvie on the cheek. "Leave it to me," she said.

"Do not let him bully you!"

Cat waved as she went upstairs to get ready for the day. It would be interesting to see what sort of mood Loic was in.

• • •

There were several large estates, similar to Loic's, dotted around the valley. Cat had gazed at them from her bedroom window, wondering which one was his.

Early blossom had started to place tentative blushes on the bare trees that lined the stony walkway down the hill. Cat hugged her wool overcoat around her against the unexpected frosty air. Sylvie had loaned her a pair of solid walking boots, and she was glad for these as she avoided the potholes that dotted the path. When she arrived at Mas d'Amiel—the name on an elegant sign on the gate—Cat could feel the combined effects of the chilly air and the sun on her face. It had probably turned pink.

She stopped at the pair of wrought iron gates that stood open at the entrance to Loic's property. There was a small gatehouse on the right, smoke emerging out of its chimney into the air, then a long drive lined with bare trees that looked to have been trimmed in that classic rectangular way that the French favored. These were flanked on either side by vineyards, spreading as far as Cat could see.

Cat began her walk up the driveway. The best plan would be to ignore any negativity on Loic's part. She was doing the right thing by helping Sylvie. That was certain. After all, Sylvie was the one most affected by Isabelle's secrets, and Cat was clearly invested in discovering the truth as well.

These thoughts bolstered Cat as she trudged up the long driveway to the house, "Mas d'Amiel." It was a charming name, even if its owner was proving to be more than a little confusing. Cat rounded a bend in the driveway and stopped.

"Oh!" she gasped aloud. She found herself standing before a three-story honey-colored Provençal mas. Three rows of symmetrical windows, their pale blue shutters open, overlooked what was clearly a professionally designed front garden, its box-hedged beds curving around a central fountain surrounded by winter pansies and early daffodils.

As Cat approached the house, she passed a handsome black-painted sign off to her right, pointing to the winery. A high stone fence, topped with wrought iron details and a lamp and with a wide gate in the middle of it, led to what must have once been the stables. Now, several small vans and two large trucks were parked just inside the gate.

Cat stopped walking when Loic appeared through the wide gateway in front of her.

"Have you been waiting long, Cat? Sorry, I didn't see you there."

This was unexpected. He looked almost pleased to see her. Cat didn't reply right away. After the way he had stormed off after his sister, she had been braced for some kind of rehashing of the argument they'd all been having earlier. And Sylvie had said he was being stubborn. But as he stood there, wearing a pair of dark green Wellington boots and an old pair of jeans, she realized he was waiting for her to speak. And unless she was mistaken, he looked almost uncomfortable.

"I haven't been waiting at all. Just arrived, in fact. It's a beautiful walk down the hill."

"Good. Good." Loic gestured with his head. "Come inside. I'll . . . er . . ."

"Look, I don't want to interrupt your work."

He stopped outside the pale blue front door, paused for a moment. "I'm sorry about my sister. She was very close to our grandmother. Losing her affected Josephine more than I realized. I understand what she's saying, but I talked to her again this morning after I spoke to Maman. We're grateful to you for your help. My mother really seems to want it, and we're grateful you're willing to do that for her. I think she sees you as less emotionally involved in it all than she is, and so young, and . . . I hope she's not putting you to too much trouble, Cat."

"No. It's okay."

Loic moved forward and opened the front door to the house. He led her into an enormous entrance hall. A curved staircase, with a more delicate version of the stable's black ironwork and a balustrade in the same intricate pattern, wound its way to the top floors of the house. It was so tempting to ask if she could have a tour. But she was here on business. That was all.

"This is my . . . house," Loic said. He seemed to be watching her.

"Well. Wow!" Cat said, turning to him, keeping her voice bright, although this hardly did it justice. "It's beautiful."

A flicker passed across his mouth. "Good."

He strode to the right—opening an enormous set of double doors—through a sitting room that opened directly off the entrance hall, and sauntered straight through the room. Two oversized cream sofas framed the room, a gilt mirror hung over the fireplace, and several dramatic pieces of modern art covered the walls. Cat wanted to linger and stare, but Loic kept going, through another set of doors and past the dining room, complete with a table that looked to seat twenty; more huge pieces of contemporary art on the walls; and another fireplace the size of Cat's apartment in Brooklyn.

Then he turned abruptly left through a swinging wooden door, and they were in the kitchen. Two black Labradors rose out of a basket in the sun underneath a set of French doors that looked out on to a kitchen garden surrounded by high stone walls.

Absently, she reached down and patted one of the Labs. He snuffled his nose into her hand. After a few moments, she turned to face Loic.

He was leaning against one of the kitchen counters that lined the wall. A long wooden table occupied the middle of the room.

"You . . . like cooking?" Cat winced at her words.

"Yeah, I do." Loic picked his Vespa helmet up off the counter.

"I'm wearing the wrong shoes. For the nunnery, and the bike." What on earth was she talking about now?

"The nuns will probably kick you out."

Cat felt a giggle coming on. "I . . . like your kitchen."

"Thank you, Cat."

There was a silence.

"I . . . should be fine with the nuns, though. It's no problem."

"None of them speak much English. Could be tricky."

"Oh."

"Yes."

Cat folded her arms. The Lab went ever so slowly back to his basket, stopping and looking up at Cat. "Hello, there," she said, moving over to give him a pat.

"It's unlikely any of the nuns are old enough to remember Isabelle's arrival in 1940," Loic said. "Our only hope is if she confided in any one of them more recently. But they're thick as thieves, they are. Will be impossible to get much out of them, I would think. Even if any of them had talked with my grandmother."

He was right, and it was hard to know what to do about it. Cat followed him out across the *potager* and through a wooden door in the wall. His scooter was parked on the gravel.

On the back of Loic's Vespa, Cat attempted to come up with a plan. If Isabelle had confided in any nuns, she would probably have sworn them to secrecy, given the trouble she had taken to keep the apartment a secret from her family. It was unlikely that any confidante from the 1940s would have passed Isabelle's story on to the next generation of nuns.

Cat clasped Loic's hips as they rounded a bend. She closed her eyes. Christian. Christian was the person to focus on right now.

She pulled back all of a sudden. She had gotten too close. Darn it, now what would he think?

But he seemed focused on the road, eyes ahead, as he charged up the hill.

"Okay, here we are." Loic stopped the bike right at a set of tall gates. A high wall encircled the top of the hill, and Cat craned to see glimpses of the nunnery rising up behind.

Loic took off his helmet. He rested it in the crook of his elbow and looked at Cat.

"Thanks for the ride."

"Let's go see what secrets these nuns can tell us."

"Great." Cat took a step toward the gates, which were bolted shut with an enormous lock. She stopped for a moment, then, slowly, turned around to face Loic.

"Bell," he said, pointing to a huge bell to the side of the gate.

"You've got to be joking."

His mouth twitched. "Need a hand?"

"I'm fine." Cat pulled on the heavy bell rope. Nothing. Not a solitary note.

Loic put his helmet down and strolled across to stand behind her.

"I'm fine," Cat said, giving the bell another heave. Not a peep.

Loic was close behind her. His arms were around her body, his hands on hers on the bell. Cat wanted to move, didn't want to move. It was only a bell. He was only helping her, and yet . . . he was quite close.

"*Un, deux, trois* . . . pull!"

Cat pulled.

An enormous peal rang out through the valley. Cat wrenched her hands up to her ears, but Loic beat her to it. His hands were warm on the sides of her bare head.

She turned to face him.

His eyes were dancing with mirth. When the bell stopped, he gently took his hands away from her ears.

"It's colder up here," Cat said.

"True. It's warmer down in the valley." Loic's dark eyes caught her own.

"Bonjour, Loic!" The gate was opened, slowly and steadily, almost right away. Had there been a nun hiding behind it the whole time?

"*Soeur* Susanne," Loic leaned forward and kissed the middle-aged nun, who held the gate open for them, on the cheek.

"What is the reason for this pleasure, Loic?"

"This is Catherine Jordan," he said. Then he went on to explain to Soeur Susanne, in French, why they had come there.

"Ah." Soeur Susanne held out a soft hand to shake Cat's. "C'est une periode difficile pour vous, non?" It is a difficult time for you, no?

"Oui," Loic said. "Est-ce un bon moment?" Is this a good time?

"Oui, oui, absolument. Entrez."

"Ah. Merci. Je . . . my questions will be *vite*!"

Susanne smiled and opened the gate.

"Glad you've got that sorted," Loic drawled behind her.

Cat felt her nerves getting the better of her. She was in over her head. She should have seen it coming. Loic was going to make fun of her the whole way.

"Soeur Marguerite keeps all the records," Loic whispered into Cat's ear. "She thought that was the best place to start. If we can establish when Isabelle arrived, then, I don't know, it might give us a clue where my grandmother came from? Soeur Susanne insists that Isabelle did not confide in any of the nuns. She worked here until thirty years ago. In the last twenty years, she only made the journey up here when she was invited to do so—to attend certain religious occasions, that sort of thing. Isabelle wasn't the sort of person who just came up for chitchat. And none of the nuns have been here for more than twenty years. Seems they're quite the itinerants these days."

"Excellent," Cat said. That this was a crazy mission was certain. What had she been thinking?

"Merci!" Cat said, as Soeur Susanne stood back to allow her to go first down a long, dark corridor. It was lit with the occasional wall sconce, but after the clear Provençal light outside, Cat had to blink a few times to adjust to the dimness.

"Keep walking," Loic said from behind.

"I am."

They passed several closed doors on either side of the passage. Susanne and Loic chatted in French until the hallway widened into a circular room. Several wooden doors with curved tops led off it. There was a rug in the middle of the floor, and a round table with a small statue of the Virgin Mary.

Susanne knocked on the farthest door to the right, turning the handle at the same time. She popped her head inside and then came back to speak to Loic.

"Sister Marguerite is at prayer," Loic said. "I told her we would wait."

Soeur Susanne kissed him on both cheeks. She said something in French and then bustled off up the hallway.

Cat hovered on the spot, folded her arms, and looked at the floor.

Loic leaned against the wall. "She thinks it's worth talking to Soeur Marguerite, just on the absolute off chance she knows anything. But it's unlikely, so don't get your hopes up. Soeur Marguerite has been here the longest, but only for just over twenty years."

Cat nodded.

"So," he said. "Have you got a list of questions?"

Cat felt a twinge of irritation. Of course, he was right.

The sound of a door closing sliced into the space, then, footsteps.

"Ah, Loic!" A nun whose wrinkled face was almost as pale as her wimple looked up at Loic. He leaned down to kiss the tiny woman on the cheeks.

"Vous allez bien?" she asked him.

"Oui, oui. Soeur Marguerite. Je vous presente Mademoiselle Catherine Jordan."

The hand that Marguerite held out was small and soft. As the nun led them into her office, she chattered with Loic. Isabelle's name came up several times, but Cat got the impression that Marguerite was only asking Loic how Sylvie was coping with her mother's passing.

When they all sat down at Marguerite's simple table, Loic explained the whole story in French. It was hard to know whether to look at Marguerite, as the older woman's eyes widened until it looked as if they would pop.

When Loic finished, there was a pause, and then Marguerite held out her tiny hand and patted Cat's.

Cat felt herself relax back into her hard seat a little

Marguerite began talking, rapidly, to Loic, her remarks punctuated with the odd shrug. Cat could see that Marguerite wasn't able to help.

Cat chewed on her bottom lip.

"Je suis desolée, Mademoiselle," Marguerite said, shaking her head.

Loic turned to Cat. "I know that my grandmother arrived here pregnant and exhausted after her escape from Paris. But that's all I know, and Marguerite doesn't know anything else. The nuns don't ask people about their pasts. It's up to visitors if they want to talk, and it is well known that my grandmother did not. They came to care about her, and she cleaned for them until she was sixty-five. That was all."

Marguerite made a comment. She sounded a little bossy now.

"Marguerite has offered that we go through the visitors' records. Like I said, it's our only option."

"It's a start." Cat followed Marguerite and Loic out the door. "Thank you," she said, turning to the nun and taking her hand.

CHAPTER TWELVE

The records office was in a circular turret, way up at the top of the convent. Sunlight streamed in through the tall windows that surrounded the room. Marguerite asked them to wait on the rug in the center of the floor.

"Presumably this was the safest place to store everything," Loic said, as Marguerite unlocked a door and disappeared into another room.

"You can see my house. Look, Cat, there," he said, pointing down to the valley.

Cat went to stand beside him. She could see the roof of his house. It was a large U shape.

"I'm looking at buying another property, that one, to the left."

"How exciting for you."

"I'm planning on turning it into more vineyards, putting another manager in the house. One of my employees is a really terrific chap. He has four children. Would get them all out of the town, kids into the countryside. Perfect for them. If he wants to do it, of course." When he turned to Cat, his face was lit up.

The door opened and Marguerite entered with two great books in her arms. Slowly, she pushed the door shut. Loic took the heavy old books from her and put them carefully on the table.

"Nineteen forty," Loic translated. "Marguerite has things to do. I can stay and help you, Cat . . . if you want."

The navy blue books were enormous.

"Café pour deux?" Marguerite asked. She sounded pleased with her work.

"Oui, merci." Cat smiled at the old woman. She turned to Loic. "I think I'll need all the help you can give me."

• • •

After three hours, neither of them had found a thing. Reading endless entries—mostly in a jaunty, upright hand, the fountain pen never smudged once—was becoming exhausting.

"I've read four months of entries and exits," Cat said. "Seemed they wrote a record every time a nun walked out the door."

Loic had taken off his jacket and rolled up his shirtsleeves. His dark head was bent over the other book. "A lot of people seeking alms, in this one." He paused and looked up. "Are you hungry, Cat?"

"Starving."

"Here." Loic pulled a chocolate bar out of his pocket. Held it out to her.

"This is good," she said, taking a bite.

"It's French."

The bar was rich, and too much for one person. "Want some?" She held it out to Loic.

"Yeah, thanks." He grinned at her, leaned forward, broke a piece off the end.

"Back to work." Cat took in a breath. Businesslike. That was what she had to be. Just because she was seated in a turret overlooking a spectacular hillside in the South of France, with the sun streaming in onto a stunning French man opposite, there was no reason to flirt. What would Christian be doing now? It would be morning there, so . . .

Another hour went by. The sun had moved again and now shone directly into Cat's eyes.

"Need to move?"

Cat slid the heavy book around to the other side of the table.

"Do you have any ideas for what we should do if we find nothing here?" Cat asked, turning to yet another enormous page full of spidery handwriting.

Loic went quite still. "Cat," he said.

Cat pushed her chair back, twisted her long hair away from her face and behind her head, and whisked around the table to look over Loic's shoulder.

He pointed at the page in front of him.

Cat's phone rang.

"Oh, darn it. I have to take this call."

"Honey!" Christian's voice was a faint scratch in Cat's ear.

"The reception . . . I can't hear." Cat moved away from Loic but kept her eyes trained on him. He had a piece of paper and a pencil and was writing things down.

Christian said something—it was unclear what, exactly. Then: "Could you put me on speaker, Cat? It might help you to hear me more clearly!"

Cat glanced at Loic. He appeared to be absorbed in the record books. "Look, can I call you back?"

Christian's reply was undecipherable.

"I'm not alone." This was in a loud stage whisper.

"No! Urgent!"

Cat moved toward the turret's door. She could hear voices outside. At least two nuns were at the door.

"Need to be quick!" Christian shouted.

"Oh, God," Cat muttered. She glanced at Loic again. He hadn't moved. Wincing, she put the phone onto speaker mode.

"Honey! What's the delay?" Christian's voice belted through the entire space.

Loic seemed to shift a bit in his chair, but he didn't look up.

"Not alone here, Christian . . ."

"Mother wants to announce our engagement in the *New York Times*. This weekend. They're doing it. Normally, they need six weeks notice!"

"Oh."

"Right. Honey, they need to know the school you attended, all your awards and achievements, your parents' place of residence, and both their occupations. Even though they're deceased. I know some of that, but you'll need to fill me in on some of the details."

Loic looked up.

Cat moved right to the very corner of the room.

"Charity events you've attended recently, Cat."

"Me?"

"Work with me. Please."

The room felt rather hot. The nuns outside laughed at something. They sounded very cheerful. Loic had put his pen down; his eyes were right on her, crinkling at the corners.

"Honey?"

"Um, can I email you tonight?"

"Cat! If we don't get it to them within a half hour, it won't happen at all."

Loic shrugged at her and grinned. He pointed to the journal in front of him, gave it a thumbs-up.

Cat gritted her teeth. "I went to Coginchaug Regional High School in Durham, Connecticut."

"That won't do," Loic said, almost under his breath.

Cat glared at him. "My parents lived there all their married lives. Didn't you know that already?"

"Did their residence have a name, honey?" Christian sounded patient.

"They need the street address?"

There was a silence. "Your father worked for the office of policy and management. Okay. Mother, Bonnie, stayed home, didn't she, honey?"

"Sure."

There was the sound of furious typing.

"Awards, then?"

"Me?" Cat paced around in small circles. She glared at Loic. "I won the bubble gum blowing contest at the Durham County Fair when I was fourteen."

Loic collapsed in a fit of laughter on the table.

Christian groaned.

Cat smiled and went on. "My mom used to cook for people in need. I helped her deliver the food. But they never gave me a prize. I never asked." She stared at Loic.

Christian went quiet. "Honey."

"Yes?"

"That's absolutely fine."

Loic sat up.

Cat smiled. "Fine?"

"I like it."

"Right!" Cat held her head up. "Perfect, then. Talk soon."

"When are you coming home? Elise's working away on the engagement party. Three hundred guests. A garden party at our place in the Hamptons. String quartet. Finger food. We wanted The Frick, but with less than two weeks, even Mother couldn't swing it. When will you be home?"

"Soon. I'll be home soon."

"I'll book you a flight tomorrow, then?"

"Christian . . . I can't."

"Could you get in touch with my assistant to book your flight, then? No longer than ten days. Although that will be cutting things a bit close. I miss you. I need you here, honey. I can hardly wait to start planning the wedding itself. Cat?"

"Yes, me too, Christian." She looked helplessly out the window at the view. A tractor wound its way through a grove of olive trees just beyond Loic's land.

"Good-bye for now," she said, and hung up the phone.

Loic pushed his chair back. "Okay, then, Mademoiselle Bubble Gum, what are you doing tonight?"

Tonight? Nothing. She should book her flight home.

She moved back to the table. "What have you found, Loic?"

But Loic stood in her way. "Have a break tonight. Come to an engagement party in the village. They're old friends of mine. We all grew up together. I think you'd have fun. In the square. Plastic chairs. Paper napkins. Entire village, communal cooking."

Cat gave him a look. He was doing it again. She wouldn't react, even though her stomach was doing a little dance of its own. "Tell me about the entry."

"Look at this." Loic rested his finger on the yellowed page of the journal. The handwriting was clear. "Albi. Isabelle de Florian arrived here from Albi. On the twenty-second of June, 1940, seeking alms."

Cat went to stand next to him and then moved slightly away again.

"Three hundred kilometers west of here. I hate to think of her walking."

"Pregnant, during the war," Cat said, her voice quiet.

"I know."

"No address in Albi, though."

"It's a lead, Cat." His voice was soft. "Shall we get out of here?"

"Yes." Cat pressed her hand to her forehead. She followed him down the stairs, while he tucked the piece of paper with the date written on it in his jeans pocket. He popped his head into Soeur

Marguerite's door and thanked her. As they rode back down the hill, he seemed preoccupied.

"Come to the party tonight," he said, as he stopped the scooter outside Sylvie's house. "Have some fun, Cat. Forget . . . everything for a few hours."

Cat handed him his helmet.

He gently pushed it back into her hands. "Pick you up at eight?"

"I really need to sort things out at home."

"Sure." Loic revved up his engine.

"Look—" Now he was being sarcastic.

"I can't hear you!" Loic shouted. He flipped the brake off and disappeared down the street.

"Oh, darn it," Cat said, aloud, to herself. She opened Sylvie's unlocked door, went inside, and stomped upstairs for a bath. After that, she would call Christian.

• • •

"Honey, I'm in the middle of lunch with clients. I've only got a minute."

Cat was in her pajamas. Sylvie appeared for the third time at her bedroom door in her third possible outfit for the engagement party in the village square. This time, she had on a stunning black wool dress. It clung to her timeless curves perfectly. Cat gave her the thumbs-up.

"You cannot stay here alone, chérie." Sylvie didn't move from the doorway.

Cat pointed at her earphones, held up the phone. "I'm so sorry, Sylvie. I've got things going on at home."

Sylvie marched across the room. "Party is in an hour. You cannot be on the phone all night. Is bad for you. Take a break, Cat. Be French!"

"I looked at three apartments today," Christian said. "The second one was the best. Closest to the park. I took Tasha and Scott with me. Tash sent you the link. Did you like it?"

"Tash likes the apartment?"

Sylvie was still there.

Christian cleared his throat. "I thought you and she had similar taste."

Cat thought about Tash's clinical minimalism. Her children did not have toys. "Oh, God, I should be home."

Sylvie threw her arms in the air and turned and left the room.

"No! Wait, Sylvie! I didn't mean that! Not at all!"

"What, honey?"

Cat lay back on the bed. "What was the apartment like?"

"Great kitchen. Good for entertaining. All white. I say we take it. We'll have to make a move now."

"Cat."

"Loic!" Cat sat up on the bed and drew her fingers up to the top button of her pajamas.

"What's that, honey?"

"Nothing," she whispered into the phone, sending Loic devil messages with her eyes. "Excuse me!" she hissed at him.

He leaned against the doorframe, looking ridiculously handsome in an open-necked shirt, black blazer, and jeans. "Everyone is going. You can't stay here."

"Excuse me," Cat said, getting up and moving toward the door.

"Should I sign the lease? What do you want me to do?"

Loic took a step inside the room. "What're you going to wear?"

"Nothing!" Cat almost shouted down the line.

Loic raised one eyebrow. "Very French."

"What? You—out!" Cat moved to push Loic and then took a step back.

He had opened the wardrobe. ". . . although this would also make a beautiful first impression." He had zoomed in on a blue

1930s vintage dress that she had hung up just in case Sylvie had proved to be the formal type. He put in on the bed.

"Christian," she said, looking at Loic.

"Look, I say we go with it, honey. It's perfect."

"Can you hold the apartment for a few days?"

"Sure, honey. But it's not clear to me why you can't just get on a plane and come home. I'll need to make a decision about it soon."

"Things have gotten more complicated," Cat said, feeling her shoulders tense. "I have to go." She hung up.

"Sorry things are complicated, Cat." Loic sounded serious, but his eyes were flirtatious.

Cat stood in the doorway of the bathroom, facing him. "Okay then. You win. I'll come to the party if Sylvie's going. But I should be home. I wish you'd just taken the inheritance and left the past alone." She shut the door, pulled the dress over her head, brushed her hair, looked at her face in the mirror. She pulled out her makeup bag.

"If you were Maman, you'd just take the apartment, and the painting, not knowing anything about it, even though it had been left to a stranger?" he called through the door.

Cat smoothed foundation over her skin and brushed on eye shadow, some blush. She worked fast.

"Is that what you'd do, Cat?"

"It's not like that."

"But it is, isn't it?"

Cat put her makeup brushes down and sighed into the mirror. Then, in a gesture she had never before used in her life, she threw her hands in the air, just like a French woman.

Sylvie got a lift to the party with friends, and Cat climbed off the back of Loic's bike at the bottom of the hill forty-five minutes after she had started getting ready. He had parked right on the edge of the market square. The buildings that framed it housed shops, apartments, and a couple of small hotels. They were all lit up. Cat looked at the enormous white tent that covered most of the square. An accordion was playing; there was the sound of laughter, the smell of meat roasting on a spit.

Cat put her helmet on the bike and ran her hands down the blue dress, straightening it.

"You'd do the same thing as Maman, Cat. I'm sure of that."

Cat looked at him.

"How many of your real friends are you inviting to your engagement party?" he asked.

Cat stopped. If he had been standing in front of her, she may have slapped him. Instead, she folded her arms.

Just then, a group of men came tumbling out of the tent. Seeing Loic, they threw their arms around him, slapping him on the back. Then they saw Cat and stopped.

"So," one of them said. "This is the beautiful Américaine, Catherine."

Loic patted the man who had spoken on the shoulder. "Thank you, Leon. Cat, I'd like you to meet Paul and Marc. Now, I'm going to take Cat inside for a drink."

"Ah, we'll be back in a minute!" one of the men shouted. "You, Catherine, have fun!" he called, blowing a kiss to Cat.

Loic held out his arm for Cat to take. He smiled and shook his head.

Cat stood there for a moment, and then she smiled back. She took his arm and walked into the party. What was the point of arguing about things, anyway? With any luck she would be back to her own life in a few days. This escapade, France . . . it would all be nothing soon.

CHAPTER THIRTEEN

Cat lost track of how many times her glass had been topped up with pastis. She had managed to eat most of the plate of food that one of Sylvie's friends placed in front of her—delicious spit-roasted meat, colorful salads, fresh baguettes. The engaged couple had both made long and raucous speeches in French. Loic had translated for her, quietly, and now, his own speech was well underway, as he would be the best man at the wedding.

"I didn't know he was best man," Cat said to Sylvie, when she appeared at their table.

"He and Patric have been close friends since they were very young."

Cat sat back in her seat, the white plastic that Loic had promised, feeling her shoulders relax. Once Loic finished his toast, to loud and long applause, the sound of happy conversations and laughter filled the tent. Though Loic's chair was empty for the moment, the man on her other side made a valiant attempt to conduct a conversation in some mangled mix of French and English that had them both in hysterics.

A group of older women brought out a cake the size of a football field, and after some loud and very out-of-tune singing, they began slicing it up.

When Loic came back to the table, a young woman leaned forward and said something to the group. Then there was a general shuffle, and the woman seated herself next to Cat.

"'Ello." The young woman's red hair was piled up in a messy bun, and her green eyes danced. "I 'ave wanted to meet you. I am Aurore, old friend of Josephine's."

"Nice to meet you." Cat smiled.

"Eh! Loic!" Aurore shouted. She said something about pastis.

"Mais, non!" Loic batted his arm at her from the other side of the table.

"Non? Pastis?" the girl shouted.

"Oui! Pastis!" The rest of the table joined in.

Aurore leaned in closer to Cat. "Is old game. We play when we are teenagers."

"Oh, goodness," Cat laughed.

The first few questions of the game, which was clearly some sort of truth or dare involving pastis, were conducted in French. Though she didn't understand a word, Cat allowed herself to laugh along with the enormous guffaws that roared around the table.

"Catherine." Aurore nudged her. "Is your turn."

"Oh, no, I don't have anything to ask."

"No. Is not that," Aurore whispered. "Is Loic, 'e 'as question for you."

"No one wants to know anything about me."

"Cat," Loic said, his eyes straight on her. "Describe your apartment in New York. Truth only."

Quiet descended on the table as ten pairs of eyes stared at her.

Cat frowned at him. That wasn't such a hard question. She opened her mouth.

"You cannot tell a lie," Aurore hissed. "If you are caught telling a lie, you are out of the game. Last man standing is winner. Loic is last man in, apart from you."

Everyone was watching her. The atmosphere seemed surprisingly tense. "I live in Brooklyn. I have an apartment there. It's small, nothing special."

"Oui."

"Okay?"

"More detail."

Cat looked at him. She had nothing to hide. The game was ridiculous, but still. "It's decorated with vintage things. Pieces that I've found in markets. I buy them, restore them, and . . . it's not cluttered, though. Just that everything is kind of special. To me. Anyway."

"They don't understand you," Loic said in English. "But I believe you."

There was a round of cheers.

Cat sat back in her seat. That hadn't been so bad.

"Cat," Loic asked her again. "We have to finish the game." He indicated the pile of euros in the center of the table.

Cat shook her head. "I just finished!"

"I already paid for you," Loic said. "One more question."

"Oh, really?" But everyone was looking at her. She smiled. "Okay."

"So, you like vintage things." Loic spoke softly.

"Yes, yes."

"I think that's true. So, why aren't you more interested in all the stuff in my grandmother's apartment?"

Aurore translated this time, to the rest of the table. There were a few mutters.

"Don't you want to just keep it?"

"Never!" she laughed.

"Liar."

Heads spun back and forth between the two of them.

"Une question de plus!" two men shouted.

"They take this game very seriously, Cat," Loic said. "They don't believe you."

"Oh, come on!"

"Tell me something."

Heads swiveled.

"Okay, Cat. Why are you marrying a New York socialite?"

Cat felt her jaw set. "I'm not doing that."

"Liar," Loic whispered. Without uttering another word, he reached out, his eyes stuck on Cat, and, slow as ever, took all the money from the middle of the table. The group erupted in loud shrieks.

"Bah, he always wins," Aurore said. "'e is annoying like that."

"Yes."

"Cat." Loic stood up. "Time to go home?"

"I think so." Cat stood up too. Immediately, all the men at the table pushed their chairs back and swamped them with kisses on both cheeks and warm hugs. A couple of the women she had spoken to earlier stood up and kissed Cat on the cheek as well.

"I 'ave enjoyed meeting you," Aurore said. "I 'ope to see you again."

"Me, too," Cat said, meaning it.

"Perhaps we can go for coffee some time?"

Cat smiled at her. "Oui," she said. "Some time. I would like that." It was unlikely, but there it was.

• • •

Cat woke early. She had tossed and turned all night. Loic's game must have affected her more than she thought. In the end, Cat decided that was exactly what it was. A silly game. It didn't matter. There was no point seeing it as anything else. She got up, pulled on her dressing gown, and went downstairs. She would make coffee and talk to Sylvie about the next steps in her research.

Loic was in the kitchen.

At the sight of him, Cat turned to go back up the stairs, hoping he hadn't seen her.

"Cat?"

Cat stopped in her tracks. Slowly, she turned around. "Hey."

"I've been to the boulangerie. Hungry?"

Cat stood where she was. Loic looked perfectly fine this morning, without so much as a hint of a hangover—although it had been hard to know whether he had drunk much last night. He had certainly had his wits about him; after winning his game, he had been perfectly able to ride his Vespa back up the hill with Cat on the back. She had not said a word to him the entire way.

Now, he seemed perfectly at ease. He strolled over to the table, carrying a plate laden with croissants and another with fruit. The mellow scent of fresh coffee wafted through the room. Cat sat down, poured herself an espresso, took a croissant and a tangerine. Loic sat down opposite her, tore a piece off a croissant, and then put it back on his plate.

Cat ate in silence. Loic seemed perfectly content just sitting there.

After what seemed like enough silence, Cat put her coffee cup down. "I want to help your mother, that's all, Loic. This is a business thing. You don't have to invite me to . . . parties, or anything."

There was a pause. "Fair enough."

"Good," Cat said, standing up. She picked up her plate and one of the platters. "And I'll have to return to Paris and fly home very soon. It's not just the engagement. There's my work, and—"

Loic was right behind her. "I've booked two tickets on the eleven o'clock train to Albi."

"You have got to be joking."

"What's wrong?"

"Oh, so you were drunk, then, is that it? Conveniently don't remember? Would you like me to remind you what you said to me?" Turning to face him now, she almost bumped into him.

"Quickest business relationship I've ever had, Cat."

"Excuse me."

Loic went back to the table and picked up some dishes. Then he stopped. "The New York society pages, Cat? Really?"

Cat pulled out the dishwasher rack too hard.

"You're the one who's going to have to fit in with him, Cat. You'll have to fit *his* mold. He won't change for you."

The room seemed to spin. How dare he feel entitled to give her advice on how to lead her life? He had never even met Christian. What right did he have to interfere?

"I wouldn't have said anything if I thought you were going to be happy."

"You don't know anything about me." Cat rinsed plates. Stacked them. The kitchen suddenly felt very small.

"I heard enough. Do you think he really cares about what you want, Cat? Has he expressed any interest in what you're doing here? Does he listen to you, or is he too busy to care a fig about what matters to you?"

Cat turned, suddenly, to face him. Then she placed her hands over her ears and glared at him.

Gently, Loic reached forward and took Cat's hands away. "I get the message."

Cat turned her back to him and resumed rinsing things off. "We should be worrying about what we're going to do if we can't find any details about Isabelle in Albi."

She would not even think about the things he had said about Christian. Of course Christian cared about her. He had come all the way to Paris to tell her in so many words. He had been delighted with the apartment. And if he wanted Cat back in New

York to help plan their engagement party, well, that was part of being engaged!

"Look. I love Christian. I just want to help Sylvie find some answers, and then I want to go home. Loic, it's my life."

Loic's eyes were on her, she knew that. Best to avoid them. But he stayed quiet, and, after what seemed an interminable silence, Cat looked up at him.

"Look at me, Cat, and tell me you're honestly one hundred percent happy." He almost whispered the words.

"Stop it," Cat whispered back.

He reached out and held her chin in his hands, gently. "Not many people would be as selfless as you with that inheritance, Cat. Honestly, they wouldn't."

"I haven't done anything special." This was safer territory. Cat cleared her throat. "You know, I think you'd do exactly the same thing if you were in my place, for instance, and Sylvie would, too."

He dropped his hand. "Yes. But would that fiancé of yours in New York do the same thing? Would he fight so hard?"

Cat had to press her lips together and turn away.

"You've gone too far," she said.

"I just don't think it sounds like he's good enough for you," Loic said.

"Excuse me," Cat said, her stomach turning and her voice uncontrolled. "I should go upstairs and pack." She moved toward the staircase. Was Sylvie still asleep? Or had she heard her exchange with Loic? Cat closed her eyes and stopped for a moment.

"I'll be returning to my old life, you know, as soon as this is done," she said, still not facing Loic.

There was a silence. Still, Cat didn't turn to face him. "I won't," he said. "I never go back." Cat blew out a breath and climbed up the stairs.

CHAPTER FOURTEEN

Cat stood outside Sylvie's house while the older woman hugged Loic hard. Then Sylvie turned to Cat and handed her an envelope.

"It is the only photograph that I have of my mother, of Isabelle, when she was young."

Cat opened the pale blue envelope and looked at the faded photograph inside. A dark-haired woman stared straight at the camera, her hair swept back off her face in a neat bun. The photo had not been softened or touched up, as so many were during that time. This was no soft-lens romanticized version of Sylvie's mother. Her features were clear.

"Great, thank you." Would she ever come back to Provence and see Sylvie? See this beautiful village perched on a hill? It was unlikely, she knew. Blossoming had spread down in the valley, and the view was a riot of pinks and frothy whites. Leaning forward, she hugged Sylvie.

"You will let me know how you get on. You will keep Loic in line."

Cat pulled back and smiled. "Yes to both. I'll do everything I can to find out the truth. Then, I'm going to hold you to your part of the bargain!"

Loic's friend Etienne pulled up outside the house. He and Loic loaded up their bags.

She had emailed Christian and left a message on his phone to say that she would be returning as soon as she could. That she had promised to help Sylvie, but . . . then it had been hard to know what to say. Now, the images of the apartment that he had emailed to her this morning came into her head again. The apartment was clinically white. Cat had looked at it, trying to see where her vintage pieces would fit. Given that it was all white, anything would match, wouldn't it? As she had looked through the photos of every room, she had mentally placed her things in spots that could work. But would Christian want to live surrounded by her precious collection of old treasures? They really hadn't discussed how her belongings would fit into their new life.

Cat shook her head. Loic was waiting at the car, talking to Etienne, his eyes stuck on Cat. She frowned and headed over to join them.

The apartment was fine. Of course it was. She and Christian would work out how to decorate it. Together.

"Ready, Cat?' Loic asked, holding the car door open for her.

"Yes," she said. "Yes, I am."

• • •

As the train wound through the South of France, then west to Albi, vineyards and olive groves gave way to greener fields, wider rivers, medieval towns. The carriage was half-empty, and, for a brief and uncomfortable moment, Cat considered moving away from Loic. But not sitting right next to him seemed churlish. They needed to be as prepared as possible for what they were about to do.

"I have a theory," Cat said, finally. "About your grandmother."

Loic leaned back in his seat. "Tell me."

"I bet her affair with your grandfather was carried out . . . mostly in the apartment. The memories were too painful. Sylvie told me your grandfather was killed during the war. But maybe it wasn't war that stopped her from going back. It was love."

"Hey, there." Loic held up a hand. "Way too romantic."

"Why?"

"Well, Cat, for a start, my grandmother was tough. She just got on with things. Second, she was not in any way a romantic. She despised anything like that. You're right about my grandfather being killed in the war, but that's all."

"Romance and love are not the sort of thing you discuss with your children and grandchildren."

"Why not, Cat? If you were happy, you would tell your children. You would tell them about their father, their grandfather. She didn't. Ever."

"It was love that stopped her from going back. I bet it's simpler than you think."

"No," Loic said, staring out the window again. "Cat. I knew her. She was the most practical person you ever met. She just got on with things, adapted to any situation, and coped. She was a master at moving on. This is why I find the fact that she left that apartment so fascinating. It's partly in character, but also not. The fact that she never went back sort of doesn't surprise me. But at the same time, hanging on to it, keeping it all locked up and secret—that's the part that's weird. So no, I'm sorry, she would have viewed romance as a weakness. It wouldn't be that."

Cat opened and closed her mouth, but she couldn't help it. "But would she have viewed love as a weakness, too?"

"It can be," he said. "If you get it wrong."

Cat looked beyond him, out the window of the train, and Loic seemed thoughtful for the rest of the trip. By the time they pulled into Albi, Cat had a plan. They would find out immediately if there was a convent in town. Most towns in France had nunneries, didn't they?

"Here we go." Loic stood up just before the train came to a stop, smiling at her, looking, Cat thought, almost conciliatory now. "How about we check into the hotel and ask them to point us to the local nunnery. Let's also have some lunch."

"My thoughts, too." She handed him down the suitcases. Then, they marched off through the station, trailing their suitcases—like any other professional team—off to do business.

• • •

The hotel was just off the main square, opposite the vast red cathedral that stood sentinel, dominating the town center. It was hard to decide whether the building looked more like a church or a fortress.

"It was built to show the strength of the Catholic Church," Loic said. "They had just defeated the Cathars."

"That explains it."

"It's terrific, Cat, don't you think?"

Cat smiled up at him. She had to admit it. His enthusiasm was endearing.

They walked off the square and up a narrow street lined with half-timbered houses, their ground floors devoted to charming artisan shops. Cat stopped several times and gazed in windows.

"So, what do you think of Albi, Cat?' Loic waited while she browsed.

"Beautiful," Cat said, her eyes drawn to the windows of a patisserie whose tidy rows of confections looked more like works of art than mundane food. Automatically, she reached for her camera.

"Cat . . ." Loic stood in the middle of the road and raised his sunglasses.

"Yes, okay," Cat said, tearing herself away from the blissful creations.

"The Albi convent is closed down," the receptionist told them from her desk in the hotel's miniature lobby.

"Oh dear," Cat said. "Is it possible to see the building where it was?"

The receptionist pulled out a map.

"Meet back here in the lobby in ten minutes, Cat?"

Cat nodded and pulled her suitcase toward the tiny elevator.

Terra-cotta tiles, warmed by the midday sun, ran from wall to wall in Cat's room. An enormous king-sized bed covered in a white quilt and at least six soft pillows sat square in the middle of the space. Cat had to tear herself away from the window that overlooked the tiny cobbled street.

Loic was waiting in the lobby when she came down again a few minutes later. It was hard not to stare at the town with its red-colored houses. The bricks appeared to be handmade, pocked with the finger marks of medieval builders, and Cat stopped to take photographs of them.

"The old convent was down this way," Loic said, leading her down yet another narrow street, past a covered marketplace. "The convent is now the Musée de la Mode. Fashion Museum. I doubt we'll find anything there."

Just as they stopped outside the entrance of the old building, Loic's phone began to ring.

"You never know . . ." Cat breathed, taking in the colorful flowerpots on either side of the entrance door, glimpsing the interior: tantalizing vintage fashion displayed in tall glass cases. Right inside the glass door was a large Chloe sign as well as a selection of what were most definitely Chanel vintage shoes.

"Maman," Loic muttered, frowning at his phone. "I'd better take it."

Cat edged her way toward the glass double doors and reached out to one of the oversized copper handles. "Take the call," she said. "I'll just . . . do some more research."

Loic stalked off down the street, phone to his ear. Sylvie's voice rang clear into the air. It was odd, hearing her so far away. Cat missed her already. But if she was lucky, she had fifteen minutes to do a sweep around this intoxicating-looking museum and ask about the nunnery that used to be here. Cat slipped inside.

The gentleman sitting at the reception desk wore a bow tie and a boater hat. Cat couldn't help it when her face broke into a wide grin at the sight of him. If she were a man, she couldn't have thought up a better outfit herself.

"Bonjour, Mademoiselle," the man said, tipping his hat to her, and—Cat was certain—casting an approving eye over her yellow 1930s coat suit.

Cat stole a glance out through the glass doors. Loic had disappeared from view. Hopefully, Sylvie would keep him occupied for a while.

"Bonjour," Cat said, slipping the entrance fee onto the desk in front of her.

"Merci. Il me semble que vous aimez la mode?" There was a definite twinkle in the old man's eye. A comrade, Cat thought. Most definitely.

Did she adore fashion? "Oui, er . . . oh, yes." She cast her gaze longingly into the museum.

With a chuckle, the man handed her an information pamphlet in English.

"Oh, merci." She scanned the front page. The museum had opened only a year ago. The owner was a Monsieur Noel Chevalier . . . none other than the charming gentleman sitting opposite her. He had collected vintage fashion for over thirty years, and the museum's current exhibition was a mixture of his own pieces and items on loan from other collectors.

"Please, enjoy. If you have any questions, I am here."

Cat wanted to leap into the museum and consume it like a gluttonous feast. But she forced herself to stop and held the pamphlet by her side, right out of temptation and sight.

"Monsieur," she said. "I am interested in . . . the nunnery that used to be here."

Right then, her own phone buzzed in her bag. She glanced at the man. He indicated to her to go ahead, take the call. It was an overseas call. New York.

"Oh, I'm sorry," Cat said, her hand perched above the "Decline" button.

"It is no problem." Monsieur Chevalier smiled. As Cat moved toward the next room, the door opened, and a middle-aged couple walked into the museum.

Cat hit the "Answer" button, putting the phone up to her ear. "Bonjour?" she asked, then winced. "I mean, hello?"

"Cat!" The voice boomed down the line.

Cat shook her head.

"It's Tash, sweetie!"

"Tash?"

"I was just calling to find out how long till you're back? And there's one other thing."

"Well . . ." Cat held her hand up to cover the mouthpiece a little. The couple, who were now at the desk, had turned to look at her with barely disguised disgust.

"Look, Tash, can I call you back?" Cat tried to keep her voice soft.

"What's that?"

"Oh, look . . ." Just as in the nunnery in Saint-Revel, the room was almost cavelike. But unlike the reception area, the only lights were on the exhibits, and clearly, the exhibits were something special. The first case contained a collection of wrap dresses in bright silks, once worn by Jackie Kennedy and Grace Kelly. In the almost eerie silence of the room, it was easy to be transported.

"So! I've been helping Chris and Marilyn out with your party! I have to say, Chris is the most divine man."

Chris? Christian hated to have his name abbreviated. And his mother had only recently asked Cat to call her Marilyn.

"It's like I'm getting to know him so much better. You know? You are one lucky girl. Actually"—Tash dropped her voice a few levels—"Scott tells me the wedding planner's an old flame of Chris's? You'd better hotfoot it back home soon, because she is gorgeous, and you know she's a Rothschild?"

Cat closed her eyes. In front of her was an exquisite Edwardian dress, its creaminess offset with intricate embroidery at the bodice, short sleeves, and a parasol. Imagine wearing that a hundred years ago in the South of France, sitting in the garden outside a stunning mas—perhaps one a little like Loic's—in the shade, tea things set up on a small table in front of you, children playing on the lawns. Like a Renoir. Cat frowned and moved away from the exhibit. What was she thinking now?

"Cat?"

"Oh, right, Tash." Cat headed across the room to view a gentleman's dark green silk coat and cravat. Eighteenth century. Solid. Sensible. Now, she could picture Christian wearing that. Much better.

"I have to go, Tash. Thanks so much for helping, but I'll be home soon. I have everything under control. I knew about the planner. I'll contact Marilyn. Don't worry about it."

There was a silence.

"Tash?" Cat hissed, moving to the middle of the dark room. "It's so kind of you, honestly."

"Sure."

The older couple had moved into the room. Cat cast about wildly for somewhere to stand. The woman stared down her extra-long nose at Cat's phone.

"Oh, Tash." Cat walked across to a sensible, high-necked black Victorian gown and looked at it. There was only one thing to do. "I was wondering . . . would you like to be one of my bridesmaids?"

This time, the silence only lasted a beat. "Hey, Cat, don't take this the wrong way or anything, but I'm thinking about the others, Morgan and Alicia, too?"

Of course.

"Of course. Sure, they can be bridesmaids, too. I'd love it." Cat noticed her voice drifting off with her last words.

Tash didn't seem to notice. "This is going to be so good, sweetie." She hung up.

Cat ran a hand over her face.

"Cat?" Loic came up behind her. "You finished?"

Cat forced herself to focus on where she was. "We need to talk to the owner."

They strolled back to the reception area.

"Ah, I'm afraid the nunnery's archives are all with the mairie," Monsieur Chevalier said, once Loic had given him an overview of the situation in French. "The only thing is . . ." His voice trailed off.

A young couple entered through the front door.

"Is best you go to the mairie," he said, finally.

"He was going to say something," Cat whispered to Loic, but he had his hand on the door. "But he was interrupted."

"Cat. Lunch first. I'm starving."

• • •

Loic supplied several of Albi's restaurants with wine from his vineyards in Provence. After he had a quick conversation with the owner of a bistro set in a medieval-looking square just near the cathedral, a waiter showed them to a white-cloth-covered table by the window in a nearly full room.

Once they had ordered the day's special, Loic at last began to talk. "So, we go to the mairie, look in the archives, and take it from there. Agreed?"

"Oh, the mairie," Cat sighed, playing with her wine glass. "Of course."

"What is it, Cat?" His voice changed right away.

"Nothing! So . . . how is your mother?"

Loic shook his head. "I don't want to burden you, but now that you've gone, it's hit her. She's realizing she'll never have a chance to talk to my grandmother about any of this ever again."

"I know. Look, I'm determined to get her some answers as soon as I can. Her peace of mind is clearly at stake."

Loic nodded. "I agree. Thank you, Cat." The wine arrived, and he raised his glass.

"So . . . how difficult was it to establish yourself in the wine business?"

Loic seemed to chuckle. "Well, it wasn't easy at first."

Cat waited a beat.

"I had a partner, at first." He smiled up at her, and she was struck again at how he never avoided her gaze. "We met studying in Paris, and we traveled after we graduated, through Europe, then to Australia. She was as keen on winemaking as I am. And we had this dream of owning a vineyard in Provence."

"What happened?" Cat asked, then, stopped herself. "Sorry. I didn't mean to pry."

"That's perfectly all right." Their food arrived; they had both ordered risottos. "Well, she decided to go back to Paris and do further study, and I . . . had the opportunity to buy the Mas d'Amiel. Victoire came down on weekends for a while, and we made all these plans. But that was all they turned out to be, just plans. Just talk. She met someone else in Paris. So. That was that. For the best, actually."

The risotto was cooked to perfection. The woody taste of porcini permeated the rice. Cat almost swooned over her first bite. "I'm sorry."

"Ah, well. Like I said, it all happened for a reason. I'm sure of it."

• • •

It only took Loic a few seconds to get them past the reception desk at the mairie and into the archives department. Cat pushed all thoughts of home into the remotest parts of her mind. Tash had persisted, texting her three times since their conversation. Could she, Tash, tell Alicia and Morgan that they were bridesmaids? Or would Cat prefer to do the honors? They only had another three hours to send a photograph of Cat and Christian to the *New York Times*. Tash had helped Marilyn choose something and they weren't sure. She sent a photograph. She thought it was a gorgeous shot but wanted to be sure Cat approved. And Elise Rothschild, the wedding planner, had also been in touch with a bossy text asking for Cat's exact measurements.

The man sitting at the archives desk shook his head. "Non, non, non," he said, and then launched into a long monologue.

Loic fired off a few questions and then turned to Cat. He placed a hand in the small of her back. "Let's get out of here," he said, turning toward the entrance.

Once they were back out in the street, Loic strode toward the square. Cat almost had to jog to keep up while he moved straight over to a free bench in a corner opposite the cathedral. He sat down, then he stood up. Walked in a circle, then came back to Cat.

"You know, I can't see any way in hell that we are going to find out the truth."

Cat slumped on the bench. "We have to." Her phone buzzed again. She put her bag down next to her.

"The nunnery closed in 1792, Cat."

Cat tapped her fingers on the bench. A wave of pigeons descended on the square. Several children ran into their midst in delight.

"It's hopeless," Loic said.

"I swear Monsieur Chevalier was about to say something."

"I don't think so. How could he possibly have anything to say when the nunnery closed not long after the revolution?"

One of the children's parents had procured bread. The pigeons crowded around the small group in the corner of the square, swooping and pushing, grabbing at the tiny crusts. Cat's phone buzzed twice.

She ran a hand across her forehead.

"I think, Cat, it's time we called it a day."

She looked up, incredulous, but he sounded serious. "All this angst is driving Maman insane. You should have heard her. Let's just leave it."

"But I can't just take all your grandmother's things."

Loic stood up, started to move across the square, paced back again. Inclined his head. In spite of everything, it was a friendly gesture.

"Come on, Cat, let's go."

• • •

The next morning, Cat packed her suitcase but her mind was elsewhere. She had hardly slept. This morning, another barrage of texts from Tash, Alicia, and Morgan had awaited her. Added to that, there was a lengthy voice message from Marilyn, asking if Cat preferred lavender silk or taffeta for her engagement dress, because wonderful Elise Rothschild, who had stepped in at such short notice, wanted to know. And would Cat mind if Marilyn gave her mobile number out to the caterers and the florists? It was the sort of endlessly polite question that Marilyn would ask.

Cat had stayed awake half the night. To take Sylvie's apartment and the family painting was more than criminal.

"Honey, stop worrying about it," Christian had said at some ungodly hour. "Come on home. I miss you. If these people don't know what a good thing is when it's offered to them, then that's their problem. The apartment was left to you. Give them a benefactor's donation; that will sort it."

"What?" Cat had laughed. "You make me sound like . . ." *one of you*, she almost added. But she stopped.

"Well, I'm sure looking forward to getting to plan the wedding together."

Cat hung up. It was impossible to feel at peace with anything.

And then Loic wasn't in the breakfast room when Cat went downstairs. She ate quickly—a bowl of fruit, some yogurt. She would have to go to the station, check out what time trains left for Paris. She would have to borrow the hotel computer this morning and book her flight back to New York. But there was something she had to do first. She wouldn't be able to live with herself if she left any stone unturned.

After breakfast, she headed back up to her room, did a final pack, brushed her teeth, slicked on some mascara, dabbed on perfume, and slipped out of the hotel. She headed straight over to the Musée de la Mode.

Cat could see Monsieur Chevalier at the reception desk through the doors. But the museum wasn't open yet. Cat approached the glass door, then stopped. If she didn't find out whether he had more to say, it was going to niggle her badly.

Another text buzzed through on her phone. Elise Rothschild. Cat held the phone up and peered at the small photograph in front of her. A mauve confection of a dress: short, tight. Cat texted back a polite "No thank you." Oh, she should be there.

Monsieur Chevalier spotted Cat. He bent down, unlocked the catch at the bottom of the door, and opened it.

"Bonjour, Mademoiselle."

"Oh, oui, bonjour, Monsieur Chevalier." Cat smiled. How on earth was she going to phrase her question?

"Vous voulez entrer? You would like to come in?" he said, holding the door open.

"Thank you. Merci." The interior of the museum sent the same frisson through Cat as it had yesterday. Its magical lighting was already on, the pieces displayed in stark beauty through the dim space.

The elderly man went to sit behind his desk. "Please," he said, "sit down."

Cat took in a breath. She was going to sound ridiculous. Of course, Loic had explained the problem in some detail yesterday, and Monsieur Chevalier had been kind, but still.

"Monsieur. My . . . friend, Loic, told you yesterday that we were trying to trace a . . . refugee who fled Paris in 1940. We thought she may have sought refuge at the nunnery, but, of course, she must have stayed somewhere else."

"Mais, oui."

"Oui. And look, it's just that I thought you started to say something yesterday and then were interrupted. Sorry if I have it wrong. I had to ask."

Monsieur Chevalier lay his hands on the desk. "So. There was nothing at the mairie?"

"The convent closed so long ago," Cat said, keeping her voice polite.

"Oui." He toyed with his fountain pen on the desk. It was exactly like the one Monsieur Lapointe had.

Cat waited.

"So. You are determined to find something out, oui?"

"I have to," Cat said.

"Alors." The old gentleman seemed to appraise her. "Well, Mademoiselle—"

"Jordan, Catherine Jordan."

"Well, this will sound unusual, but there is a woman still alive in Albi. It is known that she took in refugees during the war. I am not sure that she will be able to help you, but—"

"Try me."

"It goes back further than you think."

"Okay."

He waved a hand toward the chair opposite his desk. Cat sank into it.

"There is a story, though some people do not believe it; those who are more . . . religious are not convinced." He eyed her.

Cat stayed quiet.

"It is said that one of the nuns, one of the last nuns in this nunnery, during the revolution, had an . . . affair with a member of the royal family. An escapee from *la guillotine*. A cousin of Louis the Sixteenth."

"Really?"

"And." The gentleman leaned forward. "We have an old woman, here in Albi, who is descended from this . . . infamous nun. Of course, many people say this is rubbish. They do not acknowledge the woman as being descended from royalty, or, more importantly, even of our church!"

"Ah." And this woman had also taken in refugees. So. She was courageous and descended from a rebel—Cat liked the sound of her already. A picture of Marthe popped into her mind, and Virginia. They, too, had wanted to forge their own destinies but had been labeled as crazy, or wild. Cat shook the sound of Loic's voice out of her head. Was she forging her own path or allowing it to be planned for her? No. She wouldn't think like that. She had made her own choices. She wasn't giving up and letting others run her life. The very notion would be ridiculous.

Monsieur Chevalier pulled a small piece of thick cream paper from the top of his walnut desk. He pulled out his fountain pen and started writing in upright black script. "You can talk to this old woman. She will help."

There was an address on the piece of paper, and a name: Mademoiselle Josephine Leclair. There were people outside the glass door. It was ten minutes before opening.

"I will go to her. Thank you, Monsieur Chevalier." How on earth was she going to convince Loic not to head back to Saint-Revel? He had said he planned to book a train first thing.

The old gentleman leaned forward and kissed her on the cheek. "Good luck, Mademoiselle," he said. "I wish you the best."

On her way back to the hotel, Cat mulled over the possibilities. It did sort of make sense that Isabelle may have sought refuge with someone who had connections to the church. If they had found a pattern in her movements, that would be very helpful.

Loic was standing in the lobby of the hotel when she walked in. His suitcase was at his feet. When he saw her, he shook his head and raised his hands in that Gallic way.

Cat rushed over to him. "What time's your train?"

He looked faintly amused. "In an hour, why?"

"I have to tell you what I've learned."

There were other people checking out in the tiny reception area. A small line had formed at the desk, and a couple turned to stare at Cat. Carefully, she reached out, grabbed Loic's arm, and pulled him to the far corner of the room.

"I have a lead," she whispered. "If you have half an hour, you need to come with me now. If my lead can't speak English . . ."

Loic ran a hand through his hair. "Cat."

"Look, I know it's a long shot," she said. "But Monsieur Chevalier knows a woman who's descended from a renegade nun and a prince, or a cousin of the prince, during the revolution. They had an affair. Now, the descendant—who is still alive now, although she must be nearly ninety herself—used to take in refugees during the war. She's called Mademoiselle Leclair. I'm going to see if I can talk to her now. Come with me?"

Loic chuckled. "I thought Monsieur at the musée looked crazy."

Cat forced herself to stay calm. "Look, Loic, if I don't try, then . . . I'll never be able to live with myself."

Loic raised a brow, looked at his watch. "I have half an hour," he said, "but that's all."

"Good." Cat almost slumped with relief.

Loic looked at her, then, and a smile spread across his face. "You seem pleased I'm staying, Catherine?" He pronounced the word with a French accent.

"Oh, not at all." Cat moved toward the exit of the hotel. "Could have had any old translator."

"Could have fooled me just then," Loic said. He caught up with her and reached down, taking the piece of cream paper that Cat held in her hand. His fingers brushed hers, and she pulled away. He was studying the address on the paper. And then, her phone buzzed again. Elise Rothschild. A bright aqua dress this time, floor length, voluminous with gold shoulder straps.

"Lovely, Cat," Loic said, looking over her shoulder.

Cat put the phone back in her bag.

"I know where this is," Loic said. "It's only five minutes' walk."

"Excellent." Cat focused straight ahead.

"Half an hour," he said.

"Of course!"

• • •

Mademoiselle Josephine Leclair's house was an ancient house in a street of ancient houses. When Loic knocked on the door, Cat crossed her fingers that the elderly woman would be home. No sound came from inside, no sound of footsteps through the door.

Cat reached up to the door to knock again, then stopped. "You know, I was surprised that you gave up so easily, Loic. I was surprised you wanted out."

She didn't look at him while she spoke, and when he replied, he sounded close.

"There's no point in me staying, Cat."

For some reason, this filled her almost with despair. She hated to admit that she had come to value his company, his presence.

Loic reached out and knocked on the door again. Nothing. He leaned against the wall, and the sun shone onto the cobblestones. The buildings on either side of the narrow street looked as if they had not been touched for centuries.

"It's another beautiful day," Cat said.

"Yep."

"It's been nice getting to know you, Loic."

"Yes."

She had to do something. Otherwise he'd go, and for some irrational reason, she wanted him to wait a while longer. Perhaps Mademoiselle Leclair had just stepped out to run a quick errand. What if she were to return? How could Cat stop Loic from going right this moment?

Her camera. She took it out. He had expressed an interest in her photography. She would take some shots of him. She could send them to Sylvie. "Mind if I take some photos of you, Loic?' she asked, keeping her voice deliberately casual.

He was a dream to photograph. So good-looking, it was almost ridiculous. Cat took several shots, and then he moved away from the wall.

"Thanks, I'll send them on."

"She'll like that."

Cat put her camera back into her bag.

"Time to call it quits, then?" An odd expression passed across his face.

"Is that what you really want to do?"

"We have no choice. No leads, Cat. Nothing to keep going for. If you want to keep trying, then by all means, do so, but I can't see the point."

Cat started to walk away from the old house. The sound of her boots clattering on the cobblestones was the only sound to break the wintery silence. It was as if all the buildings were asleep. It could only happen in the Old World, Cat thought, this silence, this age-old feeling that, if you closed your eyes, you could be back in medieval times.

"Cat."

She turned back to Loic. He was still standing close to Mademoiselle Leclair's front door. An almighty rattle echoed through the silence, the sound of metal against old, heavy wood. Someone was at Mademoiselle's front door.

Cat walked back slowly, not daring to hope that it could really be Mademoiselle Leclair herself.

After what seemed like minutes, the door opened slowly. And there stood the tiniest lady Cat had ever seen in her life. Indeed, if she had not had scruples, she would have pulled her camera out and started snapping right away. The woman seemed enveloped by the height of the door. She wore a dark pink woolen suit, the skirt slightly flared, and a black brooch pinned to her breast. But it was her face that struck Cat: eyes that were like two dark chocolate drops, set among a multitude of tiny lines and indents that graced the old woman's features with such character that Cat was unable to tear her eyes away.

"Mademoiselle Leclair?" Loic asked.

The old lady, whose hair was pulled back in a haphazard sort of bun, looked up at Loic and smiled. "Oui," she said, holding out an ancient mahogany-colored hand. "Oui."

Mademoiselle Leclair insisted they come inside, waving away any explanations that Loic tried to give regarding who they were. She led them through a low-ceilinged entrance hall and then into a little sitting room with a faded pink sofa and a chair covered in miniature yellow flowers. A magazine lay open on a round wooden table next to the chair, and there was an old lamp next to this, its yellow light shining direct on to Mademoiselle Leclair's puff of hair as she eased herself into it.

Cat glanced at her watch. Fifteen minutes of Loic's precious half hour were gone.

He leaned forward and launched into an explanation, gesturing with his hands as he spoke. Loic spoke a little more slowly than usual, Cat noticed, in an effort to engage the old lady sitting opposite him.

Mademoiselle Leclair sat back in her seat. A flicker of recognition passed across her face. Loic was still.

"How much did you say?" Cat asked.

"Just asked why Monsieur Chevalier thought she might have information."

Cat nodded.

The old woman rested her hands on the sides of her chair. Slowly she pulled herself up to a standing position. Loic stood to help her. She muttered something, almost under her breath. Then she grasped Loic's arm, looked up at him, and smiled. Despite the fact that she was clearly in pain, she spoke rapidly to him.

"She is a pacifist. She took in many refugees from the Nazis. But she says she can't remember an Isabelle de Florian."

Mademoiselle Leclair still had Loic's arm. She said something else.

"She wants us to come with her to the room where she keeps her memories."

Cat followed them, laboriously slowly, down the narrow, dark hallway toward the back of the house. The walls were lined with black-and-white photographs.

Mademoiselle Leclair and Loic turned left at the end of the hallway. Cat followed them into a smaller room. Mademoiselle Leclair reached up, her hand turning on the old-fashioned light switch with a precise, decisive motion. Then she grinned at Loic. It was almost as if she was still entranced by the idea of electric light. What would happen to all of this once Mademoiselle Leclair died? Would it be sold to a couple of Parisian holidaymakers? Turned into a bed-and-breakfast accommodation? It was a treasure chest, an elusive glimpse into the past.

"These are her private records, Cat. She hid them in the cellar during the war years." Loic leaned over a chipped wooden desk.

Mademoiselle Leclair opened the brown leather book in front of him and pointed her knotted finger determinedly at the top of a page.

"Your train," Cat whispered. "You'll have to leave now . . . unless . . ."

"I was dreading catching it." He didn't look at her when he spoke, but Cat noticed his eyes crinkle a little at the corners.

Cat smiled at him and shook her head. She read the faded, sloped entries on the page. There were several entries for 1940, but no Isabelle de Florian. She scanned the list, slowly, twice.

"Isabelle should have been here in mid to late June," Loic said, his eyes on the page. He rested his finger on an entry.

Cat read the name. "But that's not—"

"Look again," Loic said, running his hand over hers.

Cat didn't move her hand. Somehow, if she did, it would be acknowledging what he was doing, so she left it where it was. "Sylvie-Marie Augustin," she read. "Three, rue Charpentier, Sarlat."

"It's in the Perigord region. Further north. On the way to Paris."

"Yes, but it's too long a shot. The name, Loic."

"Read it again."

"Sylvie?"

"Exactly."

"Really?"

Loic pulled out his wallet; he tugged, gently, at the photo that Sylvie had given them of Isabelle when she was a young woman.

"Mademoiselle Leclair?" he asked, his voice gruff. He showed her the picture.

She took the old photo in her hands and pushed her delicate plastic-framed glasses further up her nose. She held the photograph up, stared at it. "Oui," she said, after a while. "*Peut-être.*" Perhaps.

Loic took the photo back. He said something to Mademoiselle Leclair and held her hands in his own for a moment. The old woman reached up and kissed him on the cheek, letting her hand linger there. She turned to Cat.

"She wants to kiss you, too."

Cat leaned down to touch her own lips to the feathery skin of the woman who had harbored refugees, who had helped, who still—in the face of war and of all the years she had endured—was kind, welcoming.

"Thank you," Cat said.

As they emerged out into the clear air, Loic stuck his hands in his pockets.

"Sarlat, Cat?"

"I guess so."

He grinned. "Good. I hoped you'd say that."

CHAPTER FIFTEEN

It was market day in Sarlat. The entire town was covered with stalls that wound around in front of its charming rustic buildings with their steep-pitched roofs and brown-shuttered windows. It was as if everyone in the entire town had put out a table. There were arrays of gorgeous food; a cheese van; fruit stalls bursting with bright oranges, tangerines, and lemons. An entire stall was devoted to walnuts, and several tables were laden with the Perigord's famous foie gras.

Loic seemed keen to show Cat around. On the short train ride, he had pointed out various famous castle ruins perched on the hillsides.

"Come and see a proper French market, Cat," he said, as they wandered through the sunlit streets.

"You have got to be joking."

They had left their bags at the hotel.

Loic threw an arm around Cat's shoulders. "It's the weekend."

"If I keep getting distracted, I'm going to have to go straight to my engagement party after stepping off the plane!"

"Cat, listen. You're going to tell your children that you came to France and never saw our markets?"

"Yes," Cat laughed.

"No."

Cat pulled out her phone. "Rue Charpentier's this way."

"You Americans." Loic grinned at her.

"And you French."

"Be French."

Cat shook her head. She followed her map in the direction of the street she was looking for.

It wasn't far from the town center, down some narrow cobbled streets. Rows of old stone houses lined rue Charpentier. When they knocked on number three, there was no answer.

Cat waited several minutes, Loic hovering behind her. The sound of the stallholders' shouts resonated through the town.

"Whoever lives here's at the market," Loic said. "You're wasting your time, Cat."

Cat knocked again.

This time, a head appeared out of a window in the house next door. A woman with graying hair in a loose bun held the shutters open and called something in French.

Loic thanked her and turned to Cat.

"What is it?"

"The entire street, Cat, has gone to a wedding. That woman is babysitting her grandchildren while her own children are at the festivities. She's come down from Paris for the weekend to help out. No one will be back until after midnight, and then they're hardly going to be in a state to discuss World War Two. We'll have to come back tomorrow. I'm sorry."

"No, you're not."

"No, I'm not," he chuckled.

Cat bit back a smile. The market looked enchanting. Loic, she had to admit, was kind of enchanting, himself. She was in France. Why not just enjoy it? She thought of her grandmother, Virginia. Would she have strayed off task for one day? Yes.

"Take a break. Let yourself have a little fun."

They strolled back out toward the colorful stalls, where merchants were smiling, chatting with their customers. The women carried large woven baskets. Though it was winter, the sun shone.

"Okay," she said. "Just this once."

"Just this once, Cat."

By the end of the day, she had taken hundreds of shots and perused countless vintage stalls. They had spent an hour in a photographer's gallery, admiring his stunning black-and-white photographs and talking about the pros and cons of setting up a small business.

They stopped at a small bar on the way back to the hotel. Cat set her purchases down next to her on the black leather banquette and took a sip of the wine Loic had ordered for them.

"Any French woman would have demanded that I take her out for dinner by now," Loic said, turning the stem of his glass, not looking at her.

"Lucky for you, then, that I'm not French." She smiled.

"Do you like France, Cat?"

Cat leaned forward in her seat. "There's something so . . . comforting about the rhythms of life here. And yet people have such an eye for quality. Everything seems to be such a labor of love."

Loic chuckled.

"Have you ever been to New York?" she asked.

"Yes, once." He looked as if he were thinking about something. "You haven't eaten properly in France yet. The best restaurant in the region is right here in town, and I think tonight's the night."

Cat drained her wine. She couldn't do that. Shouldn't. How would she feel if Christian were going out with someone else—a stunning someone else—for dinner tonight? Because there was no denying that Loic was stunning. And he was French. On the other hand, he knew she was engaged, and he was just showing her his country, nothing more.

"Sure," she said, sitting up. "Sure. Why not."

Loic raised a brow. He stood up and helped her on with her coat. "Very well, then," he said. "Let's go back to the hotel and get ready."

But as Cat applied makeup to her face, doing her eyes as she would if she were going out at home in New York, it was impossible to push away the voice inside her head that told her this was a date. She had, of course, the perfect vintage dress for an evening at a French restaurant, and there was no doubt that the French women there tonight would be no slouches. If she wore it, she told herself, it would only be for her own benefit. Cat frowned at herself in the mirror. Who was she kidding? Any woman would revel in the way this handsome French man looked at her, and the fact that Loic was also no slouch didn't help at all.

But she was not in danger of doing anything untoward. She was engaged to a good man who loved her, and she couldn't be happier. Hurriedly, without giving the matter any further thought, she slipped on the dark green dress, left her long hair hanging loose, and put on a small gold necklace that she had bought for herself at one of the market stalls. A spray of perfume. She looked appropriate, that was all. The French were discerning, and she didn't want to look like a sloppy American.

Cat looked at her watch. Ten minutes until she had arranged to meet Loic in the lobby. She picked up her phone. She hadn't talked to Christian for a while, and the texts from the bridesmaids and Elise had waned. The quiet had been odd and slightly unnerving.

Quickly, fingers dancing over the glass, Cat sent Christian a text, telling him exactly what she was doing. Going out for dinner in Sarlat. With Loic. He was showing her around. Hopefully everything would be all sorted in the next couple of days and she would come home. She couldn't wait to see him. Cat sent it off and shut her phone.

Christian would most likely be going out to dinner, too, with his friends. Of course he would. Loic was a friend. Nothing more.

Loic stood in the lobby. He looked devastating. His white shirt was open at the collar, and the black jacket he wore only enhanced his eyes. He had changed into a pair of black trousers. When he saw Cat, she noticed the way he started a little.

"You look beautiful," he said, giving her his arm.

"Thank you." Cat kept her eyes trained ahead. "It's a . . . lovely evening, for the time of year." She closed her eyes. Stop it. *Stop gabbling. Not the weather. Honestly.*

Loic stayed quiet as they walked out of the hotel and onto the streets, which were filled with couples strolling in the cold, clear air. The restaurant was located in what had probably once been a beautiful old house on a wide boulevard. It had been restored with what looked like great sensitivity to its past. The original wall lights were still in place, gilded mirrors hung on the walls, and the parquet floors gleamed. The effect was cozy and convivial and sparkling.

"I wonder why your grandmother felt she had to change her name—that is, if we're following the right lead," Cat said. Their table was set against a window overlooking the lamplit street. People strolled past, wrapped in long coats and scarves.

"Let's not talk about my grandmother tonight, Cat."

Cat looked across the table at him. "Well . . . this place is amazing."

"Have you ever thought about taking a risk?"

"Risk? What risk?"

Their first courses arrived. Cat took a bite of her foie gras with spiced sauce and caramelized apples and almost swooned.

"Well." Loic leaned forward. "When I started my own business, my father thought I was mad."

"And look at you now."

"But it's not work. It gives me great pleasure—each and every day. And your job?"

He seemed so . . . earnest that it was impossible to tell a lie.

"I hate it," she laughed.

He laid his fork down on his plate and smiled. "You hate it? Did I hear you right?" He shook his head, and his words became softer. "Why would you do that to yourself, Cat?"

Cat avoided his eyes.

"Why are you always . . . selling yourself short?"

"I'm not," she said, but she looked up then, straight at him. There was something so honest, so . . . caring in his voice. Instantly, she pictured Christian. Had he ever spoken to her like that? Did he see how she really felt? Did he care? Cat shook this away. Of course he did. She was becoming confused, that was all. Being away from home, all the excitement with the apartment, and now being here with Loic. It had thrown her off course. She focused on tidying her napkin on her lap.

"Look," she said. "It could be a worse job."

"Why don't you create your own life the way you want it? Why do you just 'settle'?"

Cat pulled her hair back from her face. "Loic!"

"Cat."

"Look. I would love to set up my own photography studio." She was becoming rattled. She knew she shouldn't let him get under her skin, but her words were like a runaway train, and there was no stopping them now. "I would love to start my own business. Believe me. But I don't know the first thing about it, and I can't afford to leave my job, and now that I've ended up with Christian—"

"Ended up? That doesn't sound like living. It sounds like finality."

"No, it's not. Look." Suddenly, she didn't know what to say.

"It shouldn't have to be a life sentence, Cat. Don't you see? So many people exist, so few live. Do you want to look back on a lifetime of regrets?"

Cat shook her head, slowly. The lamb arrived, its herb sauce dolloped generously on top.

"This looks wonderful, thank you." Loic patted the waiter on the back. "You must have fabulous food in New York," he went on, his expression softening all of a sudden.

"There's something about this, though. It's divine." Cat picked up her cutlery. Was she glad or not for the distraction of the food? Their conversation had somehow developed a sort of urgency of its own. She half wanted to finish it, half wanted to escape from its almost compelling intensity.

Loic stayed quiet.

"Look, I admire you for doing something on your own, but it's not for me," she said.

"People would line up for you to photograph them in France. We are a nation of posers." Loic grinned.

"It's not that simple."

"Cat, my father worked for the French government all his life. He was unhappy the whole time, right until he retired. He never came home at night and talked about it, never showed the least bit of enthusiasm for what he did. Fair enough, he adored my mother. She was his salvation, and he was always loyal and loving toward her. But why not have both? Why not at least try to create both the career you love and a life filled with love? As long as you're with the right person—"

"You make it sound so simple."

"Why not? It's exactly what we need: passion for our work and love. Chanel, by the way, said something similar."

"I know." Cat ate in silence for a while. A string quartet began playing in the far corner of the restaurant. Beethoven. Cat's father had loved classical music. She closed her eyes for a moment.

When she did speak, it felt right to speak. It felt as if it was time to talk, after all these years. Maybe it was the music, maybe it was being in a strange country, maybe it was simply being with someone who seemed to want to listen.

"I had always dreamed of doing just that," she said, "but my father vehemently opposed any of my dreams. He thought it was crazy enough for me to want to be a photographer. He wanted me to study law. Had I taken the risk of setting up my own studio, started taking on my own projects, he would have disowned me."

Loic reached out a hand, then pulled it back.

"He wasn't a bad person, Loic. He just had strident views on everything—politics, religion, history, what sort of friends I should have, what I should wear when I was a teenager."

"Aha."

Cat waited for a moment. Should she keep going? But Loic was still quiet.

"I guess he just wanted me to play it safe. Oh, we used to argue—all the time. I just became so sick of hearing all his rigid views on life, you know? It might sound, I don't know, arrogant, but I sort of saw myself as an artist, in a way. I wanted to create something of my own, not just follow other people's rules. I suppose I was rebellious back then."

"I understand."

Cat drew in a breath. Should she tell him? Perhaps not, but he was such a good listener. And if she was honest, she wanted to tell him. She waited a beat. "You see, after one of our arguments, one summer night—six years ago—my father stormed out of the house. He always lost his temper if anyone stood up to him. My mother followed him out the door. She always tried to calm him down. Two hours later. Well. The police called me. I was at home, still. Waiting. And they were both dead. He had driven off the side of the road . . . sorry." She averted her gaze. "The guilt . . . I had to identify their bodies, and go to the hospital, have all this grief counseling, you know."

The waiter presented their desserts with a flourish. Cat forced herself to take a bite of the chocolate cake. But it tasted acrid in her mouth.

"It wasn't your fault." Loic reached out across the table, caught her hand in his.

Cat didn't move her hand away.

"But, you can't live an entire life just to please others. Especially those who are dead."

Something stirred in her at this. "Oh, no! No. My father would have hated . . . Christian and his friends."

Loic watched her. "So that's it, then."

Cat put her napkin down. What was he thinking now? "We should go, Loic."

Loic paused. Looked at her. Looked like he was trying to decide whether to speak his mind.

"For God's sake, don't marry Christian. Don't do that to yourself, Cat. Wouldn't it be better, much better, to do what it is that you love and to find someone who cares enough to support your dreams, someone who shares your interests? Stay with him and you'll write your own tragedy. Why would you do that?"

Cat felt hideously exposed. This had all turned into something so raw, it was physically painful. Could Loic read her mind? What was he trying to achieve? "But you don't know Christian," she said. "He's a good man."

"Is it stability that you want? Is he safe? Is that it? Do you love him?"

"Stop it."

Loic called for the bill, sat back in his chair. Didn't say anything while they waited. When he had paid and they had put on their jackets, he held the door open for Cat and she shivered as the cold night air hit them. Loic took off his coat and laid it over her shoulders. Cat took it. It seemed churlish not to accept.

But as they walked down the street, he caught her hand and stopped her, just on the edge of a pool of light shimmering from the street lamp onto the pavement.

"Cat," he said, gently lifting her chin with his thumb and forefinger. Then he bent down and rested his lips lightly on hers.

Cat shook her head. "No," she whispered, but as his lips touched hers, her entire being sprang to life. For a few moments, she gave into it, kissed him back, her hands wanting to run up and through his hair, to hold him, just as he was holding her around her waist.

It took all the discipline she could muster to step back. "That's unfair, Loic," she said, but her voice was husky, sounding almost like something she had never heard before. Like someone else's voice.

Loic was breathing hard. His eyes, intense, were on her. "Stay with me in France," he said. "Start up your own studio here. Sell those beautiful photographs of yours; take commissions that interest you, Cat. Collaborate with people who write coffee-table books. Whatever it takes, I'd support you."

Cat forced herself to take another step back. She couldn't look into his eyes. She knew what she would see there. If she looked, she would never turn away again.

She forced herself to speak. "The circumstances have been so intense for you. It's understandable that you're confused. But that's all it is."

Loic was beside her. "Never been less confused in my life."

"Please."

"So you won't risk anything, let alone your heart?"

Cat turned from him then and started the short walk back to the hotel. Tears were threatening to fall down her cheeks. It was just because she had opened up. Just because she had told the truth about her parents' tragic death. She hadn't even told Christian. He knew about the crash, but not the events leading up to it. So why had she told Loic all of that?

Cat stopped all of a sudden. Loic was right beside her. He reached out to take her hand.

"Don't be so hard on yourself," he said, his voice almost a whisper. He drew her toward him, took her in his arms again, hugged her.

For a moment, she rested her head on his shoulder, and then she allowed him to take her hand as they walked back to the hotel. What was going to happen when they arrived? Her mind spun like a whirling dervish. She would not do anything untoward. She would not.

When they did arrive outside the hotel, its golden lights streamed out through the long windows onto the pavement. But something caught Cat's eye, something other than the light.

A woman sat in a red velvet chair at a small table by the window. She was looking at them. Cat slipped her hand out of Loic's and moved around to the hotel's entrance. She reached out and rested her hand on the handle.

"Don't give up on yourself," he said.

But Cat opened the door and went inside. The woman stood up from her red chair as Cat strode toward the stairs. She wouldn't wait for the elevator. She had to get away. Fast. But the woman was walking toward them. Loic had entered too, now. *Probably admiring Loic*, Cat thought, and a tinge of sadness crept through her. She pushed it away. She put her hand on the painted bannister, had her foot on the first step, was ready to run upstairs when she suddenly became aware that Loic had stopped in the lobby. Perhaps the woman had approached him. She was determined not to care.

"Catherine? Catherine Jordan?"

A voice—clear, hard, American—came from behind her. Cat turned, full circle, too fast, raising her hands up to her flushed cheeks, both at the same time. The lobby was hot, and she still had Loic's coat around her shoulders. Automatically, she took it off and laid it over her arm.

The woman stood too close, and Cat could smell the scent of her expensive perfume. She was wearing Fifth Avenue jewelry and a kaleidoscopic blouse with a tight purple pencil skirt.

"Catherine." She held out a hand, well-manicured fingers tilted slightly down in that refined way. "Charmed to meet you. Elise Rothschild."

Cat felt faint.

Elise smiled, her tanned face forming into a perfect smile that seemed to complete the package along with her long blond hair. Loic moved up a little closer. He had his hands in his pockets. Cat handed him his coat. Everything seemed like a mirage.

"Christian found you, and here I am" Elise smiled. "It was pretty easy, sweetie."

Cat had a vision of Christian watching her through a webcam. In the restaurant—oh, dear God, outside! "Christian?"

"GPS. Isn't it romantic?"

Cat wanted to sit down on the bottom stair.

"Cat—" Loic took a step toward her.

Cat held up a hand. "I'm fine."

"You went an awful color there, Catherine. I thought you were almost going to faint." Elise sounded cheerful. She turned to Loic.

It was impossible not to sense Elise looking him up and down, putting two and two together and making six. Why had Loic decided to be so stupid tonight, of all nights? Risks and dreams? Cat wished she had never heard the words.

Something had to be done.

"Loic Archer." Loic held a hand out to Elise. "Cat's been helping my mother."

Cat felt her eyes widen and then her shoulders drop. Thank goodness. He was not going to make her look like a fool.

Elise appraised Loic like nobody's business. "Enchantée. Vous habitez à Paris?" You live in Paris?

"Non." Loic shot a glance toward Cat and winked, ever so slightly.

"Loic and I were just wrapping up a meeting, and Loic, Elise is my . . . wedding planner." She cleared her throat.

Loic raised a brow, and his lips twitched. Lips that had been kissing her, only a few minutes ago . . . thank goodness Elise *had* arrived, then!

"Loic, Elise and I should talk. Now, I think."

"Are you sure, Cat?" Loic held her gaze.

"Yes." The word came out far softer than she had intended. "Yes!" she barked.

"My, I wasn't expecting to find you with . . . such a charming French man, Catherine," Elise twittered.

Something sprang inside Cat. It was as if the entire evening had been a slow-motion dream sequence and now she was back on track. Firmly gripping the reins. "Loic, thank you so much. I'll see you . . . in the morning."

But then—how was this going to work? How on earth was she supposed to scour Sarlat—in what was likely a futile search—with Elise Rothschild, society wedding planner of the year, in tow?

Loic caught her eye once more. "Excusez-moi," he said, passing both her and Elise and climbing the stairs up to his room.

Cat felt a sharp twinge of sadness as he walked away.

But she turned to smile at Elise. "So."

"So," Elise said, drawing her hand out and inspecting her watch. "You know, Catherine, it's late. I've had a long trip. We have a lot to do. Let's plan to talk first thing tomorrow."

"I still can't believe Christian tracked me using my phone."

Elise reached her soft hand out toward Cat's again. "There's nothing wrong with a man missing his fiancée! I'm here to take you home, but before that, we're going shopping!"

"I see." Cat gnawed on her lip.

"Yes." Elise started climbing the stairs. An elegant little yawn escaped, and she arranged her fingers over her mouth. "Please, excuse me. Have a blissful sleep."

Cat took in a jagged breath. "Good night," she said.

Ten minutes later, Christian's phone went straight through to voice mail.

"Christian? You can't send people over here with no notice. Anyway . . ." She softened slightly. She had hardly been a model of propriety this evening. "I miss you. I'll be home soon. Call me tomorrow."

Cat went and stood at the window of her hotel room. Outside, the streets of Sarlat were silent, empty of all the color. Now, there was only the odd flurry of wind scattering the few leaves that still lay about, the only remnants that had not been swept away after last autumn.

Cat drew the curtains closed, took off her earrings and her dress, and lay down on her bed. She was unable to stop replaying Loic's kiss in her mind.

CHAPTER SIXTEEN

The next morning, Elise held her hand up to decline the offer of another cup of coffee. She seemed as at home in the tiny breakfast room in Sarlat as she would have been in one of New York's luxe hotels.

Loic had not appeared. Every time someone new walked into the room, Cat couldn't stop her head from swiveling toward the door. When a young couple arrived, their arms thrown around each other's waists, popping pieces of croissant into each other's mouths when they had settled at the nearest table, Cat forced herself to focus on Elise. Elise pointed at her cream folder on the white tablecloth. "Catherine, I just want to start by saying that I am so honored to be planning your wedding."

"It's Cat," Cat said, half-absent.

"Any chance that we might find some suitable . . . shops in this town? I need to get an idea of your tastes."

Cat forced herself to swallow a piece of baguette. Her mind, her treacherous mind, kept lodging itself on that kiss. The way he had held her; the streetlight, shining on the pavement, a pool of silver underneath their feet. She put the bread back on the plate with a thump. What had she been thinking? She had hardly slept.

"Because otherwise . . . Cat, I thought we'd take the opportunity to go up to Paris today. Then we'll get you home for your party in plenty of time. I promised!"

"I have some things I need to take care of here today." Cat still avoided looking at her. "Do you have some things you might like to do today? It's a beautiful town. You're in France!"

"I know France."

"Of course you do."

"We'll do the smaller designers in Paris. The last thing you want is anyone else wearing the same outfit as you!"

Cat ran her fingers around the rim of her saucer. "Did . . . Christian tell you what I'm doing here?"

"He said you were helping some damned French family sort out a will. But, I mean, I gather it's not really your problem."

Cat smiled at the thought of Christian's words. "Well, the fact is, it *is* sort of my problem."

"Yes, but this party is all about you. You can't miss your own engagement party."

"No . . ."

"Come to Paris. Once you get there, you'll forget about all of this."

Cat drained her coffee. Elise was right. Of course, her life in New York—her *real* life—should be her number one priority. It was madness to put that behind a crazy scheme that her grandmother had unwittingly involved her in years ago. But still.

She pushed back her chair. "I can't come to Paris today. But if I can't find anything today . . . then perhaps I'll come back with you tomorrow."

"Is that a promise?"

Cat stood up. "I really don't know."

It was far easier to push thoughts of Elise out of her head than it was to rid her mind of the idea of Loic. After brushing her teeth and folding her clothes and putting them in her suitcase, Cat stalked up the narrow hotel stairs to the third floor and knocked on Loic's door.

She would have to talk to him. She knew that planning what she was going to say beforehand was one thing; saying it directly to his face was going to be quite another. Cat put her ear to the door. Nothing.

Until it opened, fast. Cat almost fell inside the room. Light flooded in from the windows, which were bigger than those in Cat's smaller room. Silently, she cursed the receptionist, who had likely taken one look at Loic and given him an upgrade.

"Bonjour."

But it wasn't Loic who answered the door—it was the maid.

"Bonjour?" Cat said, her own voice slightly hysterical now. "Er . . . Monsieur Archer, s'il vous plait?"

"Non," she said. The young maid appraised Cat. "Monsieur in zis room, he checks out early. Gone."

Cat stared at the girl. "Vous êtes sur?" You are sure?

"Oui." The maid threw open the door.

"Yes, thank you." Cat scanned the corridor. "Look, did he leave any . . . messages, do you think?"

The maid folded her arms. "Mademoiselle."

Cat took a step backward and waved her thanks, her cheeks warming all out of proportion to the temperature in the corridor. She took the stairs to reception at a brisk pace.

"Excusez-moi?"

"Oui?" The young man at reception looked disheveled, as if he, too, had had an interesting night.

"I was just checking if my . . . if Monsieur Archer had left any messages before he checked out?"

The man reached down under the desk.

"Thank you," she said, when the man handed her an envelope. It had the hotel logo on it. Cat checked the reception area. There was no one about. She moved across to the window seat where she had first spied Elise. Her hands fumbled with the envelope. She felt inside. There was something more solid than a letter. She pulled it out; the photo of Isabelle slid into her hand. There was nothing else in the envelope. That was all.

"Charming," she said aloud. The man at the reception glanced at her. Cat put the envelope in her bag. Excellent.

Cat slung her bag on her shoulder. She would simply have to continue alone. But once she was out of the hotel, once she was walking up the winding streets of Sarlat again—past the old houses, through the wide town square—she stopped at the entrance to a narrow, pretty lane. The boutiques, their signs flapping in the sharp breeze, hadn't opened yet. It was too early.

Cat reached for her phone. She was not going to let Loic walk away. She was doing this for him. For his mother. She had not initiated anything. He had. She would not let him ignore her now. If she had to leave a message on his phone, well, then she would do so.

"Cat?" He answered after the first ring.

A woman walked past down the lane. A little girl swung the woman's hand; they were singing a lilting, repetitive tune.

"Morning. I'm going back to the address in Sarlat. Are you . . . still in town?"

"Cat, you know what I think? I think you have so much more potential than you know."

Cat shook her head. "Do you want me to let you know what I find out?"

"Ticket collector's here."

Cat turned into the lane, tucking herself away from the breeze that had sprung up.

"Perhaps I should never have chased down the will," he said. There was a shuffle of paper, a quick conversation in French down the phone line.

"But you did . . ." Cat knew she sounded vague. She closed her eyes. So this was going to be how it would end.

"God knows why," he said.

"I'm going to the house now."

"An entire line of mistakes won't fix things, Cat." He hung up.

Cat stood where she was for a moment and looked up the lane. A woman was opening her shop a couple of doors up.

She smiled at Cat. "Bonjour."

"Bonjour." Cat straightened her bag on her shoulder. She would go back to this address in rue Charpentier on her own. She would try to find out if Sylvie-Marie Augustin—a woman who had passed through the town seventy-two years ago, along with potentially thousands of other refugees from Paris en route to the south of France—was the same woman as Loic's grandmother.

Shouldn't be too difficult at all.

A half hour later, Cat stood before number three, rue Charpentier. The shutters were closed on both floors. For a moment, Cat was reminded of the apartment in Paris. After knocking on the heavy front door, she stood still in the silent street, listening for the sounds of movement inside the house.

The sound of scraping wood above her made her jump. Cat took a few steps back onto the cobblestones. A woman's face appeared in one of the top-story windows. She was in number five.

"Bonjour, Mademoiselle." The woman, who looked about forty, leaned out and looked at Cat.

"Bonjour." Cat smiled. "Er . . . parlez-vous Anglais?" Just then, her phone went off in her handbag. Cat glanced up at the woman, who stood there, watching her.

"Pardon," Cat said, fumbling around in her bag. If it was Loic, he might be able to help her interpret. The woman muttered something in French and retreated behind her window, shutting the shutters with a hard clang.

"Oh, no," Cat said aloud, pulling out her phone. "Please, don't go away." She glanced at the screen. Christian! "Oh, Mon dieu," Cat cried, aloud again. She answered it, double quick.

"Honey!" Christian sounded rattled, as far as Christian did get rattled. "Is Elise with you now?" he asked, his voice cutting into hers.

"No."

"God, sorry, sorry, Cat. She's damned convincing when she wants to be. Told me it seemed like such a good idea. She loves France. You could bond over the boutiques. Insisted she surprise you. Mother agreed, and . . . I've been flat-out . . . sorry." He sounded as if he were in the next room.

"I've been missing you," Cat said.

"God knows she and Mother get carried away sometimes. I'm so sorry. But you have to understand. Elise is no threat. No matter what anyone tells you."

"Threat?" The green front door belonging to the house next door opened. Cat moved toward the woman who stood in the doorway. A girl who looked around thirteen stood beside her. The girl seemed to be going out. She had a backpack slung over one shoulder. Cat moved closer to them.

"Thing is. And I want you to know this, Cat. Have to be honest. Five years ago, we had a brief, well you know, fling, Elise and I. God, should I have told you?" Christian coughed.

"Oh?"

"Mother and her mother are old friends, of course. Elise's done a few other weddings lately. Mother was impressed. It's a professional decision now, that's all."

"Look, I'm not worried, Christian. That's all in the past."

The woman was saying something very fast in French to the young girl.

"Excusez-moi, un moment," Cat said to Christian, and then shook her head at the involuntary French. "Can you hold on for a moment, Christian?"

"God only knows what you thought when she turned up like that, what must you think—"

"I have a little English," the young girl took a step toward Cat. "Can I help you?" Her words were halting.

Cat smiled at the girl. "I'm so sorry, it's my fiancé. I'll be two seconds."

The girl nodded and turned back to the woman, clearly her mother.

"Christian, I have to go. I'm just trying to . . ." There was no time to explain. To him, it was all so simple. Sell the apartment, go back to New York, offer the proceeds to Sylvie. If she took them, well and good; if not, move on. Perhaps it was a more sensible way to live. Clear-cut. Cat sighed.

"I'm looking forward to you coming back, honey."

"Oh, me, too. Look, Christian, we can talk about all of this in person soon. Don't worry. I'll call you later, okay?" She waited until he had hung up the phone.

The woman was pointing at her watch. There seemed to be some sort of argument going on.

Cat held out a hand.

"You are looking for Mademoiselle Delfont?" the girl asked.

"Oui." She would run with this.

The girl turned to her mother.

Her mother nodded.

"You are relative?"

"Oh! Friend . . . she is a friend of my . . . family." Cat blew out a breath.

The girl said something to her mother. She turned back to Cat, reddened a little, and then ploughed on.

"Mademoiselle Delfont in the . . . er . . . hospital. Sick for a few weeks."

"I see."

The mother said something and prodded her daughter in the back.

"Is pneumonia," the girl said.

Cat thought fast. "Could you tell me what hospital she is in, so I can go and see her?"

There was a heated exchange with her mother.

"Alors . . . is the Hôpital Saint-Louis. Down this street. I think turn left, er, maybe right. No, is left. Pardon . . . then you go this way some time, then you turn your right. You will not miss." The girl looked exhausted from such a long speech.

"Thank you so much." Cat shook the girl's hand. "Well done." Thank heaven for Google maps.

"Miette Perrot, et ma fille, Jacqueline." The woman pointed at herself and then her daughter.

"Mademoiselle Delfont," Jacqueline went on. "Send our . . . best wish."

"I will, thank you." Cat smiled. She looked up at the high-roofed building. "You have a beautiful town."

"Merci," Jacqueline said, a dimple appearing on her cheek.

Cat had to restrain herself from reaching for her camera and taking a photograph of the mother and daughter outside their townhouse. She waved and turned to leave. What she was going to ask Mademoiselle Delfont was a complete mystery in itself.

CHAPTER SEVENTEEN

Cat felt oddly calm as she approached the Hôpital Saint-Louis. It was in an old building, its roof steeply pitched, a turret on its corner. One day, she would like to return to Sarlat. One day. The nurses at the reception station looked surprised when she asked about Mademoiselle Delfont. An American, out of the blue? Cat knew she was going to have to be convincing.

"*Attendez,*" the nurse who understood English said to her. Wait. She reappeared ten minutes later, a young man beside her.

"Mademoiselle," he said. "Please. Come with me."

Cat rehearsed and rehearsed what she was going to say to an old lady who in all likelihood had no connection to Isabelle de Florian at all. But when the young man led her into a narrow, small room, furnished only with a sofa, a drab bunch of plastic flowers, and some magazines, Cat knew exactly what was going on.

"There's no need to tell me." The room was exactly like the one in Manhattan—even the faces on the bereavement pamphlets looked eerily similar. Cat had to force herself to focus. She would not think about her parents, would not get pulled back into that time. Her mother's scorched body. Not now. She faced the young man.

"You are a family friend, Mademoiselle?"

Cat nodded. "Ah, yes."

"We have contacted her next of kin. He is in India."

"India?" Cat whispered.

"Oui. Now, is there anything more we can do for you, Mademoiselle?"

What was there to ask?

The man turned to leave.

"That's fine. I'm fine. Thank you so much." Cat moved out of the small room, down the hospital corridor, back into the morning. The breeze had settled, but a misty rain fell now. The cobblestones were shiny. Cat drew her umbrella out of her bag and began walking. She had no destination in mind, but she needed time to think. Every now and then, she stopped, pulled out her camera, and snapped a few shots of rustic lanes with lampposts dotted along their edges, a cat winding its way around one of them. By lunchtime, she was starving.

She knew she was not far from Mademoiselle Delfont's house. Knew that the only thing to do was visit her neighbors again, see if they knew whether she had even lived in the house a long time. She'd love any indication whether the woman was even a relative of Isabelle's, or a friend. It had been an effort, all morning, to make sense of the thoughts that swirled in her mind. Loic, Christian, and now Elise. But for now, she needed to keep her attention on the reason she was in Sarlat. Mademoiselle Delfont's neighbors were her last hope.

As she walked up the street, Cat noticed a familiar figure walking ahead of her, winding her way up the street. The young girl was in a reverie, Cat could tell. As she strolled up behind her, Jacqueline turned around.

"Bonjour, Catherine! Er . . . 'ello." Jacqueline's pretty face broke into a pleased smile.

"Jacqueline, is your mother home now? Would it be convenient for me to talk to her, just for a few minutes?"

"Mais oui." Jacqueline said. "You 'ave had lunch?"

"I . . . don't want to impose."

Jacqueline climbed the little stairway to her front door and pulled out a key. "Is no problem. I will practice English with you!"

"Are you sure?"

"Oui, please. Come in. Maman!"

Cat followed Jacqueline down a long, narrow hallway to the kitchen, where Miette and a handsome man about the same age were leaning over a saucepan together, laughing. Miette turned to Jacqueline and gave her daughter a kiss. There were three other children running around the dining area, playing a game of chase. Their father joined in, catching the youngest—a small girl of about four—and holding her high in the air.

"Bonjour, Catherine," Miette said, smiling. She gestured toward the table. "Voulez-vous déjeuner avec nous?"

"See," Jacqueline said, taking Cat's hand and leading her to a spot at the table. "You can stay, you can stay!"

Once she had been introduced to the rest of the family and everyone had sat down, the conversation flew between different family members. Cat made small talk with Jacqueline, who peppered her with questions about New York. When they had finished the main course—a delicious crisp fillet of fish with tiny honeyed carrots, spinach, and a potato gratin—Cat knew that it was now or never.

"I went to the hospital."

"Oui! I will translate." Jacqueline spoke to her parents. The younger children scampered off. Bruno took a sip of wine.

"I am so sorry, but Mademoiselle Delfont died last night."

"Mon Dieu," Jacqueline said, crossing herself. She told her parents and then turned back to Cat. "Maman says that she was . . . ancient. She was very nice."

Miette and Bruno watched their daughter.

Cat put her napkin on the table. "Did you . . . know her well?"

"She used to come over for lunch, like you are, sometimes." Jacqueline hung her head.

"Sorry," Cat whispered. "I should go. But you were so kind to me earlier that I felt you should know."

"Is fine." Jacqueline wiped away a tear.

Cat knew she had to think fast. This would be her last chance.

"I am engaged," Cat said suddenly.

A sudden smile lit up Jacqueline's face even though it was pale with shock. She told her parents.

"*Felicitations.*" They smiled, raised their glasses.

"Merci. I—the thing is. Well. It's my grandmother's bridal veil. Mademoiselle Delfont was a friend of my . . . grandmother's, and she was a . . ." Bridesmaid could be going too far. "Good friend. Mademoiselle Delfont borrowed it, the veil, that is, years ago. I came all the way from New York to collect it. It meant good luck to my grandmother. And I want to wear it . . . too. So, I was wondering. I don't know if someone has the key . . ."

Cat knotted her fingers together under the table while Jacqueline translated this to her parents. Bruno cleared his throat. In his deep voice, he said something to Jacqueline.

Cat chewed on her lip. "Actually, I am wondering," she ploughed on, "if you ever met my grandmother? I think she visited Mademoiselle Delfont."

Jacqueline translated this. She looked expectantly at Cat.

"Her name was . . ." Sylvie or Isabelle, which would she have used? "Sylvie-Marie Augustin," Cat charged on.

Jacqueline smiled at her. She turned to her parents.

"Mademoiselle Augustin visit here," Jacqueline said.

Something shifted. Cat sat back hard in her seat. Miette said something rapidly to Jacqueline.

"Mademoiselle's housekeeper. She 'elp you."

"Wonderful." Cat blew out a breath of relief.

"We take you to her tomorrow. She has key. She take you into house. You find your veil. Tomorrow."

Miette stood up. Cat stood up, too.

"Non, Catherine," Miette said, when Cat started clearing plates.

"Jacqueline," Cat said, catching her just before she slipped through the doorway. "Could you, could you ask your parents if I could go and see the housekeeper today? I am in a rush . . . my engagement party . . ."

After a rapid-fire exchange between mother and daughter, Jacqueline turned to her.

"I take you there now. I am going to visit my grandmother this afternoon."

Cat wanted to collapse on the spot. Her respect for private detective work had just multiplied beyond belief.

When Cat left, Miette leaned forward and kissed her on both cheeks.

"Maman 'opes we will see you again," Jacqueline said.

"Oui. I hope so, too." Cat smiled. She waved and stepped out into the street with far more confidence than she felt. How on earth she was going to convince the housekeeper that she needed to be alone to search the house was one thing. What on earth she was looking for in the old lady's house was quite another. The only possibilities were letters or diaries. How she would read them was yet another question. But it was too late to back out of any of this now.

When she and Jacqueline arrived at the housekeeper's street, Jacqueline waited with Cat at Mademoiselle Delfont's housekeeper's front door. The house was in one of the old lanes that snaked behind the main streets of the town. The housekeeper answered the door almost right away. When she saw Jacqueline, she waved them into her entrance hall. A short conversation in French followed. The housekeeper knew that her employer had died. She hugged Jacqueline and patted the young girl on the head. Jacqueline told her about Cat. The woman made a face, threw her arms over her head as if to make a veil, and shook her head.

After what seemed like a terrible pause, during which Jacqueline appeared to be pleading with the woman while the housekeeper folded her arms and took Cat in, the thin woman finally nodded her head. "I take you to the house, in few days. I am in shock. I cannot go there now."

"Thank you, Mademoiselle, but . . ."

Jacqueline looked at her watch, squealed and ran out the front door.

Cat waited until the sound of the young girl's footsteps had retreated into the afternoon.

"You see, it is delicate. I am . . . pregnant. I need to go home to America as soon as possible. Or my wedding will be a complete disaster. I will show. My fiancé's family is . . . very strict. I will have a horrible life. If you could take me to find the veil today . . . well." Cat looked down at her 1940s pumps. Heaven help her, she was a terrible liar!

Mademoiselle huffed and folded her arms. She took a lap around the room. Then, she appraised Cat. "Wait. I will get my bag."

"Thank you. Merci." Cat offered up her biggest smile and sighed with relief.

• • •

Mademoiselle Delfont's house was higher and narrower than Miette and Bruno's house next door. There was a stairway just inside the front door. The housekeeper stayed tight-lipped as she led Cat to the kitchen, settled herself at the kitchen table, and folded her hands on her lap.

"Je vous attendrai ici," she said. I will wait for you here.

"I can look upstairs?" Cat waved a hand up the stairway. She felt as if she were a burglar.

"Oui."

Cat wiped her hands, which had become slightly damp, on the sides of her dress. The second floor was tiny, just a landing with two rooms off it. One was a bedroom; a polished wooden double bed sat hard against the wall, its bedspread white and fresh looking, along with a dressing table and an armoire. Everything was in its place. It was as if Mademoiselle Delfont's spirit had not quite left.

The room next to this was a small sitting room, its faded red sofa covered with Aztec-patterned cushions. The walls were lined with books—mostly history books and politics. On a coffee table in the middle of the floor was an old television guide, the television remotes arranged neatly next to it. Several ornaments sat on the windowsill that looked out on to the street. It all seemed well kept, organized.

Cat moved back to the small, empty landing. She looked up at the ceiling. An access door. So there was an attic. Mademoiselle Delfont could well have corresponded with Sylvie-Marie Augustin. Cat's only hope was that she had done so in writing.

There was an upholstered chair by Mademoiselle Delfont's bed. As quietly as she could, Cat carried this out to the landing and placed it under the hole. Then, taking off her shoes, she stood on it, pushed the door open, supported herself with her fingers, and peered into the roof cavity, the top of her head just above the lip.

But it was just an attic, musty with dust that hovered in the light that formed yellow strips in the otherwise dark space. Cat peered, swiveling slowly on the chair, supporting herself with her elbows on the lip of the manhole. No boxes. Nothing. She slid the manhole back into place, climbed off the chair, and put it back.

The housekeeper cleared her throat downstairs—a great harrumphing noise that echoed through the house, causing Cat to jump. She looked at the armoire and tiptoed over to it, shoes still off. The door was locked. Cat closed her eyes; the housekeeper should know where the key was. But if the woman caught her rummaging through Mademoiselle Delfont's papers, well then . . . Cat wiped a hand across her forehead.

She moved to the dressing table and eased open the top drawer as quietly as possible. Cat hardened herself against the wave of feeling that swept through her as she looked at the recently deceased woman's things. There was an old brush, lined up like a soldier in perfect formation, with three lipsticks, their lids peppered with escaped streaks of pink and red; a powder compact; and a small pot of moisturizing cream. The drawer was lined with thin brown paper. Cat lifted this up; a piece of it almost fell away from her hands as it cracked with the delicacy of age. She shut the drawer again and reached for the bottom drawer.

There was a thud on the stairway. The housekeeper's footsteps were slow but firm as she mounted the stairs. Cat pulled at the bottom drawer. The woman's steps continued.

This drawer contained a stack of unused purple notepaper; the scent of lavender shot into Cat's nostrils as she fumbled, her fingers catching on the worn red ribbon that bound the paper together. In spite of their shaking, her hands whizzed through the rest of the drawer, traveling far faster than the housekeeper's feet. Old bills, a dry-cleaning note for twenty euros, a letter, a wedding certificate, two pairs of glasses . . .

The footsteps stopped. Cat spun her head around. The housekeeper wasn't watching her. Instead, she seemed to have gone into the television room across the tiny landing. There was the sound of the woman tutting, more footsteps. Cat returned her attention to the drawer.

"Mademoiselle?" The housekeeper was coming toward the bedroom. Two seconds, one second. "I have to go, Mademoiselle. I have job in other house."

"Oui." Cat scanned the inside of the drawer. There was nothing obvious in sight. The housekeeper's laborious steps grew closer. Then she noticed that the lining didn't quite lie flush with the drawer—could that mean something? She slipped her fingers under a corner of the paper. There was a furious sound of ripping as the paper came up from where it had stuck to the bottom of the drawer.

"Damn," Cat muttered under her breath. There was something wedged under the lining. Knowing Cat's luck, it was probably a laundry bill, but she grabbed it anyway. She pushed the drawer shut with a thump and threw herself away from it, almost falling over her own feet.

"You no find this veil."

"The armoire was locked."

"No veil in the armoire."

"Oh." Cat sighed.

The housekeeper didn't move from the doorway.

"I checked under the bed," Cat said, keeping her voice quiet. "My grandmother said it might be there—"

"I clean under the bed. Each week. I clean it. No veil there."

"Of course."

The housekeeper waved her arm at Cat. "Am sorry you not find your veil," she said. "You make beautiful bride in any way. I see that." She turned to leave.

Cat watched her and felt inside her bag for the envelope that she had taken out of the drawer, tracing her fingers around its edges, then followed the housekeeper out of the room.

"Merci," she said, as they reached the front door.

"Oui." The woman held the door open for Cat. "God bless."

"*Au revoir,*" Cat said, relaxing a little at this. She turned down the street, headed toward the main square and her hotel. But as soon as she had turned the corner, she picked up her pace, trotting along, her wedge heels clacking on the pavement. The late afternoon sun shone, watery, as if it had absorbed all the morning mist and wind and was benevolent now.

Several people sat on benches in the square, reading newspapers and watching children run around the fountain. There was only one empty bench. Cat swooped over to it, sat down, and reached inside her bag and started to pull out the envelope.

"Catherine!"

Cat sat up with a jolt and closed her bag with a snap.

"I've been looking for you everywhere." Elise arranged herself on the bench.

"Elise."

"Oh, Cat, wait until you see what I found. For both of us."

"Both of us?" Elise had several bags at her feet. For a hideous moment, Cat pictured them in matching violet dresses at the party. "Oh."

"This town's not so bad, you know." Elise reached down to one of the bags. "The French just have such natural style! I mean it! Now, I'm not going to show you anything I've bought until we've both got something to drink in front of us."

"Elise—"

"Why don't we go for a coffee? No need to sit out here in the cold. My goodness, I could even go for a hot chocolate, not that I normally would, but, hey, this is France, what do you think?" Elise reached down and grasped her bags.

"Elise, I have something I need to do right now. Just give me a few minutes."

Elise looked at her, eyes wide. "I bet you can't wait to get back to New York. Oh, you must be wildly excited. A white wedding! Chris says you're a photographer! We're going to make sure this is the most gorgeous wedding ever. One people will talk about for years."

"Elise, I need five minutes."

"Now. One tiny thing. That handsome French guy you were with last night is divine. What's his story?"

"I wasn't with him." Cat felt her stomach sink.

Elise linked her arm through Cat's. "Well. Knowing my luck, he's probably halfway around the world by now. Didn't see him in the hotel this morning. Even though I had a good look, I can tell you. So, can we get back home and get this party started?"

Elise stood up and began walking toward the nearest pretty street.

Elise hadn't listened to a word Cat had said. Cat bit back her annoyance and followed the other woman across the square, shaking her head at the back of Elise's elegant woolen coat.

In the end, they chose a typical French bistro, with tiny round tables and sparkling mirrors on the walls and a bar in the middle of the room. Elise had all her bags at her feet.

"Marilyn asked me earlier about desserts," Elise said, pulling out her Blackberry and tapping a few keys.

Cat sipped her espresso.

"And, for starters, the caterers want to know if you'd like vintage-style plates for the party? Marilyn thought you'd love the idea. See, she is thinking of you. It's so nice."

Cat had to put down her coffee cup.

"I told them yes"—Elise looked up—"to the vintage crockery, if that's okay? As for what we'd serve, we thought we'd do French patisseries for dessert? A bit of France!"

Cat could only nod. Elise's kindness, and Marilyn's, only exacerbated her guilt over what had transpired the night before. But what had happened last night hadn't been her fault. Or had it?

Elise leaned down into the bag. "And this," she said, "I thought would be so perfect for the party. Is it you? I mean, if it isn't, there's no drama."

Cat couldn't help but gasp. Instinctively, her hands reached out to stroke the exquisite gown that Elise held up. It was oyster-colored silk, backless, and draped to the floor, swathed at the front. Nineteen-thirties, to a T.

"My God," Cat breathed, her heart wanting to break.

"Great," Elise said. Carefully, she put the dress back in its bag.

Had Isabelle owned something like that, leaving the apartment in Paris to go to the theater, spraying on some perfume from one of her round bottles on that exquisite dressing table? Her hair would have been done in some elaborate style, swept off her face. Or imagine her grandmother, Marthe, the beautiful courtesan. How divine she would have looked when she went out.

"My dress is completely different. I'll show you later. Now. About tomorrow," Elise said. "I thought we'd catch an early train up to Paris. Seven o'clock okay for you? I know it's early, but then we could go straight to the airport. I can get us on a connecting flight to JFK tomorrow evening. There are some business-class seats left, you know. Lucky I can pull strings. We'll have you out of here and back in New York in no time. Then you'll have a few days to get over the jet lag and be thoroughly recovered for the party."

"Elise?"

"Mm-hmm?"

"I have to . . . use the restroom. I'll be back." The restroom was right at the back of the bistro. Cat almost sprang toward it.

She had maneuvered her way through the sliding wooden door into a tiny area with a sink and then through another door to a toilet: footpads, a hole in the ground. Cat pulled the sliding door shut, holing herself up against the basin. The light in the tiny room was dim; Cat perched underneath the only bulb, which swung above her head. She peered into her handbag, feeling for the envelope.

There was a knock on the bathroom door. "Sweetie?"

Cat fumbled about in the bag, keeping her fingers as silent as she could. She hit on the envelope and pulled it out.

"It's your prospective mother-in-law. On the phone. She wants to know . . . sorry, are you finished?" Elise's voice rose a few decibels as her speech went on. Her hand was on the door. It wasn't locked.

Cat slipped the piece of paper back in her bag, fast. She opened the door, almost falling into Elise.

"Marilyn's on the phone?" Cat asked, knowing she sounded breathless.

"Moët or Krug for the engagement party? She has the wine merchants on hold right now. What do you think?"

What on earth was the difference between the two champagnes? "Better to ask Christian, do you think? I don't really mind."

"He has meetings all day. It's your call."

"Well, I think Marilyn should decide."

Elise eyed her. "Moët," she said, launching into a quick conversation with Marilyn.

"Elise, I just have to do something. Lipstick! You know how it is!" Cat moved toward the bathroom door again.

Elise stayed where she was, still chatting to Marilyn at the back of the bistro.

Cat slipped back into the tiny room. With a flourish, she reached inside her bag. The envelope was sealed.

The envelope was addressed to Mademoiselle Catherine Jordan.

Elise was still outside the restroom. "I'll use the restroom after you," she called through the door. "You know, this is getting very exciting."

Cat read the address again. It couldn't be right. Had she picked up another envelope from inside her bag by mistake? She was going insane.

"Are you done in there?" Elise whispered. "Someone else is here, too. We're going to have a line here soon!"

Cat stuffed the envelope back in her bag. Then checked it was in there. Zipped the bag closed. Cat felt almost ill with waiting, but she would have to wait.

"Go ahead," she said, opening the door, her smile bright.

"Oh, I'm okay after all." Elise linked her arm through Cat's. A man had joined the line. He reeked of beer and cigarettes. "After you!" Elise waved him into the restroom.

"Let's get out of here," Elise whispered to Cat. "And let's go plan your wedding! Drinks in the hotel? Then dinner. My treat."

"Great," Cat said, her voice growing ever quieter.

By the time they were back in the hotel, Cat had made a plan. "I should go and freshen up," she said.

"Again?"

"What?" Cat had already started moving toward the staircase, but Elise had a grip on her arm.

"Just don't tell me you're incontinent, that's all." The other girl tossed her long blond hair. "I had a bride like that a few years back. Had to rush to the ladies room during the service. Then again during the speeches. You do your pelvic floors, sweetie, don't you?"

Cat took Elise's arm this time. "Drinks, then," she said. "I'm not incontinent, Elise."

Four hours later, when Cat thought if anyone said the word *wedding* again she would quite happily hide under a rock for a year, Elise seemed to have exhausted even herself and yawned elegantly as they arrived in the hotel lobby.

"So, I'll see you at six, then. We'll need to be at the station by six forty-five."

Cat stopped. "I'll text you in the next half hour if there's a problem."

"Oh, you are so funny!" Elise leaned forward and kissed Cat on the cheek. "I'm going to love working with you."

"Yes." Cat allowed herself to be kissed.

Then she ran, as fast as decorum would allow, up the stairs and into her hotel room.

• • •

The writing on the envelope was perfectly formed cursive. People hardly wrote by hand at all anymore, Cat thought, except for shopping lists and the odd scrawled notes. She sat down on the small upholstered chair in the corner of her room and turned on the lamp above her head.

The envelope was purple—the very same color as the stationery set that Cat had found in Mademoiselle Delfont's bureau—and the envelope had been sealed neatly, right up to the border along the top.

It seemed sacrilege to rip it. One of those penknives would be perfect, Cat thought. It was the sort of envelope that begged to be opened in an elegant room in a château. A footman bearing a silver tray should have delivered it.

Cat shook her head. What should be happening was that Loic should be here. Or Sylvie. At least they should be on the other end of the phone line. For there was no doubt this was of far more concern to either of them than to Cat.

Cat reached into her bag, pulled out her phone. Treacherous thing. Did Christian know where she was right at this moment? The thought was scary. And yet he had apologized so much on the phone today, had seemed so genuinely sorry, and it was not hard to believe that Elise could be exceedingly persuasive. Look at how she had distracted Cat this afternoon.

Should she call Loic? Share this latest update with him? If only he hadn't been so silly last night. He had become carried away, that was all. She had to believe that's all it was.

Cat looked at the envelope. She owed it to his family. They should know what was going on.

She dialed and Loic picked up.

"I found something," she said.

He was silent.

"There was an envelope, in the house here, and . . . brace yourself. It is addressed to me."

"You're joking."

"No."

"What's in it?"

"God knows. The woman who owned the house had . . . just died. She was very old."

"Well, read it."

Using the sharp tip of a pen, Cat tried as best as she could not to damage the envelope as she opened it. She read aloud.

Dear Catherine,

You will have received, by now, Isabelle de Florian's will. I am a friend of hers, a close and trusted friend. Isabelle instructed me to send this letter to you at the time of her death. She asks that you contact the same lawyer again, the one with whom you have been dealing with regards to the will. There is another letter there that contains information that you will find valuable. The letter is filed with the lawyer under my name, Delfont. You just need to ask for it and show this letter with my signature on it.

Mademoiselle L. Delfont.

Cat read it twice.

"Do you want me to meet you in Paris, Cat?" Loic sounded gruff.

Cat closed her eyes. "Yes, please."

"Where, then?"

"I'll make an appointment with the lawyer and let you know. Shall we meet at the apartment at, say, ten, and walk from there?" That would give her a little time to talk to him. She had to make things perfectly clear—about herself, about her engagement. She had to be honest with him.

"We'll talk about it in person tomorrow. And Cat?"

"Yes?"

"Thank you."

CHAPTER EIGHTEEN

Cat had a little time to kill before getting to the apartment, so she decided to walk part of the way. Paris, with its sober stone buildings and gray skies, could not have been more different from the villages in the south. She attempted to appear full of purpose as she strode along the Right Bank, but she knew she was fooling herself.

Elise had gone shopping for the day. Their flight didn't leave until six that evening, so Elise had left their suitcases at a friend's apartment.

Cat was having trouble containing her anxiety. Utterly bewildered, she ran through various scenarios in her mind. Perhaps Isabelle had witnessed something terrible in the apartment and had vowed never to return. Cat still thought that Isabelle could have been so affected by her memories of rue Blanche that she couldn't go back after Loic's grandfather was killed. Maybe Isabelle's grandmother, Marthe, had asked Isabelle not to touch the apartment, or perhaps Isabelle had genuinely wanted Virginia to have it, for her own reasons. But these ideas all felt far-fetched, and none of them really made sense. They didn't explain everything—especially not the secretiveness toward Sylvie, Loic, and Josephine. Why wouldn't Isabelle have simply told them about the apartment?

It was time things were out in the open. But Cat couldn't help feeling that she was still an intruder. She was glad that she had contacted Loic and invited him to join her at the lawyer's office.

Cat tried to concentrate on the bookstalls that lined the pavement. One of the owners smiled at her, and she nodded back. The river looked dark this morning. Perhaps the sun would come out later, perhaps not. But now, the water seemed to move slowly, toward something inevitable. It seemed as if it held secrets that Cat would never know.

She turned away from the Seine and headed north toward rue Blanche.

It was almost a surprise to discover that Isabelle's building looked the same. Had she been expecting something different? But when Cat opened the door to the apartment, she gasped.

The entire place had been catalogued. Plates—hundreds of them—porcelain pitchers and cups and exquisite glass vases were stacked in neat rows on the dining table. Every pile of objects was labeled as if they were exhibits in some obscure museum. The dining chairs were arranged in one corner, pushed aside as if to make room for a ball.

But it was the person standing with Loic who surprised Cat the most.

"Bonjour," Cat said. It seemed the best place to start.

Loic and Josephine both looked at Cat, seeming so alike that for a moment Cat felt intimidated. She had to stop herself from taking a step backward.

"Anouk let us in." Josephine's voice rang through the neat, echoing space.

"Of course." Cat wandered past them, taking in the neatness of it all. The apartment had been vacuumed, and all the dust was gone. That faint smell of ancient perfume, the trace of Marthe and Isabelle that Cat had sworn was here last time, had disappeared forever.

The curtains were swept up into enormous silk knots; wallpaper still hung askew in places, while in others it remained fully intact as if in hope, perhaps, that nothing too radical would be done. Everything looked dull in the weak gray light.

"It had to be done, Cat," Loic said.

"I know."

Josephine was silent, but Cat sensed that she was watching her closely.

"Josephine, I'm so glad you've seen it." Cat smiled.

"I wanted Josephine to see the apartment," Loic said. "But I guess we should go."

Cat nodded.

"Wait." Josephine spoke suddenly. "There is something. One moment, please?"

"Sure." Cat smiled again.

"Oui." Josephine took a turn around the sitting room. "Perhaps we sit down?" She perched on the edge of the chaise longue. It was spiderweb-free now, and no puff of dust pooled in the air when Josephine sat down.

Cat moved over to sit on its other end.

Loic was watching Josephine. "What is it?"

Josephine seemed agitated now. She stood up, moved over to stand by the bed, and then came back and sat down again. "I am at a loss as to how to begin. I don't know if even I can say this. It is not simple."

"You can trust Cat."

Josephine turned to Cat, her dark almond eyes seeming as if they were assessing now.

Cat couldn't help but gaze back at her.

"Loic is in love with you."

Cat stood up.

"He has been honest, Catherine."

"Josephine." Loic's voice was quiet.

But she held up a hand. "Let me continue, Loic. Cat, you have something to say?"

Cat leaned a hand against the back of her chair.

"I apologize for my older sister. She was born like this. The fact that she trained as a psychologist was incidental."

But Josephine kept her gaze fixed on Cat. "It's you I need to talk to."

"You don't have to listen to this, Cat."

Josephine frowned. "You are engaged. You want to marry this man in New York. But you have been . . . how you say it, stringing my brother along?"

"No."

"But I am right, no? You will go back. You will do your best to forget my brother, even though you love him body and soul. You will still go ahead with your marriage."

Cat felt her breath coming in short little bursts. "Excuse me?"

"Loic deserves honesty. This is all I am saying." Josephine seemed as calm as a summer lake.

"Look." Cat felt her voice rising. "I am engaged to Christian because I choose to be. I'm perfectly happy. I'm going back to New York tonight and that is that. I can't see how Loic could have possibly thought any different. But I'm sorry if he did. I'm sorry if you think I encouraged him."

"I am not judging you," Josephine went on.

Loic moved toward the door. "I've heard enough."

"You've come all this way to see the file," Cat said.

"I didn't come to see the file."

Cat closed her eyes. "You need to find out the truth."

"Look, Cat." Loic turned and came over to stand in front of her. "If your Christian was different, if I thought he'd make you happy, I wouldn't say anything. But he can't possibly love you. Not really. He wants you to fit into his world. Society pages, wedding planners. He's not thinking about what *you* want. If you were with me, I'd want you to make your own decisions, not pander to mine. I wouldn't stand by when I know that you're miserable at that job. I wouldn't be making all the decisions about our life together—your home, your wedding, what you're going to wear—without you even there. I know you're unhappy. I can see it. I just wish you could see it too."

Josephine went over and stood by the window.

Cat shook her head. "Stop it!" she said, surprised by the sound of her own voice. "Stop it! I can't listen to any more of this. Please. Either come with me to the lawyer's office or just go."

The strength of her convictions—or what she thought were her convictions, or what were supposed to be her convictions—hit her with unexpected force. Suddenly drained, she slumped on the chaise longue.

Loic stood framed in the doorway; she could sense him, but she didn't look at him.

"Loic?" Josephine was still over by the window.

"It's no good," he said, his voice deadly quiet. "There's no point."

And he turned.

Cat closed her eyes until she heard the front door close.

Her hand shook as she brought it to cover her mouth.

"I will leave," Josephine said. "I am sorry, Cat. My brother has never loved like this before. I thought it would help to get it all out in the open. But clearly you are not willing to see the truth that is so plainly before you."

The sound of her footsteps died away. Cat gazed around, helpless, at the packed-up apartment. The entire reason she had gone to so much trouble to find out the truth had disappeared out of the apartment and out of her life.

Pain sliced through her chest, settling in her throat, lodging there until she found it hard to swallow. What was she doing? What had she done? She felt a pang of guilt at the thought of Christian. What had he done other than be himself?

Loic was just trying to confuse her. She stood up, even more agitated now. What on earth did he know about what she wanted? Good lord he had jumped to conclusions.

Cat picked up her handbag and moved past the neat accumulation that was all that was left of the apartment in rue Blanche. But as she did so, it was impossible to get the expression on Loic's face, or the back of his coat as he left, out of her head. Her heart tightened at the realization that she wouldn't see him again.

CHAPTER NINETEEN

Cat wasn't sure how she did everything she managed to do in the next few hours. If anyone had asked her, she would probably say that she didn't remember any of it at all. It was as if she might fall apart if she did not keep moving.

First, she ran through the contents of the apartment. Anouk had left an inventory. The insurance was arranged, and the Boldini was safely stored at the Musée d'Orsay. Cat checked that every window in the apartment was locked, and she closed the shutters. Finally, she stood in the cold, dark dining room, leaned her hand against the now-polished table. She would probably never come back. Once the truth was out, Cat was determined to do whatever it took to convince Sylvie to take what was hers. So. This was it then.

Though she felt a strong urge to have one last look at the other rooms, Cat locked up the apartment and left the building.

All she had to do was collect the file from Monsieur Lapointe, read it, go home, and sort the rest out from there. Presumably this information was exactly what she and Loic had been looking for the entire time, and now she had found it.

It was the end of everything.

She could return to her old life.

• • •

Cat handed Mademoiselle Delfont's letter to the receptionist at Monsieur Lapointe's office. The receptionist did not open it. Instead, she stood up and took it straight back to the offices behind the waiting area.

Four red velvet chairs were arranged around a dark wooden coffee table. Cat hovered for a while, then sat down on the chair closest to the reception desk. She reached out for one of the dated magazines in front of her and flipped through its pages, hardly noticing that the words were French.

Several minutes later, she pulled out her phone. Elise had texted. Was Cat in the taxi? *Nearly*, Cat replied. She was nearly in the taxi. She sat back in her seat and looked up at the ceiling.

"Mademoiselle Jordan?" The receptionist appeared back at her desk. "Monsieur Lapointe will see you."

Monsieur Lapointe didn't stand up when Cat entered his office. He was sitting at his desk, his hands resting in a temple shape on the antique wood.

"Entrez," he said. "Sit down."

Cat sat opposite him.

"There are several formalities, Mademoiselle Jordan—"

"My flight to New York leaves in a few hours. I should be on my way to the airport. I hope you understand."

Monsieur Lapointe stayed quite still. He looked thoughtful for a moment. "Alors."

Cat waited.

"In this case, I make an exception."

Cat took in a breath. It was impossible to know what to say.

Monsieur Lapointe handed her a legal document. "Please sign here."

Cat leaned forward, hardly noticing her own signatures, initials on the tops of scores of pages.

Monsieur Lapointe swiveled his chair toward the table behind his desk. There were several files on this table, and Monsieur Lapointe's hand hovered over one of them. He pulled out a document, put this aside, and reached inside the file again. This time, he pulled out an envelope. It was small. He handed it to Cat.

"Merci." What else was there to say?

Monsieur looked at her almost as if he seemed to be considering whether she understood the importance of what she had in her hands.

Her phone buzzed with another text.

"I should be at the airport. My . . . assistant is waiting there with my luggage." Her assistant? Wedding planner hardly sounded sensible.

"Of course, Mademoiselle. You will be in touch." He looked at the letter over his spectacles. "We have some time to sort out the tax. But not so long."

"I know." Cat stood up. Impulsively, she went around the desk and kissed him on the cheek. "The apartment will have to be sold. There's nothing I can do unless Loic and Sylvie decide to take the estate."

"I will hear from you soon."

"Thank you, Monsieur Lapointe, for everything." Cat took her letter. If she didn't get in a taxi this minute, she could miss her flight.

"I'm running so terribly late. I'll have to sort out the final details by phone. I'm so sorry I can't stay and read this with you." Cat was halfway out the door.

Monsieur looked at her over the top of his spectacles. "Catherine," he said. "It has been a pleasure, Catherine."

"Thank you!" Cat whispered. She slung her bag over her shoulder, feeling instinctively for the shape of her passport through the bag's soft leather, and raced out the office door, out into the street, her eyes scanning for a taxi.

• • •

"Sweetie!" Elise was sitting on a black plastic chair in the airport. She waved at Cat and looked hugely relieved to see her. Elise's long blond hair was tied in a ponytail, and she wore a black wool trouser suit for the flight.

"That was cutting it a little close," she said, nudging Cat as if they were schoolgirls.

Cat kissed Elise on the cheek, pushing aside the thought that all of this kissing was perhaps more for herself than for Monsieur Lapointe and Elise. It seemed necessary, a sort of balm after the appalling scene with Loic and Josephine.

There was no line for business class. Elise spoke to the woman behind the desk while Cat hovered behind her, clinging to the envelope that she didn't dare put in either of her bags. The taxi driver had carried on an extraordinary conversation the whole way to the airport, giving Cat no chance to read. He had offered boiled sweets wrapped in clear cellophane several times during the journey. If nothing else, his ramblings—half in a language Cat had no hope of recognizing, half in English—had been something of a distraction.

The thought that the letter may contain some answers was both exhilarating and terrifying. They had an hour to spare now. Cat would have to make excuses to Elise. She simply had to find somewhere quiet to give it her full attention.

But as soon as they entered the business-class lounge, it became clear that Elise was determined to start going over wedding details again.

Cat excused herself after several polite minutes and went to the restroom. It was the only escape.

There was a lounge area just inside the entrance. Cat settled herself onto a white ottoman at the far end. She pulled at the envelope, trying not to destroy it, her fingers working fast. Cat read the enclosed letter twice.

She put it in her lap, looked at herself in the mirror. Her cheeks were flushed.

She read the letter again.

It was dated 2003.

Ma Chère Catherine,

I am saddened to be informed by my lawyer of the death of your mother, Bonnie Jordan. I know that what you are taking on is a considerable burden. I understand that you need an explanation. That way, you will know what to do. My dear, I know that you will do the right thing if you are anything like your grandmother Virginia Brooke. But, I have two problems, you see. One is that I am old, and with my health the way it unfortunately is now, I do not feel that I can go through everything all over again. Second, I do not think it would be a good idea to do so. Mademoiselle Delfont, from whom you received the letter directing you to this one, will help you. You will soon understand why. You can trust her. Please contact her in Sarlat at 3, rue Charpentier.

Yours faithfully, my dear,

Isabelle de Florian.

"But Mademoiselle Delfont is dead," Cat whispered. She closed the letter, put it back in her handbag, and went back out to the business-class lounge to chat and smile with Elise as if the wedding were her only care in the world.

• • •

Elise had established herself on the largest leather sofa in the lounge and had a swath of bridal magazines set up on the coffee table in front of her.

"I thought we'd make the most of the flight. Make it into a meeting. I have some preliminary ideas here. We can get a jump-start now! I can never sleep on planes, can you?"

"I really haven't traveled enough to say," Cat said. Then, "Sorry."

Elise's face fell when Cat spoke.

After several minutes of gasping at cream gowns, silk gloves, and sparkling tiaras, Cat stood up.

"I need to make a call."

"We only have a few minutes until boarding."

"It's important."

Cat headed to a far corner of the lounge. She pulled out her phone and looked at it. Should she contact Loic again? Would he want to know that the letter was a dead end or not? The latter was more likely. What about Sylvie? Should she tell her that it seemed hopeless and hope that would be sufficient closure? Or should she think first about what to do and wait to take any action until she returned home to New York? There was nothing Cat could say to either Sylvie or Loic right now that would lead her anywhere close to finding a reason to give them back their apartment and their painting.

Cat put her phone back into her bag. Perhaps she should, after all, instruct Monsieur Lapointe to make a new will of her own leaving everything to Sylvie's family on her own death. She could just leave the entire estate, untouched, for Loic's family. But that would not give Sylvie any benefit from her own mother's estate. And there were taxes that needed to be paid in the meantime. There had to be a better way.

Cat returned to Elise, hooked her bag on her shoulder, and smiled. "Right," she said. "We have a flight to catch."

"Oh, this is so exciting. I have a good feeling about it," Elise said.

"Yes. So do I."

CHAPTER TWENTY

The engagement party was held at Christian's grandparents' house in the Hamptons. The vast lawn that stretched down to the water was decorated with a heated tent. Early spring bulbs lined the edges of the lawn, and Elise had adorned the tent with pale roses in crystal vases. Several of Cat's close friends had flown in for the occasion, along with some of her parents' friends. They were all intrigued by Christian.

One of Cat's father's former colleagues stood in a small group, looking unexpectedly comfortable among Christian's set, most of whom kept to themselves—apart from Christian's grandmother, who made a point of talking to every person at the party.

"How did you get into your line of work, Christian?" Jim Simon had worked for the government with Cat's father nearly all their adult lives.

"Oh, my father arranged it for me." Christian took a petit four from a passing waiter and popped it into his mouth.

Cat wanted to nudge him in the ribs. She knew Jim. He would jump from family support to nepotism in less time than it took for Christian to finish his mouthful.

"Having family who are willing to do one favors can be a wonderful thing."

Christian didn't seem to have worked out that Jim was being sarcastic. Cat didn't know where to look.

"Tell me, then, Christian—"

"Oh, you know what? I need to take Christian to . . . somewhere—" Cat said.

"Certainly." She could sense what Jim was thinking. She could hear it in his voice.

She placed her arm in Christian's.

"Do you think we could go somewhere quiet for a minute?" she asked him, once they were out of earshot from Jim.

Christian took her arm and strolled with her across the lawn toward a group of large trees at the far end of the garden.

"It seems odd," he said. "All these people, thrown together. None of them with a bit in common."

"Is it a problem?"

"I'd rather be alone with you."

Cat leaned up and attempted to kiss him.

"Oh, not here, Cat," he said, stepping out of the way.

"Sorry, Christian." A vision of Loic, kissing her for the first time—not caring who was watching as he took her in his arms in the street in Sarlat—swept though her head.

"I think we'd better get back to the party." Christian adjusted his tie.

Cat stood where she was for a moment. She wanted to keep him there, to explain what was on her mind, to tell him what she wanted from their life together. But Christian was already pulling her back toward the party.

"Oh, Cat. Come and meet the chairman of the bank," Christian said. "I've told him all about you."

While Cat was being introduced to the chairman of the bank, she noticed the arrival of a guest she hadn't seen for years.

"Excuse me," she said to Christian and his boss.

"Honey?" Christian's hand lingered on hers.

"I'll be back in a moment."

Cat strolled over to the small woman. She had walked confidently into the party, her hair stuck up at odd angles, her clothes a mélange of pinks, oranges, and greens.

"Nancy." Cat hugged her mother's old friend.

Nancy Wood hugged her back, then pulled away and eyed Cat and her oyster silk dress up and down. "You're not repeating the mistake your mother made?"

Cat laughed and shook her head. Always straight to the point. She had learned to take that on the chin with Nancy years earlier. "Nancy, when you meet Christian, you'll see that I'm doing exactly the opposite."

Nancy sniffed at the passing waiter with his silver tray of champagne. "Any gin?"

"Of course, Madam," the waiter said. "I'll be right back."

Nancy folded her arms. "So you really know what you're doing, my girl?"

"Of course." Nancy had been a sporadic visitor in Cat's childhood home. Though she had always made it clear that she disapproved deeply of her old school friend Bonnie's tragic marital choice, she had kept up a sort of stalwart presence in Bonnie's life. She had never lost her interest in her friend, and had tried to support her despite her feelings. Cat had always adored Nancy.

Now, the idea that sprang into Cat's mind began to blossom into a fully formed plan. Why hadn't she thought of it before? She had spent the last forty-eight hours pushing thoughts of France and the apartment out of her head. Had promised herself that she would focus on her engagement, at least for the weekend. But here was an opportunity, and Cat was going to take it.

"I have a little problem . . . Nancy, I wonder if you can help." Cat took Nancy's arm and led her away from the party to a quieter spot on the edge of the lawn.

It was hard to know where to start. But Nancy was quick; she would understand. Cat gave her a rundown about the situation in France.

"So, you see, I'm stuck," she told Nancy. "I still want to make things right, but I don't know who could possibly help me. I was thinking, I know it's an incredibly long shot, but did you know my grandmother Virginia very well?"

"Loved her," Nancy said.

Cat waved at Tash, who was gesturing for Cat to return to the party. She turned back to Nancy. She probably had two minutes at the most.

"Okay," Cat said. "When you were there, did she ever talk about her time in Paris? Did she ever mention anything at all?"

"She was fun. I remember that. Irreverent. Used to drink gin in the bath."

"Yes."

"That sort of thing. There was an endless parade of people through the farmhouse. She ran a sort of salon, if you could call it that, in the countryside. Always interesting people around whenever I went there. Her husband knew that Virginia needed fun, needed company; otherwise, she'd flee. It was an endless house party. She liked great conversation."

"Any particular friends you can remember?" Cat spoke quickly. "Any . . . one that she might have confided in?"

"Yes."

Cat waited. She felt her pulse quicken, even though she knew it was unlikely this would lead anywhere. "Of course, all Virginia's friends would have passed away years ago. We never kept in touch with them."

Nancy gave Cat a look. "Of course you didn't meet them . . ." she said.

Cat felt her insides tighten.

"Lillian Fitzgerald's still alive," Nancy said. "She's over ninety, of course, and I can't vouch that she'll know anything. But she was one of Virginia's best friends—bit of a fixture, I would say. Last I heard, she was in a nursing home in the Village. Corner of Thompson and Becker."

Cat leaned forward and hugged Nancy hard.

"It's worth a try," Cat said. "I have nothing else left."

"Everything's worth a try, except a bad marriage." Nancy patted Cat on the shoulder and waved at someone she knew.

• • •

That night, Cat located Lillian Fitzgerald's nursing home on the net. Visiting hours were between ten and twelve each day. Cat made her way to Thompson Street in Greenwich Village at five minutes to ten the next morning.

The nursing home was above a bank, at the corner of two of the neighborhood's typically narrow streets. The trees were just starting to form their first buds. Cat was tempted to stop at one of the Village's tiny cafés for a coffee and a fortifying piece of cake before she attempted to broach the past with Lillian Fitzgerald. But there was no time to waste. Cat had never met her, of course, and—scour her memory as much as she liked—she had no recollection of her mother ever mentioning Lillian's name. It was a long shot, but if Lillian had been a close friend of Virginia's, then it was at least possible that she might have heard of Isabelle de Florian.

Cat rang the nursing home's security bell and waited outside. A uniformed nurse appeared at the glass door, looked at Cat, and let her inside.

"You're in luck. Mrs. Fitzgerald is awake," she told Cat in the elevator. "We don't disturb the residents, as a rule, if they're sleeping."

Cat followed the nurse down a long corridor and into a room overlooking the street below. The sun shone in, and the elderly woman sitting on a chair peered at Cat through a pair of large-framed glasses.

"Never seen her before in my life," Lillian Fitzgerald said with a strong New York accent. "But I know exactly who she is."

Cat breathed a sigh of relief, and the nurse slipped out of the room.

"Sit down, Catherine." Mrs. Fitzgerald pointed at the other chair in the room. Her hands shook slightly, and her legs looked like a pair of tiny pins under the crocheted blanket on her lap, but her face looked as sharp as a razor.

"Virginia was my closest friend," Lillian Fitzgerald said. "Awful shame she died so young. Not many people you can trust, Catherine. Some people just can't keep their mouths shut, but Virginia could. That's rare, and I've missed her something awful."

"Mrs. Fitzgerald, I've just come back from Paris."

"Call me Lillian." The old lady perked up in her seat.

Cat gave Lillian a quick summary of Isabelle, her family, the will, and the apartment. "So, what I want to know is whether Virginia—my grandmother—ever spoke with you about her time in Paris."

"If I could still wolf whistle, I would." Lillian said. She regarded Cat for a moment. "Oh yes, she spoke of her time in Paris."

Cat stayed silent.

"There were three of them, you know. Virginia Brooke, Isabelle de Florian, and her grandmother, Marthe."

"Marthe was still alive, then."

"Sounded to me as if that Marthe was the craziest of the bunch!" Lillian chuckled. "Now, I don't want to shock you, Catherine—"

"But Marthe was a Parisian courtesan. There was a painting of her in the apartment. It's a Boldini . . . that's another story."

"Never heard of him."

Cat had to bite her lip. She waited for Lillian to speak.

"As I understand it, the three of them had a whale of a time living together in Paris." Lillian chuckled. "I don't have to tell you what Marthe got up to when she was young, Catherine. Absinthe, the Moulin Rouge . . . Virginia said Marthe was once the toast of Paris. Well, in certain circles, of course! Men adored her. Important men, you know. She was selective with her charms; nobody's fool, Virginia said. I hate to think that it was the only way she knew how to improve her lot in life, you know. But there we are."

"Now, that Marthe de Florian took to our Virginia like a duck to a smooth lagoon. They were both free spirits. Both fiercely independent. Terrific women. Isabelle, Virginia said, was a real darling. So, so different from Virginia and Marthe! But that was what Virginia adored about Isabelle, apparently, her simple outlook, her honesty."

Yes, this made sense. Fit in with Sylvie's descriptions of her mother.

"Do you know how Virginia met Isabelle and Marthe?"

"Only the Lord God knows the answer to that. But I do know that Marthe and Isabelle took Virginia under their wings while she was in Paris. I think Virginia was entranced by the whole setup. The pair of them. The ex-courtesan and her sweet granddaughter. Virginia told me about the clothes, the jewels, and the fancy French furniture in that apartment. You know Virginia's house back here was stuffed to the gills with all that antique stuff too? She loved it. Apparently your mother, Bonnie, sold it all off when Virginia died. Your father wouldn't touch any of it with a barge pole. He didn't trust it one bit."

"I see," Cat said, her heart falling.

"As far as I know, when Marthe dropped dead just at the beginning of the war, Isabelle was devastated. Virginia stayed in Paris for a while. Those two girls continued to live in the apartment just as it was, without Marthe. When it looked like France was going to go under, Virginia came back home. Her folks insisted. She tried to carry on just like she had in Paris when she got to New York, don't you worry." Lillian winked. "When I met her here, we had a lot of fun. But I know she missed Isabelle."

"Isabelle kept her grandmother's apartment just as it was after Virginia left," Cat said. "We just can't understand why she never went back."

"Well, Virginia spoke of Marthe, too, as if she were the fount of all free womanhood. I think both she and Isabelle adored the old lady. I'm not surprised they kept all her things untouched."

"Yes."

"You look like Virginia," Lillian said. "I'd know you anywhere. She was a stunner, and so are you."

"That is very kind, but—"

"I have no idea why that Isabelle locked up her apartment and never went back to it again, but I'll tell you, Catherine, I know this: Isabelle de Florian was Virginia Brooke's closest friend. Virginia used to talk of Isabelle nonstop. Then one day, she never mentioned her name again."

Something stirred through Cat, jolting her a little. "Why would she do that?"

"Because, my girl, Isabelle de Florian broke Virginia's heart."

"Really?" Cat watched the old lady. She didn't want to say too much, had to keep Lillian on track.

"No matter how many times Virginia wrote to that darned Isabelle, the French girl never wrote back. Virginia's letters to Isabelle were returned—again and again. If you think Virginia could trace her friend in France, then think again. Virginia hunted down death notices after the war. Nothing. She even considered hiring a private detective, but finally she had the common sense to realize that if Isabelle didn't want to be contacted, then the only thing to do was respect it. Virginia never mentioned Paris again."

"I see." So Isabelle hadn't wanted to be contacted, then?

"Virginia blamed herself, Catherine. She thought in the end that it must have been something she had done that had upset her friend. Oh, Virginia went over countless scenarios with me. But that will you've got is something else! If only Virginia had known about it."

"Now there's a risk Isabelle de Florian will break her own daughter's heart, too, unless I do something about it," Cat said. "Her daughter, Sylvie, is refusing to take what's hers, unless I can prove that Isabelle wanted to leave everything to Sylvie rather than to me. Sylvie thinks Isabelle must have had good reason to leave it to me, but I know it's killing her."

"There's nothing prouder or sillier than folks who think they know someone, even those closest to them."

Cat sighed. "The fact that Isabelle went to the trouble of calling herself Sylvie-Marie Augustin is telling."

"I can't give you anything else, young Catherine."

"Thank you. You've been very helpful."

"And if you do find an answer about that Isabelle, well. All I can say is that if I ever see my old friend Virginia when I leave this earth, I will tell her that she was left a legacy by her old friend. That's what I'll say."

Cat stood up. She went over to Lillian and kissed her on her tough old cheek.

"It's been a pleasure to meet a friend of my grandmother's."

Lillian chuckled. "Like I said, you're her spitting image. It's made my whole day."

Cat felt herself grin. She waved and went back out onto the street.

• • •

Cat hadn't had the heart to move everything out of her own small apartment yet. She often slipped back there when Christian was working out of town. A few weeks after the engagement party, he had to go up to Boston for work for a whole week. Cat moved back to Brooklyn on the Sunday evening when he left. She woke early the next morning, far too early to start getting ready for work. As usual, the first thought that popped into her head was of France.

At least she had not woken in the very early hours, images of the apartment—and even more vivid pictures of Loic—overtaking her mind. This had become a ritual to which she was almost resigned. She would wake around three o'clock in the morning, feeling overwhelmed, and start to question everything. Should she have stayed longer in France? Spent more time going through everything in the apartment herself? What if there was some hidden journal there, or another letter from Isabelle, written just before she left, explaining everything? Cat should have stayed on.

But she couldn't have stayed. It wouldn't have been fair to Christian. Christian! Late at night, she would tear herself apart thinking about what she had done. Granted, nothing really serious had happened with Loic, but what had she been thinking? Poor Christian. He deserved better, and she was determined to make it up to him.

It was easier when he was away. She hated to admit it, but she slept better in her old place. But what did that suggest?

Sometimes even during the day she found her mind wandering. When she had especially difficult clients or was faced with the mundanity of yet another corporate portrait, she distracted herself by looking at her photographs of France. She told herself she needed to sort them all, but whenever she pulled them out, it was impossible not to glance at the ones of Loic. And when she did . . . well. Then she would think about what he had said.

A couple of times, she had even looked up studios for rent. But the idea was ridiculous. How would she begin to take up such a huge task? She knew nothing about running a small business.

Cat climbed out of her bed. She needed to look through all the information she had about Isabelle and Marthe one more time—something she somehow never had time for when she was at Christian's apartment in Manhattan. Christian had made it clear that he thought she should forget about the Paris apartment. He thought it would be best to either sell the place and invest the money toward their future children's school fees or try one last time to offer the inheritance to Sylvie and, if she heard nothing back, to go ahead with his first plan.

This was all sensible, Cat supposed, but she couldn't let it go. Not yet. She felt as if she owed it not only to Loic, Sylvie, and Josephine but—in a persistent sort of way—to Virginia and Isabelle as well. This was their legacy, their story. And she couldn't bring herself to turn her back on it.

• • •

Cat made a list of possibilities while having breakfast. She had been unable to come up with anything new. The only new consideration was that Isabelle had cut Virginia out of her life. Why had she done this? Had a man come between them? But Virginia would surely have confided such a thing to Lillian.

Something else, then, something more serious: something that Isabelle couldn't discuss even with her own daughter.

Cat stood up. She moved over to her computer and turned it on.

Monsieur Lapointe's latest email popped up on the screen. He reminded her of the death duties. They needed to appraise the apartment and take into consideration the considerable value of the painting, and she then had only a few months left to pay sixty percent of the value of the inheritance to the French government, given that Sylvie had refused to accept it.

Monsieur Lapointe went on to say that it was now time to prove that the title had gone to the beneficiary of the will. He was keen to complete his attestation immobilière.

Cat wrote a quick reply and then clicked over to the Internet.

She couldn't shake off the idea that something serious could have happened in the apartment. Something so traumatic that Isabelle had never wanted to return, to talk about it, or even to let her family know the place existed. If so, could it have been reported in the newspapers at the time? With no other leads, it was all Cat could think of to try.

It only took five minutes of research to work out that if anything had been reported in 1940 in Paris, it would most likely have appeared in the main newspaper from the time, *Paris-Soir*. But the archives were not available on the Internet.

So. Who could help her now? Cat picked up her phone, looked at it for a moment, then dialed Paris. Anouk Tailler listened to Lillian's information with the same calm demeanor that she had undoubtedly applied to her inventory in the apartment.

"I will check the archives of *Paris-Soir* for 1939 and 1940. I have been there before. They are all on microfiche." There was a pause. "I don't know that you are onto anything, but it is worth to check this out."

"It could have been something serious, Anouk."

"I will go there this afternoon. It is no problem."

Cat hung up. She collected her coat and bag and decided to walk to work.

• • •

Anouk called a few hours later. Cat was photographing a baby, organizing endless poses on tiny chairs and in the flowerpots that she detested but her boss loved.

"I'll be thirty seconds. I'm so sorry, but I have to take this call," Cat said. She would never normally interrupt a photo shoot, and the baby's mother looked so disappointed that she finished the shoot and let Anouk's call go to voice mail.

As soon as the client had left, Cat grabbed her phone, slipped into her tiny office, and closed the door. Anouk had left a brief message asking Cat to call her right back.

"I have found something." Anouk sounded urgent when she answered the phone. "I will translate from the French. This is June 10, 1940. 'The body of a young woman has been found in an alley on the Right Bank. The body has been identified as that of Camille Paget, the maid of the late Marthe de Florian, the infamous demimondaine who died late last year. The murder is under investigation.'

"There is nothing else. No reference to it again. I have checked every paper for the next year. After the occupation, the Nazis took control of the newspapers, anyway. So."

"Oh, dear God," Cat said. "Thank you, Anouk."

"It would have been a terrible thing to happen to Isabelle. She had recently lost her grandmother and, you say, her friend from America. It could explain, I suppose."

"Maybe."

"But you say that Isabelle de Florian never contacted your grandmother for the rest of her life? And why would she not tell her daughter, Sylvie, that her maid was murdered? Is not such a secret."

"My thoughts too, Anouk. I'll need to let the family know what I've found out—and see what it could all mean."

"Good luck."

"I'll need it."

"Call if you need me." And with that, Anouk hung up.

Sylvie was not as efficient at picking up the phone as Anouk.

"Chérie," she said, her voice sounding weary down the line.

When Cat had explained what she had learned, Sylvie sighed. "Chérie, this is all so much to take in. I am wondering whether I knew my mother at all."

"I don't know if we'll ever be able to fully understand what life was like during the war," Cat said.

"Oui, but I still maintain that my mother must have had a good reason for not changing her will."

"But what if she did change it, Sylvie? The attestation immobilière is about to go through. Once I've paid the inheritance tax, I won't have anything to give back to you. I'll have to sell the apartment. But what if your mother changed her mind at the last minute? We have to find out."

"I cannot see how she could have changed anything, chérie."

There was a silence.

"How . . . is Loic?"

"Well, if you want the truth, he is not fine."

"I'm sorry—"

"He knows his own mind, chérie."

Cat chewed on her lip.

"I'm sorry. I should not have said that. How is your . . . engagement going?" Sylvie coughed.

"Great!"

The older woman was quiet for a moment. "I will let you go."

"Sylvie, I'll keep you posted."

Sylvie was gone with the click of a button.

• • •

The following Sunday evening, Cat had everything to do with rue Blanche spread out on her kitchen table. She was expecting a call from Christian any minute to say that he was back in New York. For the five-thousandth time, Cat went over all the evidence in her head. Rolled it around until she came back to the beginning, which was that she didn't know much.

But when she read Isabelle's letter once again, something struck her.

Of course.

How slow she was.

Isabelle had wanted Cat to talk to Mademoiselle Delfont about the past, but Mademoiselle was apparently around the same age as Isabelle. Isabelle had covered her tracks like a professional, so she must have counted on the possibility that Mademoiselle Delfont could also be dead.

The phone rang.

"Honey!"

Cat checked her watch. On time. "Welcome home, Christian! How did it go?"

"Rather well, actually. Better than I thought. Sorted everything out for the bank, and I want to celebrate. I'm in a cab. Dinner, honey?"

"I'm . . . well. I'm at home."

"Fine, see you there."

Cat shook her head. "I mean I'm in Brooklyn. At my home."

"I'm sad to hear you call it that."

Cat took a turn around the room. "I'm right in the middle of something. I need to sort it out. Sorry."

"I'm sad to hear that, too."

"I'm sorry to make you sad."

"That's good to hear," he laughed.

"But I have to do this."

"Cat, it's that damned French thing again? Why can't you just sell the apartment, pay the death duties, and get your own life back on track? If the de Florian woman doesn't want the inheritance, I don't see what the problem is. You're making things too complicated, Cat. Keep it simple."

"I was supposed to talk to Mademoiselle Delfont, but she's dead."

"We've been over this. I say that would have been nothing. Maybe she's got some old necklace for you. Let me buy you one instead."

"I'm going to call Paris now."

"Paris? It's midnight there."

"I've thought it through."

"Do what you have to do. I'll see you later." He hung up the phone.

Cat dialed Monsieur Lapointe's mobile. Maybe she was insane, phoning a Frenchman at midnight, but Monsieur Lapointe would not answer his phone if it did not suit him to do so. She was sure he would turn it off if he was asleep. The man was meticulous.

"Mademoiselle Jordan?" He sounded wide awake.

"I'm so sorry to call you so late."

"I have been at the theater. It is no problem."

"You are very kind, Monsieur. I have an idea. A big one, maybe . . ."

There was the sound of a click. A door closing, perhaps? Cat imagined Monsieur Lapointe in a wood-paneled study deep in his Parisian apartment. He would have changed out of his theater outfit and into a pair of striped pajamas, navy velvet slippers, and a paisley smoking jacket—pure silk, of course.

"Monsieur," she said, shaking the picture from her mind. "It has struck me that Isabelle de Florian would not have instructed only Mademoiselle Delfont to tell me the entire story. What if something had happened to Mademoiselle Delfont? Which it has. Isabelle would have made sure there was another source of information for me or . . . for my mother."

"Oui . . . peut-être." Perhaps. Monsieur Lapointe did not sound convinced.

Cat took a breath. "Don't you think that Isabelle would have left more information somewhere? After all, this is a woman who disappeared for seventy years. She never contacted her best friend in America. And yet Isabelle tells me only that Mademoiselle Delfont will help me—but not that she will tell me everything."

"Oui . . ."

"She says she can't go through it all again, that it wouldn't be a good idea. Don't you see? Where else would she have left information but at her lawyer's office? Monsieur, could you possibly look for a file under the name of Virginia Brooke or Bonnie Jordan?"

"I would have to go into the archives to do that."

Cat closed her eyes. "Monsieur Lapointe, where are the archives?"

Something changed in Monsieur's voice. "Mademoiselle Jordan, most of my work is very dull. You will understand therefore that with this, I will make an exception. I will go to my office this minute. Our archives are stored in a special room behind the building. They are in perfect order. I will do a search."

"You're not in your pajamas?" Cat would have hugged him if he were in the room.

"Of course I am not in my . . . pajamas! I will call you either way."

Cat slumped back on her red sofa. She wrapped herself up in her peacock scarf, and she settled down to wait.

Christian called again.

"I was hoping to see you. I'm sorry I was frustrated," he said.

"I'm sorry too. I had a lead. I wanted to follow it up."

"I'm here now, at that Italian place we went to last week. Morgan and Michael are here, too. You're sure you won't join us?"

"I wouldn't be good company for you." She would make herself some toast.

Half an hour later, her phone rang. "Monsieur Lapointe?" Cat grabbed at it.

Someone was at the door. "Oh, excusez-moi." Cat dragged herself to answer it.

"Cat!" Elise stood with a clutch of takeout boxes. "Christian told me you weren't going out for dinner with them, so I thought—"

Cat allowed Elise to kiss her on both cheeks. "Elise, this isn't a good time."

But the other woman was in the apartment. "I've just been at the gym, so I thought Chinese takeout?"

"My dear Mademoiselle, if you will permit me," Monsieur Lapointe said down the phone. "I have found something."

"Were you happy with the engagement party, sweetie?"

"Elise . . ." Cat held up the phone.

"Oh! Sorry to interrupt!" Elise didn't sound sorry at all. She popped her takeout boxes on the kitchen counter. "Do you mind if I get some plates out?"

Cat waved at her to go ahead.

"There was no file under the name of Bonnie Jordan," he said.

"Oh."

"No. But, Catherine, I do have a file under the name of Bonnie Brooke," Monsieur said. "It is marked private and confidential. Only for her."

Cat closed her eyes. Of course. Virginia had died in 1978. She was relatively young, only sixty-three years old, when breast cancer had cut her life short. Bonnie had married Howard two years later.

"Chow mein okay?"

Cat nodded at Elise and blocked her free ear with her other hand. "Are you able to open it now?"

"I am afraid I can't do that," Monsieur said. "I am sorry." He cleared his throat. "You will have to come to Paris. The formalities."

"Oh, please, Monsieur."

CHAPTER TWENTY-ONE

The plane arrived at five-thirty in the morning, Paris time. Cat had slept only sporadically, distracted by thoughts of Isabelle and Marthe. How Cat would have loved to meet them both. And then there had been other thoughts, thoughts about her grandmother.

The taxi arrived at Cat's hotel well before business hours had begun. Cat had booked her room for the night before she arrived, and having taken a shower, she fell into a deep and exhausted sleep for three hours. When she woke, the first thing she heard were birds. She was in Paris, and it was spring.

This time, Monsieur Lapointe did not keep Cat waiting in the reception area. As soon as she entered the building, he appeared at the front desk to escort her into his rooms. His assistant, as before, witnessed the signing of all the documentation, but Monsieur moved ten times faster than he had before. Cat felt light-headed, as if everything were unreal.

Monsieur dismissed his assistant once everything was signed. The envelope in question sat in front of Cat on the desk. It was fat, and yellowed with age.

"Would you like me to translate?" Monsieur Lapointe asked, one hand on the envelope. "Or would you prefer a proper translator?"

"In the file, Mademoiselle, there is a very fat envelope. There are forms that must be signed and witnessed. Can you get a flight in the morning?"

Did Monsieur think New York was just a stone's throw from Paris? Cat looked at Elise. "There is someone who could get me on a flight," she said.

"Call me as soon as you are booked."

"Monsieur?"

"Oui?"

"Thank you!"

Elise was, unsurprisingly, helpful. "I've been a member of all the airline clubs since I was a kid. Give me ten minutes, Cat."

Cat was surprisingly hungry, even after the toast. Elise had Cat's computer screen open. "The earliest flight I can get you on is at four-thirty tomorrow afternoon to Charles de Gaulle. There is a seat. Do you want it?"

Cat nodded. She would take two days off work.

"And now for the important stuff," Elise said. She pulled a swath of samples out of her bag. "We are going to have such a fun evening, sweetie!"

Cat took a large sip of her wine.

Cat smiled. "Monsieur, I would love you to read it. The only thing is . . ."

Monsieur coughed. "I could not reach Monsieur Archer. As they have first right of refusal regarding the property, I had to . . ."

"That was exactly my question."

"However, with your permission, perhaps I could send him a copy of the information we have in this file."

"Whatever it is, it will have to go to both Monsieur Archer and his mother."

Monsieur coughed. "You are ready? Some café, perhaps?"

"Thank you, Monsieur, no café."

Monsieur cleared his throat. He opened the envelope. Inside was a thick sheaf of thin, typewritten pages.

"Mademoiselle," he said. "The document is in English."

Cat reached out a hand. "Then," she said, "I will read it to you."

March 29, 1978

Dear Bonnie,

I wanted to write a cover note to this document in which I have done my best to put into writing all the things that my friend and confidante Sylvie-Marie Augustin told me while we met for coffee last week in Avignon. Sylvie-Marie asked me to translate all of this into English and then type it up in order to explain it all to you, Bonnie. I took extensive notes that I read and re-read during our talk just to make sure all of it made perfect sense.

I was very happy to help my dear friend Sylvie-Marie out when she learned through her lawyer of the death of your mother, the late Virginia Brooke, during the winter in Connecticut. As a fellow American, I was fascinated to learn about Virginia and her wonderful joie de vivre. Suffice it to say I wish I had known her, Bonnie. She must have been a very special woman and I am sure you miss her so very much.

I know you must have been confused when you received the will and especially flabbergasted to learn that you have inherited such a legacy! There is no doubt on this earth that you will want to know why you are now in possession of an apartment in Paris.

Sylvie-Marie so wants you to understand the events of the past that she asked me to act as a backup for her at the time of her death. We have gone to the extra precaution of writing everything down for you in case anything happens to me in the meantime.

I have known Sylvie-Marie Augustin since the war. I was, as they used to say, something of an unusual girl myself. My father was a magistrate in Boston, and I inherited all his interest in politics and history. Unfortunately as you would know, the fact that I was a girl in those days didn't help my ambitions. The situation in Europe during the 1930s fascinated and concerned me especially, and I found myself wanting to do something—anything—to help.

Had I stayed home in America, I could see my life turning into an endless round of meaningless tennis games and tea parties with some suitable husband who would bore me to tears. I wanted none of that. It seemed like everything that mattered was happening across the Atlantic, so I sailed there on my own and arrived in Paris in 1938. Although I had some money of my own, I secured myself a position as a secretary in a legal office. I had studied French in school as a girl and put it to good use. But it was the evenings in Paris that brought things alive. People were talking politically and drinking far too heavily, and what with one thing leading to another, I soon wended my way into a group of anti-Fascists who were determined to do something about the rise of this type of government in Europe.

As you must know, when the Nazis invaded Paris, there were people who needed to get out of France. I helped convey them from one safe place to another, and later I wound up working for the French Resistance. These were both the best and the worst years of my life.

I fell in love with a fellow maquisard, *a French Resistance fighter, with whom I worked, and soon after the war, we married. I have spent the rest of my life in the Perigord region. I still take a great interest in politics and ended up teaching the subject at our local university. Now, I will try my hardest to convey all of this important information to you in the best way I know. I have added in a few details of my own, given my understanding of the times of which I write.*

God bless, my dear,

A bientôt

Louise Delfont.

Taken from my notes, as told to me by Sylvie-Marie Augustin, February 1979

Dear Bonnie,

The first thing you must know is that the apartment that you have inherited in rue Blanche belonged in the late nineteenth and early twentieth centuries to Marthe de Florian. Marthe was a demimondaine, in other words, a courtesan in late nineteenth-century Paris. This meant that her way was paid by her many gentlemen clients. But these were not just any gentlemen, mind you, they were only of the highest social and political classes—or they were so fabulously wealthy that their backgrounds didn't matter.

Marthe did not come from a wealthy background. In fact, she worked as a lowly seamstress in Paris when she was a teenage girl. The hours and working conditions were very tough. Marthe never spoke of her childhood except in passing, and only as a slip now and then. By the time she was twenty, she had given birth to two sons. She never mentioned who their fathers were. One of the boys died as a baby. Marthe kept his tiny clothes in a locked wardrobe that she would open once a year. The other son was Isabelle de Florian's father.

One can assume that one of Marthe's many gentlemen clients bought the apartment for her when she was still in her twenties. Her rise to fame and fortune could have been gradual, or it could have been dramatic and sudden. Perhaps she was spotted somewhere running a dress to an important client in Paris. Perhaps someone was struck by her beauty and natural grace and tempted or even lured her into a way of life that would change her world forever.

No matter. Marthe de Florian adopted a lifestyle that was both glamorous and risky in the extreme. She was plied with exotic gifts, money, absinthe, and most likely an assortment of exotic drugs.

Perhaps her life could best have been described as a balancing act, hovering in a tight spot between vulgarity and glamour. But you have to understand, my dear, that back then all of Paris wanted to see and be seen. It was fashionable even among the conservative upper classes to be theatrical during the Belle Époque.

The beautiful portrait of Marthe that will no doubt strike you when you see it was done by some well-known artist, apparently, who was in his turn so struck by Marthe's charms that he had her sit for him and gave her the portrait to keep.

It was these gifts that furnished the entire apartment as you see it now and set Marthe up for a most luxurious life. As well as entertaining her gentlemen clients, she worked as a highly paid actress and made appearances in famous dance halls and exclusive clubs. Men would compete to dress her for the theater and would bask in the shock that it caused to be seen with her by their sides. Demimondaines were not accepted by upper-class women, and yet they were so infamous that nobody dared question their right to exist. It was a halfway modern world in which everyone still had a place, but there was great change brewing. That was the next generation's story.

By the time Virginia knew her, Marthe was well into her seventies, and she was more interested in overseeing the life of her granddaughter Isabelle than anything else.

Marthe was determined from the beginning that Isabelle would not suffer the same indignities that she, Marthe, had had to suffer when she was young. Isabelle's own mother had been a middle-class woman whose family had not approved of her marriage to Marthe de Florian's son. As a result, they would have nothing to do with the little girl after her young parents' untimely death, and Isabelle was raised by her grandmother in rue Blanche.

From the very start, the young Isabelle had only the most beautiful of clothes, attended the smartest girls' schools, and was encouraged to have the most charming of companions. Most of these, I am told, accepted Isabelle into their homes, though there were apparently several families who would still never admit Marthe de Florian's granddaughter into their salons.

In 1934, Marthe decided to take Isabelle to Lake Geneva in Switzerland for the summer. They set off to stay in a chalet for several weeks. This was where they met Virginia, who entranced both Isabelle and the elderly Marthe to the extent that they all became inseparable.

Isabelle was petite and bubbly, with dark curls and laughing brown eyes. As you know, Virginia was exactly the opposite, a tall, willowy blonde whose considerable beauty and delicious spark soon caused more than a ripple among the young men in Switzerland. Isabelle and Virginia, or "Virginie" as Isabelle took to calling her friend, made quite a dazzling pair, and it wasn't long before countless young men were fighting over them both.

Marthe watched over the girls as they frolicked their way through a summer filled with boating parties on the lake, picnics, and visits to the charming Swiss villages nearby, followed by evenings spent dancing on the broad terraces of the fashionable resorts.

When summer ended that year and it was time to go home, Isabelle was so distraught at having to say good-bye to her dearest Virginie that the only way she could cope with her return to Paris was to bring Virginie with her. Marthe approved thoroughly, of course.

So they returned to the apartment, where Isabelle and Virginia shared the bedroom off Marthe's own, bringing a sort of renaissance to the apartment in rue Blanche. They were looked after by Marthe's own lady's maid, the young Camille Paget. Again, the apartment was filled with gentlemen callers, but this time they were much younger, far more earnest, and less discreet. Those were wonderful years for both young women. Isabelle adored her friend, and they traveled in Europe several times together, but most of the time they lived it up in Paris.

By 1939, Virginia was receiving letters from her concerned parents, who wanted her to return to the safety of the United States. Finally, they insisted that she sail home. But then Marthe became ill. The influenza that had taken both of Isabelle's parents when she was just five years old sank itself deep into Marthe's old lungs. She developed pneumonia in November 1939. Tragically, she died a week before Virginia was booked to sail home.

Distraught, alone in Paris with neither a close relative nor a friend to her name, Isabelle grew up fast over the course of that agonizing winter. The gentleman callers stopped visiting soon. There was no fun talking to a girl who never showed the dimples in her cheeks. As the war gathered momentum during the first half of 1940—and as it seemed more and more likely that the Nazis were going to move into France—Isabelle felt there was little to live for, even if she did survive the war.

She made her will, leaving Marthe's estate to the only friend she adored and fully trusted: Virginia Brooke.

At that point, Isabelle was living alone, with only her maid, Camille, to keep her company in the apartment. Isabelle went into a sort of decline. Without Virginia, there was little to entice her out of the apartment at all.

Camille Paget was set with the task of looking after Isabelle, but with Isabelle in her condition, Camille started to go out more regularly in the evenings herself. She had always been allowed to go out if she didn't have any duties at night with her mistresses, but this became a regular occurrence once Virginia had gone.

Camille was a very different girl from Isabelle. She had grown up in Honfleur, the only daughter of a family of timber merchants who had worked in the industry for generations. Camille's mother had worked as a lady's maid herself at château Montagnac, which is a beautiful château, just outside Honfleur, standing to this day. Camille's parents had married young, and when her father went away to the First World War, leaving his young wife, Camille's mother Marcelle Paget, pregnant with Camille, nobody guessed that such a vital, bright young man would be killed in the Somme. Antoine Paget was twenty-four years old when it happened, and Marcelle never fully recovered from the shock.

Marcelle gave birth to Camille and went back to live and work at the château. Camille was raised by both sets of her grandparents, the Paget family and also the Bouchards—her mother's family. They were proud people, hardworking families who had hoped that the bright and clever Antoine would work his way up in the timber industry someday. His untimely death—like so many other untimely deaths during that terrible war—was met with such sadness on the part of his parents that they never fully recovered.

It was in this atmosphere that the young Camille was raised. Like her father, she excelled at school. She saw little of her mother, who had withdrawn back to her old life, hardly acknowledging her child. Camille had hopes of becoming a teacher when she turned sixteen and was keen to continue her education, but fate was to step in again and change Camille's life for the worse.

Although Camille's mother had never taken much interest in her daughter, Marcelle had always paid all of her daughter's bills. When Marcelle died in 1934, Camille lost all hope of continuing her education. There was no one who could afford to fund it, and Camille knew it was unlikely she would find work during the Great Depression. Her only option was to take on work as a maid, having helped her mother at the château. Camille insisted on going to Paris, despite her grandparents' angst, in order to maximize her chance of securing a position. There was nothing available for a girl with no experience as a servant in Honfleur.

Camille still cherished a hope that she could study at night to train as a secretary, now that the chances of becoming a teacher had disappeared with her mother's death. Camille was sixteen years old when she climbed on a train and said good-bye to her grandparents for the very last time, not realizing that she would never lay eyes on them again.

Paris was everything she had hoped for and not at all as she had expected. After three months of unemployment and life in a boarding house, Camille finally secured an interview at a private home in the ninth arrondissement with a lady and her granddaughter. That lady was Marthe de Florian, and her granddaughter was Isabelle. Marthe had always found it difficult to secure a lady's maid, as her reputation still preceded her.

When Marthe laid eyes on Camille, she seemed very pleased indeed. Camille had olive skin and dark eyes, just like Isabelle, but where Isabelle was all roses and dimples and smiles, Camille had a beautiful, serious, thoughtful face, framed by long, straight dark hair. Marthe seemed struck by the girl's discretion, and she was convinced that Camille would not ask inane questions about the apartment.

Camille was hired immediately and moved in right away. Her duties included dressing both Isabelle and Marthe each morning, tidying their rooms each day, taking care of their wardrobes, and attending to any mending that they might have. If the ladies were going out in the afternoon, Camille helped them change their outfits. Soon they came to rely on Camille's good taste and handed off the selection of outfits completely to her. She would choose evening gowns, manage their wardrobes, and supervise the daily maids who came in to clean and sometimes even the cook. She ran errands for her mistresses, all over Paris and they came to find her indispensable.

As well as having some evenings free, Camille had one afternoon off each week, during which she busied herself with the secretarial course that she had planned from the outset. She carefully saved up her francs and made smart purchases with any spare money that she had saved.

She finished the secretarial course, but Camille didn't leave her post in rue Blanche. She was so attached to Marthe, Isabelle, and Virginia that she didn't have the heart to leave them in the lurch. They were almost like family to her, and she was well looked after by them. Camille kept putting off the idea of being a secretary, but she kept in touch with the girls with whom she had studied at night.

Some of them had jobs now, and that meant they had a little money to spare on having fun. They encouraged Camille to go out with them to nightclubs and dance halls on her free evenings. Camille was young, and this was Paris in the Jazz Age.

Camille and her friends favored a dance hall on a narrow street on the Left Bank. It was at the top of a flight of external stairs, and those floorboards in that hall creaked to the sound of fun and laughter almost every night. Young voices chattered a mile every minute. So many of them were about to be obliterated by another tragic war. But when the music played and they danced, for a few hours they could forget about that specter. There was always an accordion player and sometimes a band.

The soldiers were absurdly handsome in their uniforms. They would stand around the bar, pretending to have terribly serious conversations. But they were really only boys.

There was one young man who was altogether different. Camille could feel his presence whenever he was in the room. There was something about his dark face—an earnestness tempered by the most devastating twinkle in his eyes and a smile that could melt chocolate.

It was hardly a surprise that he caught the interest of all the girls. But the men crowded around him too, almost as if they were hanging on to every word he said.

The first night he was there, a young woman approached the group of fellows who were standing at the bar. This young man refused to dance, but Camille swore he caught her eye and smiled at her, and when he did, oh my goodness.

Camille lost interest in all the other men. It was as if they were nothing anymore. They just faded completely in her eyes. She was bored by her companions' whispered conversations. On the nights that he wasn't there, Camille felt as if the entire place were empty of anything that mattered.

This strange state of affairs went on for some time because Camille didn't have the courage to speak to the man. She was too scared to break the enchantment between them in case it wasn't real.

A couple of times, one of Camille's friends asked who he was, where he came from, but the soldiers were secretive. They would just smile at the girl and tell her that he was nothing to worry their gorgeous minds about.

But there was no doubt in Camille's mind that something momentous was about to happen. Although she tried to focus on her job and on all the things she was supposed to do, she found her thoughts turning in a hopeless spin, no more so than when she lay awake in her small attic room at night.

When he walked over her way one night and stopped and introduced himself as Zach Marek, Camille felt her heart rate skyrocket. When he smiled right at her, it was all she could do to take the hand he offered and walk with him to the dance floor.

Once they started to dance, Camille never wanted to stop. The way Zach took her in his arms was so gentle, so unlike any of the other young men, who all seemed immature boys in comparison.

When Zach asked if she was coming back the following evening, Camille knew that she wanted to see him every evening for the rest of her life. Zach drew her close, and a few nights later, when he walked her home and kissed her outside the apartment in rue Blanche for the very first time, Camille knew she was in love.

They danced, they joked with all the other young people at the dance hall. Camille's friends accepted that they were a couple, and yet she knew that he was holding something back.

In the summer of 1939, two months into their courtship, Zach asked her to meet him at a bistro because he wanted to talk. When they had finished their meal, Camille learned what she had suspected he was hiding from her all along:

Zach told her he was a Jewish refugee who had escaped the Sudetenland on the eve of it becoming part of Nazi Germany. His family had been glassmakers in that region for generations.

Now, Jewish people in his homeland were being attacked in the streets, Fascist organizations harassed them, and synagogues were being burned to the ground. Zach was a medical student. Realizing that he would no longer be able to study or live in peace in his own country, he fled. He only just managed to escape before all Jews were barred from leaving. Furthermore, by late 1938, the Nazis had ordered that all Sudetenland refugees leave Paris and London.

At the time, Zach was helping at a hospital in Paris, dodging the authorities, working undercover. He was respected and needed there. They both knew that Hitler would not spare France. They both knew that there was no way Zach could avoid getting involved, and they both knew that his situation was more than precarious—in fact, it was a danger to them both.

In late 1939, Camille was approached and told that if she informed on her Jewish lover, Zach Marek, the Nazis would not deport him, but otherwise he would be dealt with immediately. It was entirely up to her. They gave her twenty-four hours to make her decision. Camille had never been so terrified nor so determined in her life.

Camille agreed to spy on him for the Nazis, but she fed them only lies. The game that she played to protect Zach became more and more deceptive and more and more dangerous as the year wound on. She did not tell Zach a word of this because she knew he wouldn't let her take such a risk for him.

By May 1940, Camille knew she was pregnant. On the same day she learned this wonderful and complicating news, she was on her way to meet Zach when she was stopped not by the Nazis but by French government agents questioning her activities with the Germans. Camille, who was becoming more and more adept at protecting Zach, told them the truth once they had identified themselves and shown sufficient proof to satisfy her.

She agreed to report back to the French authorities exactly what was going on with her Nazi contacts. In return, the government agreed to allow Zach to remain in Paris rather than deport him to one of the camps they had now established in the South of France for foreign Jews.

May turned to June. Isabelle was growing increasingly agitated. Her grandmother had died. Camille was often absent but appeared distracted even when she was there. She felt entirely alone. The sound of air raid sirens had wailed over Paris, and there were bombings in the city in early June. Isabelle couldn't take Marthe's precious things with her, but it was clear that she was going to have to flee. In a panic, she called Marthe's lawyer. When he came to the apartment, Camille let him in, then worked in the kitchen while Isabelle discussed her will with him. Isabelle told the lawyer to leave everything to Virginia if anything happened to her.

Camille delivered the signed document to the lawyer's office two days later, and Isabelle told Camille to pack for their escape to Spain. Several families that Isabelle knew had left already, their car roofs loaded with every imaginable and useless thing.

Camille packed mindlessly. She had contacted Zach, but every time she spoke to him, every time she went to his apartment, she was terrified of being followed by French or German agents.

She continued to pretend to work for the Germans. It was lucky she was smart, but her balancing act was of the most precarious kind. She reported to the French every question that the Nazis asked her. She met with them in the most obscure places and at the most obscure times of day and night, always alone.

But it was the threat of the Nazis that kept her awake at night, and right before the eve of the invasion of Paris, everything went terribly wrong.

Isabelle believed that her train ticket out of Paris was going to get her directly to Spain. But Camille knew better: she had read reports of soldiers barricading the stations. Isabelle was not going to leave Paris on a train. By then, the only way out of Paris was on foot.

Isabelle took one suitcase, and Camille packed her things too. She had no choice but to go with Isabelle now, but she planned to return to Paris and to Zach as soon as she knew Isabelle was safely out of Paris. Camille knew it would only endanger Zach further to tell Isabelle anything about him, so she had kept her relationship with him quiet. Zach was planning their escape, too, and had promised to wait for Camille until she returned, hopefully that very night, as soon as she had found safe traveling companions for Isabelle.

They were walking down one of Paris's charming cobbled lanes, suitcases in hand, headed for the station—at Isabelle's insistence—when three men turned into the lane.

The assassins shot Isabelle dead in the confusion and the last-minute panic that had consumed Paris on the eve of the invasion. Isabelle. Camille gasped as she realized that they had killed Isabelle instead of their real target—herself. Two of the men started to shout. Had they realized they had gotten it wrong? The last thing Camille saw of her mistress was the beautiful girl's terrified eyes, asking Camille the question that her lips could no longer form. What had happened?

Camille was vomiting on the side of the alley, but the third man shouted at her: go! As he dragged Isabelle's limp body off to the side of the lane, Camille made one last move toward her mistress, wanting to check to see if Isabelle was alive or dead, but the man pointed his gun straight at Camille's head and shouted at her again to get out.

This marked the beginning of Camille's war.

Camille lumbered toward the Seine, dragging both her and Isabelle's small suitcases to the tiny apartment that Zach had rented on the Left Bank. The disgust, the guilt, the anger, and the shame that she felt at Isabelle's death were all rolled into one great cloud of shock. She fought her instinct to crumple—or to jump off one of the bridges into the Seine.

As she made her way up the stairway to Zach's apartment, everything was silent.

The thin walls of the old building were not reverberating as they usually did with the sounds of families talking loudly in the tiny apartments that ran off each floor. Nor were there noises of pans and pots clinking as housewives carried out the jobs that took up their days.

As Camille climbed further up the narrow staircase, lugging the suitcases behind her, she fought the sickening sense that things were about to get worse. When she arrived at Zach's floor, she grew nauseous again.

His door was flung wide. Camille didn't have to do anything more than stick her head inside it to know that everything had been stripped. The mattress in the corner had been thrown half off its frame and hung, suspended, like Paris itself on the eve of the invasion.

Every drawer in Zach's tiny kitchen was hurled open, too. His cooking things had been thrown on the floor; the spatula that he had often used to make herb and cheese omelets after they had made love leaned against a cupboard door. Zach's clothes were strewn over the floorboards, pockets wrenched inside out, their random shapes casting desperate patterns on the Turkish rug that Camille had helped him choose at a market the year before.

Camille clung to the doorway, her hands slick and shaking. Her mind, which had become a haze of its former self, knew that she should go to the hospital where Zach worked. He would be there. He had to be. She turned, her hands grasping the suitcases again as if they would save her.

Someone was coming up the stairs. Camille pulled the suitcases into Zach's apartment. There was nowhere else to hide. His was the only flat off the minute landing. She closed the door, soft as a whisper.

The person knocked.

"Bonjour?" It was a woman.

Camille stood sentinel in the middle of the room. Could the person hear her breathe?

Bonnie, I have something that I need to add to my letter. What I am going to tell you may come as something of a shock. That is because the woman standing outside Zach's apartment was Louise Delfont.

"Monsieur Lapointe?" His assistant popped her head in the door.

Cat and Monsieur Lapointe jumped as if woken from a dream.

"Je suis occupé," he said. I am busy.

The assistant rattled off something urgent-sounding in French.

Monsieur leaned heavily on his desk. "I have a meeting that I had forgotten about. Oh, mon dieu. This is . . ." He looked at her. "Can you please wait thirty minutes?"

Cat put the letter down on the table.

She nodded.

She took the opportunity to get some air and wandered out into the street, still deeply immersed in the past. She had seen photographs of the Nazis marching down the Champs Elysées on the day of the occupation of France. June 1940. It had been summer then, warm, time for the seaside, for picnics in the countryside, not time for an invasion—if ever there was such a time. Nothing could have prepared her for the personal horrors that citizens on both sides must have endured. And nothing could have prepared her for the fact that it looked like Loic's grandmother was not Isabelle de Florian at all, but instead the girl who had been reported dead in the Paris newspapers: Isabelle's maid, Camille Paget.

• • •

"I think we will read on and talk afterwards," Monsieur Lapointe said half an hour later when they had settled back in their respective chairs in the office.

Cat took out the letter.

The government organization I was working for at that time had been alerted that Zach had been removed from Paris, along with other foreign Jews. We were watching Camille's activities as well as we could, given our resources and the panic. We knew that we had to remove her from Paris before the Nazi arrival.

Having been to the apartment on rue Blanche and found it empty and shuttered, I went straight to Zach's apartment. Camille wouldn't let me in for a long time. I had to convince her that I was working for the French government, or what was left of it. When she finally let me in, I told her that she would have to pack what she wanted to take with her in either her or Isabelle's suitcase and that she could ask no questions. There was no time. Camille was in terrible danger as a spy. She knew too much. There was only one obvious solution, and we both knew it. She was shaking and frantic, but she quickly sorted through Isabelle's few things. As she did so, she told me about Isabelle's murder.

I took the other suitcase and all of Camille's documentation.

Now, it was crucial that no one could know that Camille was still alive.

She took all of Isabelle's documentation, the stash of photographs that Isabelle had brought from rue Blanche, and a few of Isabelle's elegant clothes. I helped Camille into one of Isabelle's unfamiliar dresses, then we left the apartment and I accompanied her out of Paris.

We went first to the government building where I worked. Trucks had been removing things for days—people, documents, everything. I provided Camille with false documentation and a new name that we had assigned for her, Sylvie-Marie Augustin. I had a difficult job convincing her to leave the city; she was convinced that she should stay, race to the hospital. I had to almost force her to abandon the idea.

We were supposed to catch a truck on the outskirts of the city, but when it didn't show up, we began walking. We were only two of thousands of desperate Parisians clogging the roads. We spoke little.

Only once we had left the perimeter of the city did I tell her that I didn't know where Zach was, other than that he had been sent south to one of the camps for Jewish refugees. Camille hardened further. She told me that she would go to the South of France and find him.

We walked and caught occasional rides on government trucks when I could sweet-talk the drivers into giving us a lift. Finally, I left Camille at a government house in Rennes. She made her own way to the South of France.

Camille went to Sarlat, then southwest to Albi. Later we learned that Zach was placed in a holding camp at Rivesaltes, so close to Albi, before being transferred to Auschwitz. It was tragic. Camille made her way across to Provence instead, following a false lead. When she could travel no more, she sought refuge in a nunnery, in a small village called Saint-Revel, for her confinement.

That was when she took on Isabelle's name. Even the false name Sylvie-Marie Augustin was too dangerous, given the nature of our government at the time. You see, false papers could sometimes be identified as such. They had access to everything and, having "worked" for both the Germans and the French, she was still not safe. She was worried for her child's sake. Camille hid and took on the task of working for the nuns. She gave birth to a baby girl and called her Sylvie. I don't know whether this was done wittingly or not, but the use of the code name, along with that of the false Isabelle de Florian—whose story I knew—helped us to track her down later on.

The war intensifying and now a mother, Camille could not leave in order to search for Zach. She did all she could from her place of refuge, but she got no answers to her inquiries.

By 1942, I had started working for the Resistance, and through my contacts I was able to discover that Zach Marek had been rounded up by the Germans and taken to Auschwitz. He'd traveled by train from the holding camp near Albi for several days with no water, no toilet facilities, no food, jammed in a stinking carriage so packed they could not even sit down. Those who survived—and Zach did—were gassed almost immediately on arrival.

And so that was the end.

After an extensive search, I located Camille and her baby daughter, Sylvie Rose, to relay the tragic news to her. I remembered Camille, and I felt determined to help her, to at least find out what had happened to Zach. I knew she would leave no stone unturned until she found Zach, and I felt she had the right to know the truth.

After this, Camille became determined to join the Resistance. She planned to operate under her code name, Sylvie-Marie Augustin, and to do this, she had to move out of the nunnery. Camille bought a small apartment in Saint-Revel.

I always wondered how she managed to pay for it. Camille only told me recently that she had taken Isabelle's jewelry when she swapped suitcases in Zach's Paris apartment, jewelry that had belonged to the famous Marthe de Florian. Isabelle had packed the most valuable pieces, including a pair of diamond earrings, a sapphire necklace, and a ruby bracelet that her grandmother had worn nearly every day.

Camille had planned to return it all to the apartment after the war, but when she saw that the jewels would be far better used for helping the Resistance, she didn't hesitate to sell them all.

Camille sold the pieces for a fraction of their value in Aix. No one questioned that Isabelle de Florian would be selling such items, especially since Camille was wearing Isabelle's elegant clothes. Shortly afterward, she burned those and destroyed Isabelle's photographs. With Marthe's Belle Époque jewels, Camille managed to buy a safe apartment in Saint-Revel for those unfortunates running from the Vichy government or the Nazi occupation or both.

Camille housed Resistance workers, parachutists, and refugees trying to escape across the border. Camille's English grew stronger during the war, and she became a valued and reliable contact for us. She did not take ridiculous risks—she had a daughter, after all. She was steady. We could trust her, just as Marthe did.

However, I know now that Camille was terrified that she would be incarcerated for stealing not only her former employer's name but Isabelle's valuable jewelry collection. Furthermore, Camille had not reported her mistress's death. I know that this will haunt Camille to her dying day. One thing was certain, and that was that the only way she could justify moving forward was to do whatever she could to stand up to the people who had killed Isabelle and Zach.

After the war, after the heady liberation of France, Camille came to me in Sarlat and begged me not to reveal that she was not Isabelle de Florian. I was the only one who knew, and if anything were to happen to Camille, Sylvie would be alone in the world and vulnerable . . . just like Isabelle had been. Camille saw it as the great failure of her life that she had not been able to protect either Zach or Isabelle. She would not let her daughter out of her sight.

But Camille's deceit—or what she still sees as her deceit, no matter how noble her aims—is something she refuses to pass on to the innocent Sylvie. She feels that it would only further the deceit to have her own daughter inherit from Isabelle when they are no relation to each other—and when Isabelle unwittingly sacrificed her own life for Camille. I know Camille feels it was her own actions that killed Isabelle.

Camille never trusted the world in which she lived after that war. Like so many others, she did not trust that she could share what had happened with those she loved—she didn't believe they could understand the decisions that had to be made at that time unless they had lived through the terrible period themselves.

I know that Camille acted as she did to protect those she loved—Zach, Isabelle, and Sylvie. So Bonnie, there it is—a full and true accounting of why you are the rightful heir to the apartment in rue Blanche.

Camille sends you her blessing and asks that you do what is right for everyone.

A bientôt, my dear.

Louise Delfont.

CHAPTER TWENTY-TWO

Cat had sent a copy of Louise Delfont's story straight to both Loic and Sylvie while she was still in Paris, explaining that they were all tied to this story now and that she still felt she should not accept the entire inheritance. There were taxes that needed to be paid, and she offered to work something out with them. But months had passed, and she had not heard a word back from them.

It seemed that the only thing to do was to regard her time in France as much like a Boldini painting: ethereal, beautiful, and over in the swish of a second.

Shortly after that second trip to Paris, she and Christian had moved into their new apartment, which was a few minutes' walk from Central Park. Cat and Christian had settled into a rhythm that suited them both. The surprising thing was the friendship she had formed with Elise. Cat had taken to having breakfast with Elise a couple of mornings a week. As summer approached, they had started running together through Central Park. Elise was the only person, apart from Christian, with whom Cat had shared the entire story behind her apartment in Paris.

Cat hadn't yet figured out what to do about any of it. She couldn't bear the idea of selling the apartment, and as for the painting, it was still safe in the Musée d'Orsay's archives. Cat decided to give it a few more weeks—to wait until the tax situation was pressing and urgent to see whether Loic or Sylvie got in touch before she made a decision.

She still thought of Paris far more than she should—almost all the time, if she was honest with herself—and that meant thinking of Loic, too. But her wedding was in three weeks, and she was determined not to let her memories of him derail that.

She and Christian had taken to having a late breakfast together on Saturdays. Cat would spread the newspaper out on the coffee table in the apartment's all-white living room.

Cat scanned the financial section, not stopping to read about the latest deals in any depth. But as she turned a page, something caught her eye, and she read the article properly.

"No."

Christian looked up at her, his green eyes curious.

Cat scanned the brief article in front of her. "Billy Walker's lost everything! His company develops treatments for restoring cancer patients' immune systems. But that's not all. He was going to donate part of his profits toward funding treatment for a sick child. I read about it. The little boy is only three. He has no hope without vastly expensive treatment. Billy Walker had pledged to pay it all—and now his fortune's gone up in smoke. Something's wrong when that sort of thing happens."

"You sound like a walking advertisement for the guy."

Cat scanned the article again. "Christian. My grandmother died, too young, of cancer. My mother died, too young, in a car accident that was not her fault, and so did my father . . . this child is three. How many more lives could Billy Walker have saved? There's no rational explanation for simply cutting his business down. No good reason why one person who wanted to help should lose everything when there are so many success stories centered around greed. Sorry, Christian. I just find this so sad."

Christian cleared his throat. "Cat, you're the one who is being irrational. You're too emotional. Billy Walker got too big for himself, that's all."

"How?" Cat put the paper down.

Christian stood up, went over to the kitchen, rinsed out his coffee cup.

"I mean, everything he was doing was aimed at helping people. Sometimes I do wonder about this planet, Christian."

Christian planted a kiss on her forehead. "You're too emotional, Cat. Why don't you go for a run or something? I'm off to the gym."

"He started his company from scratch! His aim from the outset was always to help people. His mother died of cancer. I've read interviews with the family he was going to help. He was going to help other children as well."

"Cat, if you don't pay off your debts, you lose your company. Be reasonable."

"Surely if he was going through a rough period, someone out there could have helped? I mean, we live in New York, for goodness' sakes!"

Christian picked up his sports bag. "I'm looking forward to dinner. New wine list, apparently. See you then."

Cat waved, but she pulled out her laptop.

• • •

The restaurant was decorated for Christmas. Tasteful wreaths lined the walls, and the open fireplace threw out the scent of burning pinecones. Everyone seemed to be in a good mood, and there was a buzz among their friends about Cat and Christian's wedding. Elise, who seemed to have become a proxy member of Christian's inner circle, sat next to Cat.

"Sweetie, we've put your name down for four committees at four top schools. It's all going in the right direction for you." Elise threw her right arm around Cat's shoulders and squeezed.

"How strategic you are, Elise."

"Once they know you, your children are far more likely to get in. I know all about these things."

Christian's eyes flickered over their way. "Elise is doing a brilliant job."

Elise smiled at him. "Cat's one of us now."

Cat put her wine glass down on the table carefully. One of them? "Elise," she said. "Can you tell me exactly what you mean when you say I'm becoming one of you?"

There was a silence around the table.

"Oh, you're a wonderful person." Elise patted Cat on the shoulder. "Don't get me wrong. It's just that you're starting to shake some things off. You know, you don't act so awkward around Christian's friends anymore, and you seem more comfortable around his family. You know what I mean."

Cat lifted her napkin and folded it, ever so slowly, placing it down on the table in front of her. She stood up. "Excuse me," she said. "I am suddenly very tired."

"Cat." Christian smiled at everyone. "Prewedding nerves. Sorry, everyone. Cat's under a lot of pressure. I'm sure you understand."

Elise launched into a story about a bride who had threatened to jump off the Brooklyn Bridge if she couldn't ride up the aisle of St. Barts on Park Avenue accompanied by an entire cavalcade of Harleys. Everyone laughed and the conversation picked up.

"Everything okay, Cat?" Christian reached up to where she stood behind him and tried to take her hand.

Cat pulled her hand back. "You know what, Christian? I thought about that Billy Walker thing all day. I did some more reading about the little boy. Aren't you at all affected by it?"

Scott and Eric appeared to be listening in.

"Not now, Cat."

Cat felt flushed. She looked across the table at Christian. "It's heartbreaking."

Christian lowered his voice to a whisper. "That Walker fellow had it coming to him, Cat." He enunciated each word with care.

"So you are saying that we shouldn't care?"

A hush fell over the table.

"Be quiet, Cat."

"What did you say to me, Christian?"

Christian leaned forward, closer to her. "Be quiet about the Walker business. Do you hear me?"

Cat felt herself blanch. "No," she said.

"We picked up the company's assets for half their market value last night. All the bank needs to do is wait six months, sell the assets, and we'll make twenty to thirty million on the sale of the patents alone. Cat, the bank is paying your way. Without it, there'd be no fancy wedding, no apartment near the park. Do me a favor and don't complain about it, please."

He settled back into his seat. "What were we talking about?"

Cat folded her napkin and put it on the table. "Excuse me."

"Going to the restroom?" Elise stood up.

"No. I am . . . way too hot. I'll see you all later—"

"Tomorrow," Elise said, as quickly as a rabbit. "Brunch with your in-laws. My apartment. Can't wait."

"Right." Cat rested a hand on the back of her chair.

"Cat!" Christian sounded jovial. "I'll come with you."

"No. You haven't finished."

"Sure, honey?"

"Positive."

"I won't be late." He moved over to her and kissed her on the cheek.

Cat swayed out of the restaurant and onto the warm street outside. Her sense of disappointment at the realization that Christian's kindness only appeared to extend to his social circle had affected her far more than she had realized. Not only did he not care about the effects of Billy Walker's downfall, he had orchestrated the whole thing and hadn't told her so this morning.

How could she possibly marry a man who had caused a philanthropist to lose everything? How could she have been so naïve as to allow Elise to take her under her shiny wing?

One of *them*? That was the last thing Cat wanted to be. She stopped dead on the sidewalk. People skirted around her. She had no idea why she had allowed herself to be so swept up by the idea of love or the idea of romance or the idea of a perfect family or the glamour of their wealth, their confidence, their power, or whatever it was. But she now saw the truth in a stark, clear way that had eluded her before.

She suddenly knew what had to be done, and she set off toward the apartment with determined strides—and a sudden feeling of liberation.

CHAPTER TWENTY-THREE

A month later, Cat was sitting in an auction house in Manhattan. She was newly single and back in her old apartment in Brooklyn, whose lease, thankfully, hadn't been up yet. Once she'd seen the light, she'd moved swiftly. She knew it was hard on Christian to cancel the wedding, but she also knew she was doing them both a favor—even if he didn't realize it just yet.

Taking action on that front had inspired her to further action. With a few quick phone calls, she had arranged for the sale of the Boldini. The auction in Paris was about to begin, and Cat was listening on the phone.

"We have several interested buyers." The now familiar voice of Monsieur Olivier Gireau, her advisor from Sotheby's, came down the phone line.

"Bidding is starting at two hundred thousand euros." Olivier's voice was low.

The reserve was not far above this. When he had carried out his appraisal of the portrait, Olivier had advised that it was a sound price for a Boldini.

"We are up to three hundred thousand euros."

That was it, then; the painting was sold. She had done it. That amount might not be able to save the little boy Billy Walker was helping, but it was better than nothing.

But Monsieur continued. "There are ten interested bidders, Mademoiselle. They are taking it up in ten-thousand-euro lots. Mademoiselle! One of them just jumped it by fifty thousand euros. We are now up to four hundred thousand."

"Five hundred thousand euros. One has dropped out. Another is consulting on the phone. He has waved to continue, so five hundred fifty thousand. Still going, and to six hundred. We have three aggressive buyers. Two look nervous. One more has dropped out at seven hundred thousand. He is leaving the room. Unbelievable. Two of the bidders are dealers. They both look nervous. Nine hundred thousand! Two more have dropped away. The two dealers are both on the phone. Neither of them has bid for a while. Yes! One of them is back in. One million euros. He looks confident. But no! We have one of the more aggressive buyers back in. Thought so. One point two million! And continuing. One point three! The dealers are out. There are three left. This is passion. The painting sits there. One is consulting with an advisor. I know him. The advisor shrugs. The buyer is back in! One point five. . . one point six. . . one point seven . . . oh! Oui. One of the three is out. We are down to two. I think money is not the problem here. It is labor of love."

Cat closed her eyes.

"It is at two million euros. Okay. We are taking bids of ten thousand euros. It is on at two million, ten thousand. And two million, fifty thousand. One man is wiping his brow. And the other bidder has come back in! At two point one million! The first man sits down. He is out! You have a buyer! You have sold! Two point one million euros! The owner is jumping and hugging his wife! This is fantastic for a Boldini! Mademoiselle? Are you there?"

Cat almost collapsed into her chair. "Sure," she whispered. "I'm here."

Later, Cat wrote two checks out. The first was to the Tax Department of France. It was only the first installment, but it was a start. Monsieur Lapointe had arranged decent terms for her, and she would do her best not to sell the apartment in rue Blanche, not to mention all of Marthe and Isabelle's personal things. She would look after them as long as she lived. Cat hoped, however, that as many people as possible could enjoy the Boldini and that its sale might give a dying child a chance.

She put the second check in an envelope, hand wrote the address, and sealed it tight.

CHAPTER TWENTY-FOUR

The photograph of the dressing table needed a slight adjustment in the way that it hung, but otherwise, everything else was ready. The dressing table was still one of Cat's favorite shots, if she had to choose. Everything still looked as if Isabelle had just slipped out for a walk along the Seine. The perfume bottles—their bases lined with faint traces of old scent—were askew, the delicate silver brushes were caked with dust, and the mirror into which Marthe must have gazed every day was tarnished in spots where the glass had given up the effort against the passage of time. Everything seemed to be waiting for Isabelle to come home.

Cat had wandered around her Paris Time Capsule exhibition several times now, checking every last detail in the gallery before opening night. As much of the proceeds as she could manage would go to the little boy who now, thanks to the donations of several people, had started to receive the treatment that he needed to live. Then there was the next tax installment to pay to the French government.

Cat surveyed the shots she had taken outside the apartment—the early photos she had taken on the Left Bank on her long lunch break the first time she met Monsieur Lapointe. These were arranged around the exhibition to provide some context for the interiors of the apartment. The entire exhibition had a faded air, as if it, too, were tinted by the past. The photographs—with their pale golds, faded greens, and varying shades of brown—seemed to blend with each other into a harmonious whole.

It was strange having so many people wanting to talk to her but wonderful to know that they wanted to talk to her because of a shared love for Paris, for old treasures, for the past, for the lives of Marthe and Isabelle de Florian, for children's lives, and for the future.

Cat surveyed the crowd, which consisted of a mix of young and old. She was surprised at how many people had turned up just to see the works of an unknown American photographer, and that they seemed genuinely interested in the photographs. But the apartment had gotten a lot of press with the Boldini sale, and it seemed to have captured the imaginations of so many.

So many people had questions for her. Many of the guests were keen to see the apartment for themselves. If Cat offered guided tours of rue Blanche, she was sure she would make a fortune. But she would not do this. Marthe and Isabelle's world was as sacred to her as her own. And Loic, Sylvie, and Josephine deserved their privacy, too.

Still others wanted to know about the relationship between Marthe and Boldini. Had they definitely been lovers? Had Marthe fallen for any of her gentlemen clients? Did Cat know? How explicit had the love letters in the apartment been?

And then there were the questions that pierced Cat's heart, questions that she would never answer. Why had Isabelle de Florian abandoned the apartment for all those years? And why had she never gone back . . .

By the time the final visitor left, Cat was both exhausted and exhilarated. There were a pleasing number of red dots on the photographs, and the gallery owner had several interested buyers who were keen to visit over the next few days. The exhibition was likely to be a sellout.

And in her hand, Cat held a publisher's card. He was interested in compiling her photographs of the Paris apartment into what sounded like a gorgeous coffee-table book.

Cat drew on her coat. Snow fell on the pavement outside the gallery. It was hard to believe that it had almost been a year since she first received that parcel from Paris. The manager of the gallery held the glass door open for her.

She took a final glance around the gallery, as if willing him to be standing by one of the photographs, willing him to walk over to her, put an arm around her, walk her home.

What had she expected? She must stop fantasizing. Enough was enough. It was time to move on.

She had written to Loic, telling him about her idea; she had included him in her plans, offered to give either him or Sylvie any of the photographs they wanted, including the ones she had taken in Saint-Revel, in Albi, in Sarlat, and at Camille's convent.

Cat had not expected any reply, but it was the gesture that seemed important. Although—if Cat was honest—it was far more than that. It always had been. She just hadn't seen it.

She had to accept that his silence meant he was no longer interested in her. She had told him she had broken it off with Christian. When she didn't hear back, she had come to understand that he must no longer care. Cat walked out into the freezing street, making her way through Brooklyn back to her own apartment, which was now her home again and perhaps would be forever.

She had thought about going to Paris for a few months after she had ended things with Christian but knew that it was too soon. Anouk was taking care of things. She had planned for the apartment to be cleaned and aired regularly until Cat decided what she wanted to do with all the furniture. She turned into her Brooklyn street. Her scooter sat out in the cold, thick with powdery snow.

Ubiquitous decorated trees, their tiny yellow lights iridescent, shone out through people's windows onto the silent street. Cat put her cold hands in her pockets and walked toward her own front steps.

She stopped, hard, a few feet from her building. Someone was standing on the step.

"Cat?" Suddenly he was before her. Her heart started to dance when his brown eyes caught hers.

"Game's up, I'm afraid."

Cat took a step closer. "Did you receive my letters?"

"After I received Louise Delfont's letter, I went away for a while. My staff don't open my personal mail, you know. But I arrived home yesterday. I came straight here."

"Opera in Milan?"

"Czech Republic. Honfleur."

Cat reached out, instinctively, and took his freezing hand.

"None of Zach's . . . my . . . family survived. But I found my grandfather's old home. And as for Camille, well. She was an only child, but it was good to walk where she must have walked. I owe you a great debt of thanks. For what you did for my family. You never gave up."

Cat looked out across the street. A man with a small dog on a leash turned the corner and approached them. As he passed, he smiled at them both.

"But the future's safe for you all. There's you, Sylvie, and Josephine," she whispered.

Loic reached forward, tucked a tendril of hair behind her ear. "I heard the painting sold for a fortune. And I heard what you did with the money. Camille would have been proud of you, Cat."

"And Sylvie?" She didn't want him to take his hand away.

"Oh, Maman. Well. You could do anything and she'd still adore you. You see, she fell for you the moment you walked into her life."

Cat looked up at him. "Would you like to come in?"

His hand trailed down to her shoulder. Cat took out her key. He slipped his hand into hers as they moved up the steps. She stopped at the door just before turning the key.

"I still have the apartment in Paris, you know. I'm trying so hard to keep it. It has so many . . . beautiful things."

"I know, Cat," Loic said.

"And I have a tax bill that I'll never pay before I'm dead," Cat laughed. She opened the door into the living room.

Loic stepped inside. "Why do you want to keep the apartment in Paris?"

She turned to face him. "Because of Marthe, of Isabelle, Virginia, Sylvie . . . but most of all . . . because of you."

Loic's voice was soft. "Would you consider an investor? Someone who'd meet you halfway? With all of it: the tax, rue Blanche . . . everything?"

"Only if that person was you, Loic."

He was closer now. She reached out, put her arms around his waist.

Loic seemed to be looking over her shoulder. Cat turned and laughed.

"I see that Mickey Mouse found his way home. You didn't send for the ostrich?" he asked.

"If there's one thing I know now, it's that some things . . . some people just don't fit together. But others do. The ostrich definitely belongs on rue Blanche. But Mickey . . . well. He'd been patient, living so far from home for such a long time. I thought I'd bring him back . . ."

Loic still held her hand. Slowly he raised her fingertips up to his lips. Her fingers were warm now. There was no longer any reason for them to be cold.

AFTERWORD

Marthe de Florian was a courtesan and actress during the Belle Époque in Paris. Her apartment was discovered in 2010, having been abandoned for seventy years. Ghostlike photos of the rooms in the apartment spread like wildfire through the Internet, but I was fascinated by the story: Why had the apartment been locked up for seventy years after the owner fled Paris on the eve of the Nazi invasion?

As for Giovanni Boldini, he was the leading portrait painter in Paris during the Belle Époque. Boldini was discovered to have painted the portrait of Marthe de Florian that was found in the apartment in 2010. Other than this, all my characters and story are fictional and entirely inventions of my own imagination.

ACKNOWLEDGMENTS

The production of a book is often described as analogous to that old saying about entire villages and one child. However, *Paris Time Capsule* will always be linked with a journey for me. Along the way, I have met, come to know better, and had the good fortune to work with some of the very best of people and friends.

I am deeply grateful to my editor, Jodi Warshaw, at Lake Union Publishing for her enthusiasm for this book and for all her hard work in bringing the novel to its fruition. Huge thanks to Christina Henry de Tessan for her nurturing approach to the editing process; working with Christina led me so much further than I had anticipated—I discovered much, not only about Cat but also about myself. Thanks to Christy Karras for her detailed copyediting and to Elsie Lyons for capturing the spirit of the novel with her gorgeous cover design. Thanks to Gabriella Ven den Heuvel for always being there, and thanks to Thom Kephart—I am looking forward to working with you.

Huge thanks to my amazing publicist and friend Tracy Balsz, and to my agent, Peter Giagni—I am so honored to have the opportunity to work with you both on another exciting version of *Paris Time Capsule*.

Thanks to Nas Dean for her support with the indie version of the book; thanks to Jessica Kaye for her sound legal advice, to Miriam Connor for reading my work before it is sent anywhere else, to Jeannie Johnson for her enthusiasm in the early days, and to Cornerstones Literary Agency. Special acknowledgement and thanks to Robert McKee and to Margie Lawson—I feel so fortunate to have been able to learn from you both.

Heartfelt thanks to my friends, especially to Melanie Milburne for her unstinting love and support, to Kelli Jones for her daily texts and for the chats, to Kym Jose, Fiona Calvert, Lisa Roberts-Scott, Kerry Sculthorpe, Di Jackson, Ann Cripps, Simone Bingham, Michelle Barker, Harry and Val Stanton, and to those lovely moms who helped me by driving my children about when I was under deadline with this book. Thank you to Jasmin Emerson and Craig Keane, whose help and support allowed me the time to write. To all my other friends and also to the many friends with whom I chat most days on Facebook, you know who you are—thank you.

My writing journey was sparked and nurtured long ago by my late mother, Helen, who read to me throughout my childhood; she then threw every marvelous book that she could find my way during my teenage years. Her final words to me were "do your writing." To my ex-husband, David, who was my partner and best friend for twenty-four years until just recently: I thank you. To my sister, Jane, you are one of the most intelligent and strong women I know, always there when things are tough. However, like any proper tale, I am sure that this one will only awaken a new beginning. To my beautiful children, Ben and Sophie: I adore you both. This book is for you.

Thank you for reading this novel.
For more information on *Paris Time Capsule*, and to learn about the release of the second novel in the Paris Time Capsule series, please visit Ella at
www.facebook.com/paristimecapsule
or
www.paristimecapsule.com.

ABOUT THE AUTHOR

Photo © 2014 John Stewart

Ella Carey is a writer and a Francophile who can almost claim Paris as her second home. She has studied French since she was five and has degrees in music and arts, majoring in classical piano, modern European history, and nineteenth-century literature. Writing has always been Ella's real passion, but she has worked in various other guises. As an emerging author, Ella has had her work published in *The Review of Australian Fiction*. She has traveled to France more than a dozen times and drew on her many experiences there when writing *Paris Time Capsule*. Ella knew straight away that the fascinating true story of the abandoned apartment was a perfect fit for her, with its blend of history; impossible, decaying romance; and mystery—not to mention Paris. Ella released *Paris Time Capsule* as an indie book in 2014, and it rose to number 10 on Amazon in the US. This revised edition is now released with Lake Union Publishing. A feature film screenplay version of the book is in development. In her spare time, Ella walks her dogs along the beach, studies French, sings in a rock choir, reads, loves to visit art museums, and collects every beautiful book on Paris that she can possibly find. She is hard at work on her second novel, which is also set in Paris. Ella lives with her two children and two noble Italian greyhounds, which are constantly mistaken for whippets.